Rhanna at War

CHRISTINE MARION FRASER was born in Glasgow
during the war years. At the age of ten, she
contracted a very rare disease which terminated
her education and put her into a wheelchair
where she has been ever since.

A keen reader and storyteller, and with a vivid
imagination, she first got the idea for the story
of *Rhanna* while on holiday in the Hebrides.
Rhanna at War is the second book about this
magical Hebridean island.

Christine Marion Fraser lives in Argyll with
her husband and daughter.

Also in Fontana by the same author

Rhanna
Blue Above the Chimneys

CHRISTINE MARION FRASER

Rhanna at War

FONTANA/Collins

First published in 1980 by Blond & Briggs
First published in this revised edition by Fontana Books in 1982
© 1980 by Christine Marion Fraser
© 1982 in this revised edition by Christine Marion Fraser

Made and printed in Great Britain by
William Collins Sons & Co Ltd, Glasgow

To Ray, Cathie, and Ethel,
friends as well as sisters

AUTHOR'S NOTE

While I have tried to make the raids over Clydebank on 13th March 1941 as authentic as possible, there may be some discrepancies. According to statistics from German sources there was no bomber squadron I.K.G. 3 over Clydebank on 13th March 1941.

I wish to express grateful thanks to Alastair Ashfield, John McKee, Walter Muir, Harry Wilson D.F.C. and Ian Forsyth (the ancient mariner) for invaluable information on various subjects throughout the book.

C. M. F.

CR

Abbey ruins

Dunuaigh

Cave

Croynachan

Sgurr na Gill

Burnbreddie House

Sgurr nan Gabhar

Biddy's
Cottage

Downie
Pass

Sgurr nan Ruadh

NIGG

Slochmhor

M
U
I
R

Dodie's
House

of RHANNA

Murdy's
House

Kirkyard

Loch
Tenee

Schoolhouse

Todd the
Shod

Sgor Creags

PORTCULL

Caves

Port Rum Point

Ranald's
Boats

Y

Croft na Beinn

Ben
Machrie

RÙMHOR

PORTVOYNACHAN

Hamish's/Mathew's
Cottage

Loch
Sliach

Laigmhor

Bob's
Biggin

Y

SOUND   OF   RHANNA

PART I

RHANNA
March 11th 1941

CHAPTER 1

Shona McKenzie stood with her arms folded on the rails of the steamer and watched with quiet elation as the tiny island of Eriskay in the Outer Hebrides appeared on the horizon in an ethereal haze of mist. The landmark of Eriskay meant that in less than half an hour the boat would reach Rhanna and Shona's pulse quickened at the thought. Soon – soon she would be back on Rhanna, amongst all the dear people whom she had known all her life and who were as much a part of her as the very soil of the island itself.

She lifted her face to the sky, shut her eyes and breathed deeply, letting the salt-laden air wash into her lungs. Aberdeenshire had been lovely with its rivers, glens and majestic mountains, but she had missed the sea, hardly realizing how much till this moment of sharp air, wheeling gulls and warm winds gently rippling the surface of the blue water. It was an extremely mild day for March. At other times in the same season the sea could be a boiling fury with gales throwing waves forty feet and more into grey lowering skies. But no matter the weather, she loved her native land and had never thought she could ever leave it for more than a week or two at a time. But that had been before the war, before her childhood sweetheart, Niall McLachlan, had been badly wounded in the massacre of Dunkirk . . . and before her father had married Kirsteen Fraser, who had once been her teacher in the little school at Portcull.

For many years it had just been Shona and her father living at Laigmhor, the big rambling farmhouse in which she had been born. Just herself and her father had meant a lot of loneliness, but it had also meant a lot of shared confidences and a warm feeling that the happiness of one depended on the happiness of the other. Now there was another woman sharing her father's life, and Shona wasn't quite sure of her own feelings on the matter. She loved and respected Kirsteen, had done ever since the day the two of them had met in the little village school, Kirsteen as a young teacher just starting in her new post, and Shona, a small motherless mite of five years feeling desolate and lost in a strange new world. From the beginning she had wanted Kirsteen Fraser to take the place of the mother she had never known and it certainly had looked that all her dreams were about to become reality when she was eleven and her father had announced his intentions of marrying Kirsteen. But tragedy had befallen Laigmhor round about that time. Mirabelle, the dear motherly housekeeper who had reared Shona from birth, had died suddenly, then her father had lost an arm in a terrible accident when out searching for his brother, Alick, in the treacherous waters that swirled round the Sgorr Creags. And Kirsteen, believing that he would no longer want to marry her because of his pride, had sailed away from Rhanna carrying his child.

But all that was in the past. In the autumn of 1940, after a lapse of almost six years, her father had been reconciled with Kirsteen and she had come back to Rhanna with his son. The boy, Grant Fergus, with his black curls and dimpled chin, was unmistakably Fergus McKenzie all over again. Laigmhor had become a real family home where life and laughter abounded and where love embraced them all in a glowing little circle. Yet, despite all, Shona had felt an intruder. She had been still in the turbulent grip of some very recent crises of her own and had known she wasn't yet ready to adjust to a newly acquired little brother and another woman doing all the things at Laigmhor that had once been her ritual alone.

The idea of leaving home for a time had come slowly and conflicted greatly for a period with other instincts that would not let her relinquish, even for a little while, her beloved island. But she had felt strongly the urge to do something useful in wartime and notions of patriotism and feelings of superfluity continued to grow till eventually she had sailed away from Rhanna, a slender girl, not quite eighteen, wearing her uniform pinned with the Cross of St Andrew.

Now she had been ordered to take some leave: she had thrown herself into the job with such dedication she was physically exhausted. The leave had come unexpectedly, giving her just enough time to dash off a letter to Niall, who was at a college in Glasgow training to be a vet. At thought of Niall and of the letter she gave a little start of dismay. She had written the letter in great haste but had she remembered to post it? A rummage through her handbag revealed almost instantly that she hadn't and guilt raged through her. She loved him very dearly and her joy at returning to Rhanna was tinged with sadness that he wasn't here to share the holiday with her. What would he think of her for writing letters that she didn't post on time? At this very moment he would be thinking she was still working away in Aberdeenshire when all the time she was sailing over the sea to Rhanna. It had been a pact of theirs always to let the other know exactly where they would be so that each could think of the other in that particular setting.

Shona's friend, Babbie Cameron, came swaying over the deck towards her. Babbie was not a good sailor and despite the calm crossing had suffered from seasickness for most of the journey. As a result her normally glowing face was a sickly white colour, though nothing could take away the dazzling bright sheen of the sunlight on her red hair. Nor could it completely quench the sparks of mischief in those green, amber-flecked eyes that had the translucent look of a clear sea freckled with seaweed. They were odd eyes, dreamily masking a million secrets, yet they sparkled with soft lights of laughter and kindness. Babbie was five years older than Shona and though they had known each other only a short time, they were already firm friends. It was unusual for Shona, who had never been one for girlfriends. Most of her childhood had been spent playing with boys, especially Niall, and as a result she had always been something of a tomboy. She got on well with men; with them there were no petty little jealousies or frivolous gossip such

13

as she had sometimes encountered with girls. But Babbie was different. She was sensible, honest and great fun to be with.

When Shona had first started her nurse's training with the St Andrew's Ambulance Corps, Babbie had taken her under her wing, always ready with helpful advice yet never too superior about it. Yet despite her open honesty and frank remarks, there was something very mysterious about Babbie. She was reticent about her private life, both past and present, yet this very enigmatic side to her only made Shona like her more. She felt that there was always something that was going to be new about Babbie, no matter how long she might know her.

'Haven't you found your sea legs yet?' Shona chuckled. 'If Canty Tam saw you now he would say you were a Uisga Hag – that means a sea witch. I thought I'd better warn you about such things now, for you'll hear plenty about them on Rhanna.'

Babbie smiled ruefully. 'A sick witch might be more apt. I can always tell people that instead of sailing to the Hebrides I spewed my way across.' She looked at the letter fluttering in her friend's hand. 'Is this you throwing guilty secrets into the sea?'

'Och, Babbie, I'm a silly bitch right enough! This is the letter I wrote to Niall and just remembered I'd forgotten to post. What will he think of me posting letters from Rhanna that ought to have been posted from Aberdeen? It's not as if things were all that good between us just now, certainly not good enough to allow mistakes like this.'

Babbie eyed her friend thoughtfully. Shona was a stunningly beautiful girl, delicate and slender with huge blue eyes and a thick mass of naturally waving auburn hair. Sometimes she looked like a small girl who had lost her way in a dark wood and didn't quite know how to get out of it again. She was looking like that now, tremulous and forlorn, yet the proud tilt of her head was defying pity or well-meant advice.

A few minutes of silence passed while the gulls wheeled and screamed above the ship's funnels and a crate of chickens covered by a tarpaulin clucked morosely in a corner. Nearby was a jumble of mail bags, paraffin drums and a mountain of coal which would keep the Rhanna folk supplied for two months or more.

'This Niall of yours,' Babbie said carefully, breaking the stillness, 'you've told me often enough how much you love him, yet . . . you also hint that things are not as they should be between you. It's none of my business I know but – '

'Ay, you are quite right, Babbie,' Shona interrupted angrily, 'it is none of your business. I'll have enough of the Rhanna folk prying into my affairs without you starting as well!'

'I'm sorry, really,' Babbie said turning away. 'I was always too outspoken. My sister was forever giving me rows for it. Forget I mentioned Niall and . . . everything.'

Shona was immediately sorry for her outburst and she gripped Babbie's hand tightly. 'Och, I'm the one who needs forgiveness . . . by a lot of people I love most. My temper always lets me down. Father says it's a family failing, and how right he is. All my life I've had to fight it and just when I think I've won, it comes right back at me and hits me between the eyes. I do want to talk about Niall . . . and before we get to Rhanna there's something I have got to tell you or nosy old Behag or one of her cronies will tell you for me. I've kept putting it off because I didn't know what you'd think of me . . . innocent little Shona McKenzie with a past as black . . . as black as that coal there! Oh God! If only it was possible to wind the clock right back!'

Babbie looked slightly uncomfortable. 'Shona, you don't have to tell me anything, we all have our secrets and the right to keep them as such. I won't listen to Behag or anyone else for that matter. You can trust me.'

The anger in Shona's blue eyes changed to a look of tenderness. 'I know that, Babbie. That's one of the things I like most about you. But I want to tell you . . .' She looked out to the sea and her knuckles turned white as she gripped the rail. 'I have to talk to someone and I hope – when you've heard all the gory details you'll still want to be my friend.'

She took a deep breath and gazed unseeingly over the glistening blue reaches of the Sound of Rhanna which they were just approaching.

'Last summer, just about the time of the Dunkirk evacuations . . . I . . . gave birth to a baby . . . a little boy, Niall's son. Niall was in France at the time and I thought he was dead. We got word from the War Office that he had gone missing, presumed to be killed . . . and I ran and ran over the Muir of Rhanna to a cave, our cave, Niall's and mine. No one could find me, they searched all day and all night. During the search my little dog, Tot, died trying to find me. That may seem a trivial thing to you but oh God how I loved that dear little spaniel with her wee pot belly and her white muzzle! I got her as a present for my fifth birthday and we grew up together. She died and my little boy died . . . was born dead . . . and all because of my stupidity. If I hadn't run away he might be alive now, but I thought Niall was dead, you see, and I couldn't bear to think about that, didn't believe it really, but of course I was living in a child's world, trying to pretend that things weren't true when they were going on all around me. I did it when Mirabelle died and when Father lost his arm and I did it again when I was giving birth to a tiny baby boy with Niall's fair hair and Niall's life inside him . . . And the guilt inside me is all the worse for knowing that I made Niall make love to me before he went away to France. I thought he might never come back and I wanted something that was his to hold on to! I made a mess of everything and I feel so guilty all the time. The lovely things I had with Niall, the innocence, the freedom of the carefree love we had between us – all has been ruined because of me. We were children together, before . . . before I turned it all upside down and now I can't look at Niall without feeling soiled, without feeling that our love has been ruined. I still love him, there never has been nor ever will be anyone else yet . . . oh, I can't understand it myself . . . but I don't want to let him kiss me or touch me or even *look* at me too closely because I think he's looking at me with accusation in his eyes. Och, he's not of course but I just *feel* he is and until I get rid of that from my mind then . . . things can never be the same between us.'

The tears were pouring unheeded down her face now and her breath came out in shuddering sobs. In a great rush of compassion Babbie took her into her arms and stroked her burnished hair. 'There, there now, have a good greet, it's the first step to healing that proud little heart of yours. I'm glad that you told me, if only to unburden yourself a bit . . . and I'm honoured to be your friend. Things will come right between you and Niall. I know they will, it will just take time, that's all. Here, take my hanky and give your nose a right good blow. It's my best linen one so don't blow *too* hard!'

Shona obediently blew and even managed a smile at Babbie's typically nonsensical words. 'Och, Babbie, it's me that's honoured to have *you* for a friend,' she said with a watery sniff. 'It's a good job we're the only ones at this side of the rails or I would have given more than just you a free show. I'm sorry for being such a crybaby but I feel a lot better, better than I did a whily back anyway. Here's your hanky back and don't worry, I'll wash it with my very own fair hands when we get home to Laigmhor.' She looked quizzically at Babbie and said hesitantly, 'I've talked a lot about myself and you've listened even though you look greener than a green Uisga Caillich. What about you, Babbie? I get this funny wee feeling that you hold yourself back all the time. You laugh a lot and talk a lot of daft nonsense but I think . . . the real you is hiding about somewhere under all the surface things.'

Babbie waved an airy hand. 'Ach, you and your funny wee feelings. I've already told you I was brought up in an orphanage in Argyll and that's all there is to it! Nothing exciting about my background at all.'

Shona's gaze held Babbie's for a long time before Babbie looked away with feigned interest at a seagull strutting over the deck. 'Maybe it was at the orphanage that you learned to hold yourself back,' Shona said softly. 'For you do it all the time, Babbie Cameron. I am not the only one to be sewing

17

myself up and throwing away the scissors, as Mirabelle used to say.'

They both laughed and Babbie said gladly, 'Well, thank goodness, a Mirabelle saying from you means we're going to get away from all this serious talk. You invited me back to Rhanna with you for a rest, remember? And a rest I mean to have with a few of these ceilidhs you talk so much about and a crack or two with all those marvellous characters you've talked yourself blue in the face about ever since I met you.'

She pointed suddenly over the water. 'Look, isn't that Rhanna? It certainly looks like your description of it.'

A blurred mass of blue mountains had appeared on the horizon and Shona laughed aloud with pure joy. 'Yes, that's Rhanna! That's Rhanna! I told you it was beautiful, didn't I?' She had spread her arms wide as if to embrace the distant island to her breast and in her moments of surging happiness her face was a glowing cameo, full of childish delight and unrestrained love. It was the part of Shona that was best known to those who knew her best, an untamed wild spirit that had roamed free through the solitary wide spaces of her childhood. It was the part of Shona least known to Babbie, but now Babbie knew that she was witnessing the emergence of the real Shona. She felt the mood washing into her and despite the fact that a crowd of passengers had come round to watch the island looming nearer she too spread her arms to the heavens and shouted, 'Yes, yes, Rhanna *is* beautiful! The loveliest Hebridean island in the world!'

'Ach, you are a daft pair o' lassies right enough!' grinned one of the crewmen who was fiddling nearby with the ropes. 'It is a well-known fact that Barra has the rest of them beat. You can ask anyone that.'

'And is it not yourself who spends more time on Rhanna than anywhere else, Malcolm McKinnon?' Shona dimpled mischievously.

'Well now, and that is only because most of my brothers were daft enough to go and get themselves married to Rhanna lassies. A man has to go where his relatives are, indeed just.'

18

At the harbour of Portcull there was the usual air of restrained excitement whenever a boat came in. Men shouted instructions to each other, small boys darted to catch the ropes, chickens clucked, sheep bleated, engines churned the water till the waves foamed and slopped against the pier.

Shona's eyes raked through the throng on the jetty and almost immediately she spotted her father's jet-black head among the rest. 'Father!' she cried ecstatically though she knew he couldn't possibly hear her above the general din. But as soon as the gangplank was lowered she flew downwards like a young deer, almost colliding with Erchy the Post on his way up to collect the mail. 'Erchy, the very man! Would you put this letter into the outgoing mailbags for me? I forgot to post it on the mainland.'

'Indeed I will just,' Erchy grinned, glancing at the address with the usual curiosity displayed by the islanders. 'To young Niall, eh? 'Tis surprised I am you weren't after delivering it to him in person. It will be a whily now before he gets it.'

'Yes – I do know that, Erchy, and feeling bad enough about it as it is so don't you go rubbing salt into the wound.'

Erchy scratched his sandy head with a stubby finger and gave an apologetic grin. 'Ach well, I'll put it into the bag right away but don't ever say a word to old Behag or we'll never hear the end of it for she would have you goin' through all the palaver of postin' it proper in the pillar box an' then have me pickin' it up . . . mind you . . .' he rubbed his square chin thoughtfully, 'I'd say she has been so taken up wi' the contraption this whily back that she has no' been up to her usual sniffin' about like a starving bloodhound.'

'The contraption?' Shona exclaimed, puzzled.

'Ay, a radio thing wi' tubes sproutin' everywhere an' enough bits o' wire to make a fence round my vegetable garden . . . But look now, I have no time for idle bletherin'. You'll hear all about the contraption in good time. It's nice to see you home again, lass . . . and . . .' he gave a shy, sidelong glance at Babbie.

'My friend, Babbie Cameron,' Shona said quickly.

19

'Pleased to meet you indeed, Miss Cameron.'

'Just call be Babbie. Better to be informal from the start.'

Erchy looked at Babbie's exceedingly comely figure and his eyes gleamed. 'Ay well, right enough now, I'm no' a body for all this polite way o' doin' things myself. I'll be seein' you around then . . . Babbie.'

Shona was already at the foot of the gangplank struggling her way through people and a collection of horses and carts that had assembled at the pier to collect the coal and other items from the boat. Soon she spotted her father's black head bobbing and beside it the fair one of Kirsteen.

'Father!' Shona threw herself at Fergus and he laughed through the smother of auburn hair against his face.

'Hey, steady on. I'm just about choking to death and there's a whole lot of people gawping at us.'

'Ach, to hell with people!' Shona cried gleefully. She turned from her father to hug Kirsteen to her then she stood back to survey them both. They were a handsome pair with Kirsteen's corn-coloured hair a startling contrast to Fergus's jet-black locks. His sideburns were almost white but this only added to his powerful attractiveness. Kirsteen looked small and very feminine beside him, her fine-featured face alive with pleasure at seeing Shona. She had such a look of deep contentment in her blue eyes that Shona felt a sudden rush of gladness in the knowledge that the look sprang from the fulfilment that Kirsteen had with her father.

Fergus surveyed his daughter's pinched little face and said gruffly, 'It's just as well you're home for a time. You could do with a bit of fattening up.'

Babbie came struggling towards then, laden down with luggage. 'You left me to carry all this,' she accused Shona. 'You ought to know I'm far too lazy to enjoy such punishment forbye the fact I'm supposed to be here for a well-earned rest.'

'Oh, I'm sorry, Babbie,' Shona said with an apologetic grin. 'I was in such a hurry to get down to these two. This is my fa—'

Babbie held up her hand. 'I know who they are. God, girl,

20

you've described them to me so often I see black-haired men and golden-haired maidens dancing in my dreams.' She stretched out a friendly hand. '*I'm* Babbie Cameron and I can only hope to heaven you got Shona's letter telling you you were about to have an unexpected guest. She has a habit of forgetting to post minor little things like letters!'

Kirsteen laughed. 'Short notice but enough to allow me to air the spare room and beg a pheasant from Robbie Beag.'

Fergus extended a cautious hand. He was always very aware of his missing left arm when first introduced to strangers, but he needn't have worried about Babbie. She took his hand, and shaking it warmly said, 'Now if we had both been left-handed this might have been a bit awkward, but we're not so it isn't and I'm very pleased to meet you, Mr McKenzie.'

The ludicrous statement put Fergus immediately at ease. Babbie had brought his disability straight into the open and looking at her steady green gaze and generous smiling mouth he knew that here was one girl who would never be accused ot beating about the bush.

A small figure detatched itself from a snowy-haired gnome sitting on the harbour wall and Grant Fergus came racing to throw himself at Shona though he was careful to check the immediate vicinity to make sure that no young male companions were there to witness such a 'cissy' demonstration. His sturdy little arms wound tightly round Shona's neck but for a moment he couldn't say anything. He adored his recently acquired big sister and her leaving Rhanna had caused him a good deal of anguish, though not by one word had he conveyed his feelings to anyone.

Shona felt a swift rush of love flooding into her heart. 'Shouldn't you be in school, you wee wittrock?' she asked breathlessly.

'Old Murdoch let me out for ten minutes seeing you were coming home,' he imparted off-handedly. 'Old Joe was telling me stories till the boat came in and I got so interested I forgot all about you.'

'Well, thanks a lot,' Shona giggled.

21

He looked up at her with dark solemn eyes, the mirror-image of his father's. 'I have to get back now . . . sums. I hate them! I wish I was going out fishing with Ranald . . .' His grubby little hand curled into Shona's and squeezed it tight. 'I'll see you later if I'm not too busy . . .' He threw a laughing glance at Babbie and darted off through the village towards the school.

The others began to move away from the harbour towards Glen Fallan. Shona gazed rapturously at the peaks of Sgurr nan Ruadh and asked, 'Anything new happening on Rhanna? Erchy mentioned something about Behag having some sort of contraption.'

Fergus threw back his head and roared with laughter. 'Ay, you could call it that right enough. Our postmistress is very full of her own importance these days. She is in charge of a wireless transmitter and we all have the feeling that she is just waiting to report some momentous event in order to cover herself in glory.'

Everyone smiled at Fergus's words and Babbie said, 'It might be that this contraption thing will keep her back from all the idle gossip I hear she's so good at.'

'*Nothing* will keep Behag from that,' Shona said fervently.

'And nothing will keep me from the dinner that Kirsteen has spent the last two days preparing in your honour,' Fergus said. 'C'mon, get a move on you two.'

They were a happy throng walking up the winding Glen Fallan road to Laigmhor, which lay amongst the shaggy winter fields where there was nothing but a few early cross-breed lambs to suggest that spring was just waiting to creep slowly out from its long days of slumber. Shona talked and laughed with the others, but all the time her eyes were on the chimneys of Slochmhor in the distance. This was where Niall had lived and she looked towards the house longingly with pain in her eyes.

PART II

CLYDEBANK

March 13th 1941

CHAPTER 2

Young Niall McLachlan slumped over the books which were spread out before him on the table in his cramped little lodging room on the fringes of Clydebank. He had embarked rather adventurously into reading a long chapter on bovine milk fever. With his chin cupped in his hands he plodded on doggedly, occasionally shuddering out an involuntary yawn. His cheery little Glaswegian landlady had just relentlessly filled him with a hearty meal of thick broth followed by an enormous helping of mashed potatoes, fluffy dumplings and mince. 'Ma Brodie', as she was known to young and old alike, was a thrifty soul who could conjure magical meals from apparently very little, the limitations of ration books no obstacle to her culinary prowess.

'How do you do it, mo ghaiol?' Niall had asked once, and she had put a finger to her lips and winked a knowing eye.

'There are wee ways, son, wee ways a body has,' she had said mysteriously and hastened away without enlarging on the subject.

Niall, well aware of the existence of the 'Black Market' but less aware of how it worked, had wondered if this endearing woman could be involved in such a thing. But in the end he had decided it was none of his business because she enriched the lives of those around her with endless kindly gestures. She always seemed to be hastening across the landing with a pot of steaming broth for gentle snowy-haired Miss Rennie whose bony frame suggested a spartan existence. And Mr Maxwell, the cantankerous widower one flight below, also found his life the richer by thick slices of dumpling and other tasty tit-bits. 'It'll be *her* tit-bits *he'll* be after,' Iain Brodie had winked to Niall and roared with laughter at his own ludicrous suggestion.

The Brodies had taken the young, handsome Gael to their

hearts, delighting in his soft lilting tongue, his inherent politeness and his talk of the Hebridean island of Rhanna that was his birthplace. Their only son lay in a distant grave in France, killed in the very battle in which Niall had been wounded, and his heart wept for them and their unspoken suffering. He felt honoured to sleep in Tim's room and to use the things that Tim had used in life.

Undoubtedly Niall was happy living and working in Glasgow and seldom wasted time pining for dear familiar people and places, but occasionally his thoughts would drift, carrying him far over the western seas to Rhanna. It was a place where time itself seemed to stand still and the dour but fun-loving inhabitants retained a child-like innocence in their approach to life. Yet they were a powerful people, full of character and a strength of endurance born through the never-ending battle to reap a living from the harvests of land and sea. In amongst the dust and fumes of city life, Niall often found if difficult to remember the clean, wind-fresh air of Rhanna but sometimes it came to him in the diluted form of memories till he could almost smell the wild sweetness of tossed-heather moors, the nectar of summer fields, the piquant perfume of peat smoke, and, above all, the tang of salty sea. And of course there were the sounds of the Hebrides, the hill sheep bleating from mossy slopes, the ever-present sigh of the Atlantic Ocean, the gentle autumn winds rattling the seed pods of the gorse, heather bees buzzing . . .

Niall's elbows slipped and he sprawled into his heap of books. He'd been at it again, day-dreaming about Rhanna. Lately he seemed to be thinking about it more and more. He dearly longed to see his mother's bonny face, his father's brown eyes lit with a smile, the lively dark-haired nymph who was his little sister, Fiona, already using her feminine wiles to wheedle people round her little finger. But he wasn't sure when next he would be home because as well as being a student at the vet. college he was also a part-time member of Britain's Civil Defence, and with the Germans forever trying to get a foothold on British soil the country was alert and

26

wary. It had been stipulated that anyone in a war-connected service should remain in their own locality.

Although Niall felt that the training he had received in the Regular Army was being put to some use, there were times when he felt a great sense of frustration and an anger against the enemy for rendering him unfit to take an active part in battle. By nature he was a pacifist and didn't believe in marching blindly into a foray for the sake of dying for King and Country. But in the exuberance of youth he felt he was of the stuff that went into one battle after another, always, in the height of his dreams, emerging unscathed and ready to start again. But he had fallen almost before he had begun his posting to Northern France in the autumn of 1939. After that it was only a matter of time before the Allied armies made the withdrawal from Dunkirk.

The horror of Dunkirk often tore his dreams apart till they became nightmares, but his daytime thoughts were even more vivid and real. He remembered now and lived again in the smell of unwashed flesh, the blood and guts pouring from the wounded. No one really knew what was happening, and some were too sickened and dazed to care. Like weary flocks of sheep they had been organized on to various embarkation beaches to await in a terrifying cacophony of noise the boats that were to take them home. Smoke, dust and acrid fumes filled everyone's lungs till it seemed it would be impossible ever to breathe clean air again. Thousands of men had been taken from the beaches but thousands more still had to wait. Moreover the place swarmed with French and Belgian troops and, adding to the congestion, hordes of empty-eyed and hopeless refugees. Niall now watched it all again with a feeling of utter despair. He felt that nothing was being achieved, that the fighting and killing was all in vain. He felt vulnerable and hopelessly inadequate and, seething with passion, knew that he would gladly tear apart a German soldier with his bare hands.

The voice of his mother came to his mind like the rippling little wind of a storm warning: 'How will it feel killing a man, Niall? You that never hurt a living thing in your life?'

He had shuddered then, hating a war that turned ordinary men into savage beasts. And while the hate churned inside him, an explosion rocked the ground nearby. When the smoke and dust cleared he looked round to see one of his comrades dying, blood spewing from a gaping wound in his neck. He was but a boy of eighteen with a light sprinkling of fuzz on his chin and it had worried him that his downy beard wouldn't grow into the wiry stubble of manhood. Lying together in the cold, dark trenches, he and Niall had laughed together as they dreamed up all sorts of ridiculous beard-growing potions. Looking at the round boyish face, Niall knew that the dawn would never break again for a life so young.

The youngster, nicknamed Billy Boy by the older men, shivered as the finger of Death loomed over him. His filthy uniform had been shredded to tatters by the blast, and Niall tore off his own battle-jacket, and pushed Billy Boy's arms into the sleeves in a rough frenzy of fear. 'This will keep you warm, Billy,' he choked harshly, the sob at the back of his throat making his whispers of reassurance sound rough. 'I'll get help, you'll be fine in no time.'

But Billy Boy reached out a smoke-grimed hand to grip Niall's arm. 'Don't – leave me to – die alone. You know there's no help for me now.' A weary smile touched his white lips and he looked up into the smoke-blackened heavens. 'I'll finish off growing my beard up there . . . though . . . I think it won't matter . . . any more.'

The feeble little joke was lost in the wisp of a sigh, and the long curling lashes of a young boy who had fought like a man and was dying like one, closed over eyes from which sight had already departed. In seconds he was gone, his head a dead weight on Niall's arm, the blood of his life still rushing from the hole in his neck. Niall rocked on his heels in an agony of grief but one of the older men came and tore him away. They stumbled along the beach together while above them the air attacks continued, the planes of the German Luftwaffe zooming in and out of the pallid smoke-clouds, dropping bombs with a fiendish certainty that they were bound to hit some target, be it human or otherwise.

Suddenly Niall felt the ground ripping apart and the sound of an explosion coincided with a searing pain in his head. He heard the older man screaming in agony and saw the blood seeping through the fingers held to his eyes. The world was a spinning blur of red, and the agony inside his head made him want to vomit. Before he sank into a thick blanket of nothingness he felt a rush of gladness that it was over and he could forget a world where power-hungry fanatics took away the freedom of peace-loving people.

But, Niall thought, coming back to his present state, it hadn't been over for him. He had lain unconscious in a military hospital in England and no one had known who he was because his identity disc had been blown from his neck and the rest of his personal belongings had been in the jacket he had given Billy. When he had finally come back to the living world he learned that his parents had believed him to be dead and that Shona, his childhood sweetheart, had given birth to a little stillborn son. In the agony of thinking him dead she had stumbled over the Rhanna moors to the place that had been their secret hideout since early childhood. There, near the old Abbey ruins, was *their* cave, set into a heather-clad hillock called Dunuaigh. In it they had placed precious bits and pieces, there they had aired their childish dreams, had argued and laughed the years away till finally, in the passion of their youth, they had loved in a world-spinning union of body and soul. He had taken away her virginity and with it her childhood. She had been just sixteen then, he eighteen, and after the warm sweet days of their intimate loving he had gone away to war leaving his seed in her, a seed that had grown into a tiny son never to know the sweetness of life.

On his return to Rhanna they had both been overwhelmed with the joy of their reunion yet there had been a subtle change in their relationship. They had both suffered in their different ways. His war wound had left him almost totally deaf in one ear, but he could live with that. It was the memories of war he couldn't take. They had changed his peaceful soul into a restless spirit that yearned for revenge, both for himself and Shona whose experiences had robbed her of a lot of her gaiety and spontaneous affection. But it was too late now for regrets, too late to change what had happened . . .

The words on the pages blurred and his head sank on to his chest, the light from the gas mantle turning his hair into threads of gold. Under the fair strands at his neck stretched the tightly-drawn tissue of an ugly scar which split the curve at the base of his skull and distorted the delicate lobe of his left ear. Slowly he lifted his head and looked at the picture of Shona on the dresser. It had been taken during the Indian summer days of their breathless loving when she had still been a child. The picture was in black-and-white but he could see it in vivid colour; her slim, graceful body draped over a sun-warmed stone amidst the heather, the blue of her dress against the blue October sky, her long auburn hair vying with the bronze of the bracken . . . and her eyes, those incredible blue eyes of hers, filled with the love of life. He got up to snatch the photo to his breast, his thoughts carrying him away again, back to the cave on the Muir of Rhanna where first she had given her lovely body to him. He could see it now, the whiteness of it against the creamy wool of the sheepskin rug, her hair spread out in fiery strands, her eyes full of child-like innocence . . . until he had taken it away from her . . .

Since then she had once made a brief visit to Glasgow but she had been uneasy and out of place in the bustling city. Her discomfort had made him feel awkward and unnaturally polite, while deep down inside he had felt love and sadness churning themselves together. His proud, spirited lass had looked like a timid rabbit caught out of its burrow and he had known that she couldn't wait to get back on the train which would carry her away from smoke and noise and return her to green fields and purple mountains. But at the station he had taken her in his arms to kiss her and she had melted against him, her tongue touching his, and for a brief moment they had been, in spirit, lying on a bed of heather on the Muir of Rhanna, the bees buzzing in a frantic gathering of nectar, the sheep bleating from the wild summer mountains.

But then a nearby train had released a hideous bellow of impatient steam and they had jumped apart, the precious moment lost, and a few minutes later, her face hovering forlornly at the window, she was gone from him in a busy huffing and puffing and clattering of pistons.

The memories engulfed him so entirely that he forgot his studies, turned down the gas mantle and went to the window to pull aside the thick blackout drapes. A pale moon rode brilliantly in the vast spaces of the universe. He could picture it hanging over the Sound of Rhanna, weaving a pathway of rippling light over the deep Atlantic waters. He wondered how it would look to Shona in the grandeur of Aberdeenshire. Was she perhaps at this very moment peeping from her window to see the silvered ribbon of the Dee winding down through the glens . . . perhaps thinking of him as he was of her even while she looked at the sloping shoulders of the Grampians outlined against the sky?

The only things outlined for him were monotonous rows of houses with stack upon stack of chimney pots rising in the sharp silhouette of urban starkness. The long reaches of the Clyde estuary were hidden from his view by streets of tenement buildings. The subdued murmer of town life reached up from the street below. A dog howled unharmoniously with a wailing baby in the flat above. Somewhere in the backcourts a dustbin lid clattered and feline yowls of outrage followed as a well-aimed tackity boot found its mark. From the kitchen came the indistinct murmur from the wireless. Ma Brodie made a point of listening to the 9 o'clock news every night on the BBC Home Service. He knew she would be ensconced cosily by the range, her stockings rolled to her ankles, nursing one of the many cats which frequently adopted the house. Every so often she would murmur 'ay' by way of sympathy for the things that people were having to suffer in wartime.

Niall's reverie was broken by the thin wail of the air-raid sirens which suddenly pervaded the house. Ma Brodie raised her voice to shout, 'Would you listen to that! These poor souls in London are getting it bad. The sound of the siren is even coming through on the news!' Out of the blue, the Brodies' large ginger tom, known in the neighbourhood as Ginger Moggy, appeared in Niall's doorway, his fur on end and his green eyes narrowed to slits. He glared at Niall, his nostrils aflare with fright, and then shot under the bed to crouch there, howling and spitting. The sight of the terrified animal triggered Niall into action, for he realized that the sirens were not coming through the radio but were sounding in the immediate vicinity. Quickly he donned his coat and tin helmet and snatched up the case containing his gas mask. Outside on the landing there was a low murmur of voices and the sound of one of two doors banging on the landings above, but Niall knew that many of the residents of his building would not go down to the shelter. The experience of previous alerts had taught him that many of the residents would simply huddle under anything they considered might keep them safe, unwilling to leave the deceptive security of their homes.

Ma Brodie was in the lobby clutching a huge suitcase in which she kept her most personal documents. Her best coat and Iain's Sunday suit were still on their hangers, draped over her arm. She was always thus prepared for an air raid. 'C'mon, son,' she said stoically. 'I have everything that means anything to Iain and myself. If anything happens . . .' she paused for a moment, her thoughts on her husband out on fire-fighting duty. 'Ach, but it won't, it will likely just be another false alarm. I'd best get over to Miss Rennie and see if the auld scunner is hiding under her bed again.'

Niall went back to his room, grabbed Shona's picture and stuffed it into his gas mask case. As a last thought he reached under the bed for howling Ginger Moggy and bundled him inside his roomy coat. Ma Brodie was on the landing helping tottering old Miss Rennie downstairs. But the old lady was loath to go.

'Joey, I must take Joey with me,' she protested. Joey was Miss Rennie's talkative budgie and the wailing sirens had excited him greatly. Boisterous cries of 'Mammy's pretty boy!' echoed from Miss Rennie's flat, and Ginger Moggy stirred in the depths of Niall's coat. Viciously, he clawed at Niall's chest till he was free, and bounded with a triumphant flick of his bushy tail through Miss Rennie's door.

'Joey!' the old lady cried and broke away from Ma Brodie to totter unsteadily back into the flat.

Niall was feeling uneasy. It was his duty as an Air Raid Warden to make sure that everyone was in safe cover, and something told him that tonight's alert signalled the real thing. Ma Brodie was seeing to Miss Rennie once more, so Niall bounded upstairs to check on the others before going off to his post. The top flats were empty but for one. Inside, sprawled in a shabby armchair, was Blackie O'Riordan, renowned for his drinking bouts and subsequent brushes with the law. He was drunk now, an almost-depleted bottle of cheap wine hanging precariously on the end of his fingers. At sight of Niall the slits of his eyes widened in glazed recognition.

'Young Niall! All dressed up like a soldier! Will you be havin' a drink with me?' Without replying, Niall yanked him to his feet.

'Will you stop pullin' at me!' Blackie yelled.

'C'mon now,' Niall said persuasively. 'The sirens are howling like blazes.'

'Up the sirens! I don't give a damn. Let the bloody Nazis fly about all night for all I care. I hate the bastards! They shot me out the stinking war but it'll take more than the crap Luftwaffe to chase me out my own house!'

Niall pushed his shoulder under Blackie's oxter but the brawny Irishman was built like a plough horse and tore himself free. His huge hands flew out and Niall found himself being propelled to the door and all but thrown out on to the landing, after which the lock shot home accompanied by a shower of abuse.

Finding himself alone on the landing, the blackout

shutters on the windows muffling the sounds of the outside world; the stairs, lit only by the feeble flicker of a gas mantle, eerily deserted; and the high walls seeming to lean ever closer in claustrophobic conspiracy, Niall took the stairs two at a time, anxious to leave behind the ghostly confines. He followed the sound of friendly voices and soon found that everyone had crowded into the stuffy kitchen of the bottom flat because no one particularly favoured the damp brick shelters in the backcourts. Familiar faces wore cheery masks of composure. Gentle little Miss Rennie had the patiently resigned look of her generation, in the midst yet apart from the rest, her frail old arms clasped protectively round Joey's cage on her knee. Niall quickly realized that the stern dissatisfied countenance of Mr Maxwell was missing.

'He's maybe went to visit his sister in Dumbarton,' someone suggested, but Niall ran out and back up the steep dark stairs. Bursting into the widower's house he found him comfortably ensconced under the kitchen table, a pillow at his head and a blanket tucked round his bony frame. A little Thermos flask stood conveniently at his elbow together with a large, tea-stained Queen Victoria Coronation mug.

'I'm stayin',' he told Niall bluntly. 'I'm no' goin' down to that house with everybody reekin' o' sweat and smokin' like lums.' At that moment the softly insidious drone of the first wave of German night-raiders wafted into the room. Niall cocked his good ear upwards and Mr Maxwell put a horny hand to one of his large lugs, moulding it into a wrinkled trumpet. 'They're comin',' he said incredulously. 'It's for real right enough.'

'Ma Brodie has dumpling and pancakes downstairs,' Niall said in a persuasive rush.

'Ach, all right, anything for a bit peace . . . but mind now, if that auld Jennie Rennie and her damt budgie are down there I'm for comin' back up.' He crawled stiffly from under the table and allowed Niall to assist him downstairs and into the crowded kitchen.

Despite everything, the inconvenience, the apprehension, it was a jolly company. The teapot was already to the fore and Ma Brodie was cutting thick slices of juicy dumpling. She slipped a generous portion into a bag and pushed it at Niall. 'Eat this when you have a meenit, son,' she ordered sternly. Then her face relaxed into a warm smile and she gripped his hand tightly. 'Take care, my laddie, the tea will be on the stove when you get back. You're like my own son . . . remember that.'

He stooped to hug her briefly, sensing her unspoken fears. 'Don't worry about me . . . or Iain. He can take care of himself.' At the utterance of the words a strange fear gripped his heart. He looked at Ma Brodie's smiling, kindly little face and on an impulse he stooped to kiss her check. 'Take care, Ma,' he said softly and then turned to abandon the warmth of the kitchen for the cold black streets. There, anonymous shadows flitted, felt rather than seen. The dark shape of a baffle wall loomed and he stopped for a moment to lean against it and to look up into a sky torn apart by the furring vapour-trails of the German bombers. The ragged silhouette of the town was already sharpened by the orange glow of fires. High explosives were falling in the lower parts of town, and fountains of smoke and flames licked into the sky. He watched the planes tearing past, small dots thousands of feet above, divorced from the earth by the power of engines, yet so easily able to tear it apart by the force of explosives. Panic closed in on him. It was here! It was real! No need now to go to war, it had come to him and to thousands like him. Incendiaries were raining down. One landed at the close entrance and he dashed foward to kick it away then he began to race towards his post. His thoughts were bitter, and the nerve-shattering experience of Dunkirk came to mind again in vivid snatches. Smoke and acrid fumes made his eyes smart with tears but they were also tears of anger at the destruction and grief that he knew the German Luftwaffe would leave in its wake. 'Nazi swine,' he murmured softly, the words, spoken in his lilting tongue, full of an uncharacteristic hatred in a boy who had never hated anyone in his life.

CHAPTER 3

The shower of incendiaries that came spitting out from the planes of the Luftwaffe, Third Air Fleet, were profuse enough for some to find their way into inflammable areas of industrial sites. The black spaces of the surrounding open fields pushed the orange flames into a giant torch which greedily began to devour the little town and spread thin curls of oil-laden smoke eddying through the streets. Another wave of bombers was arriving from the east, bearing down like evil birds of prey against the cold, pale sky. Within seconds they were dropping altitude and more bombs were falling, together with parachute mines, allowing no time for people in the target-area to sort out one thought, one fear, from the other. Enormous craters split the tarmac, blowing water mains and gas mains to smithereens. Because three Auxiliary Fire Service Stations had been put out of action earlier in the evening, the problem of dealing with the Clydebank inferno was overwhelming. Many of the hydrants were dry and the firefighters were driven to use the muddy water filling the craters.

Niall, working with a rescue party clearing the debris of a crushed tenement that had received a direct hit from a 500-kilo bomb, had lost his gas mask. He breathed in choking dust and hot smoke till his lungs were raw. Someone pushed a dirty hanky at him. 'Here, tie this over your face or we'll end up rescuing you!' Quite unexpectedly they had come upon a pile of battered corpses that were so twisted and bloody it was difficult to believe they were people. From out of the heap of dead flesh a terrified voice cried for help and they extricated a young woman, pulling at her arms as gently as they could, trying to ease her free from the ensnaring bodies that held on to her legs like the sucking mud of a bog. 'She's the only one in this lot,' said one of the men. 'Dear Jesus! There's dozens of them gone!'

A squad of rescue workers raced up, filthy spectres with reddened eyes and pale lips showing through the grime. 'The next street!' panted one. 'We need some hands!'

Niall ran, and somehow he knew, even before he turned the corner, that the place he called 'home' in Glasgow was no more. All of the façades of the buildings on his street had been sheared off as if someone had taken a giant axe and split bricks and mortar down through the centre. The portions of the front walls which had been blown away ludicrously exposed all the little domesticities of family life. In one kitchen an elderly couple were seated at the table as if about to eat supper. They had been killed by a bomb-blast which had left them whole but sucked all the air from their lungs.

Two houses along to the right, underneath the great mound of smouldering debris, were buried all the people whom Niall had helped to 'safety' just a few hours before. Old Mr Maxwell's table stood sturdy and intact amidst its humble surroundings. In the kitchen above, Miss Rennie's rocking chair sat by the jagged ruins of the range. On the mantelshelf china plates remained unbroken, on the smashed hearth a plaster dog lay on its side, its painted eyes staring out from the ruins. The Brodies' bedroom lay fully exposed to the elements. All the furniture was intact but the bed mat had flipped upwards to drape over the wardrobe and a lamp shade hung from a brass bed knob on the bed end. Eerie sights, made spine-chillingly macabre by the curious whims of blast.

Blackie O'Riordan stood at the edge of his kitchen on the top flat, waiting to be rescued. A torrent of abuse, directed at the bombers in the vaults of the heavens, drowned out the instructions of the rescue squad.

Some of the dead had been blown into the air and had landed so far from where they'd first been struck it seemed they might have been dropped from the sky. They littered the road like broken dolls, arms and legs twisted beneath them. But had they been dead when they were blown into the air? That was the question that drummed into Niall's brain as he stared around him in disbelief. He looked at a crumpled ball of orange fur lying on the cracked pavement and realized it was Ginger Moggy stretched in a pool of his own blood, his lips drawn back over his fangs in a grimace. He had suffered a painful death. Above him, alive by some freakish escape, Joey perched on a crazily-leaning lampost, feebly muttering 'Good-night Mammy! Mammy's pretty boy.'

Miss Rennie's broken body was being lifted from the rubble, the jagged spars of Joey's cage embedded in her chest. Light pink bubbles of lung-blood oozed out of the little holes.

Half-sobbing, Niall ran to the heap of masonry and began to tear at it with the strength and blindly unthinking rage of a bull. Voices roared at him to be careful and several pairs of hands tried to pull him away but he shook them off and went on with his demented searching. There was no whimper of life from the piled rubble, nothing to tell him that a soul still breathed. He found Ma Brodie quite suddenly. Her eyes were open, gazing up at him out of the debris.

'Help me get her out!' he shouted desperately, but the other men were already pushing aside lumps of jagged stone, carefully freeing what was left of Nellie Brodie's diminutive frame. The teapot was still clutched in her hand, and fragments of a teacup were embedded into the flesh of her arm like crazed paving. Her rib cage had been smashed, and splinters of bone stuck through the gay, flowery apron Niall had given her at Christmas. It was soaked in blood which had congealed quickly in the powdered dust and crushed brick that had caved in on top of her.

'Ma Brodie – mo ghaoil,' Niall whispered brokenly and gently closed her eyes. He knelt beside her, too shocked to move. Deep within the crazily strewn heap of glass and masonry there came an almost imperceptible little sob. Holding his breath he cocked his good ear and it came again – the stifled ghost of a human voice. 'Someone's alive in here!' he called to the long line of men who were expertly shifting rubble in the fashion of a human conveyor belt. They scrambled towards him and carefully began the arduous task of rescue. An hour later they came upon a small boy, so petrified he was unable to move or speak, his life saved by a massive beam that had jammed above him to form a wedge-shaped tunnel. Niall was slim and agile yet neither he, nor any of the other men there, were able to wriggle in through the narrow gap.

'Haud on, I'll get in there.' Johnny Favour, named so because he was always willing to lend a helping hand, appeared at Niall's elbow.

'Johnny! I thought you were having a night with Shirley Temple!' Niall grinned, feeling a great sense of unaccountable relief at seeing Johnny's familiar, friendly face. He had changed his creased tweeds for a rather shiny navy-blue three-piece suit with a watch chain hanging from the pocket of his waistcoat. But he still wore his battered cap as proudly as a king might wear a crown.

'I left the wife at the La Scala,' he explained cheerfully. 'She'll be safe there and I'll be better use here.' He squirmed out of his jacket and handed it to Niall. 'Guard it wi' your life, son, it's my best. I'll get in beside the bairn and try to hand him out.' He disappeared in through the small opening, and a moment later his voice floated out. 'I'll need help, the lad canny move. I'll start making the hole bigger from this side. We'll shore it up with some bits of wood.'

Fifteen minutes later Niall was able to crawl in beside Johnny. The child lay in a bed of suffocating dust. He was a ghostly little figure with his face and hair coated in white plaster but Johnny was saying things that made him laugh and one side of his face bulged with toffee from Johnny Favour's trouser pocket. His legs were pinned under a lump of concrete but he showed no pain and Johnny whispered to Niall, 'At a guess I'd say the poor wee bugger's legs are crushed. I'd be a lot happier if he was greetin'. Then we'd know he was feeling something. C'mon, let's get to work.'

The job of freeing the child was painfully slow but eventually his torn and bleeding limbs were exposed. Both men knew the child would never walk again.

'Sod it!' Johnny drew a grimy hand across his face. 'Sod the bloody lot of them!'

A First Aid party had arrived. One peered through the opening. 'Can you get him out to us? We've got an ambulance waiting.'

'Pass us a blanket,' Johnny said tonelessly. 'He's shivering a bit.' They wrapped the child carefully and then, at Johnny's insistence, tucked the shiny navy-blue jacket round the small shoulders. 'You're a wee man now, son,' Johnny grinned down at the boy's pale face. 'And just to prove it . . .' he whipped off his battered cap and placed it on the child's head. 'There you are. It's maybe no' much to look at but it'll keep your brains warm.'

The little boy peeped out from the peak that came over his eyebrows. 'Ta, Johnny. I'll wear it when I'm playin' football – well, when I'm doing my goalie. Goalies always wear a cap.'

'You do that, lad,' Johnny said. 'Get going now. You get out first, Niall. Take his shoulders.'

In a short time Niall was placing the boy into the arms of the First Aid party who bore him quickly away. Niall felt dizzy with relief. At least one small life had survived the holocaust, but what of the others? The boy's parents? Old Mr Maxwell with his little Thermos flask and his assurances that he would be safe under the kitchen table. He would still be alive if he had stayed there! And Ma Brodie! The dear, big-hearted warmth of such a wee body – dead – and for what? He remembered the teapot still clutched in her hand, a symbol of a life that had cared unstintingly for everyone she met. What of Iain Brodie? Coming back exhausted from the fires. Back to what? His wife, his memories, all gone forever in a senseless waste of everything that made life tick sweetly for the average home-loving man.

The ground trembled suddenly and the tunnel from which Johnny was just emerging caved in. He made no sound as he was first smothered in dust and then crushed under the tons of rubble that came down on top of him. When it finally settled there was no whisper of life and the men knew that Johnny had performed his last favour.

Niall's mind was going numb with shock. He stared at the

dull gleam of Johnny's watch chain caught among the bricks, and everything swam in a watery mist. The rescue squad were telling him to get out of the danger area but he barely heard. He was thinking of the senseless waste of good lives. Just a short time ago some faceless nonentity had pressed a button and a bomb had dropped. The mind that guided the hand would forget quickly each press of the button, giving no concrete thought to the agony and grief invoked by just the flick of a finger.

If Niall's own thoughts had been more rational, if he hadn't been so emotionally exhausted, he would doubtless have exercised more care in his movements. But his tiring feet were clumsy and he slipped on loose masonry. The beam that had saved the child dislodged from its precarious hold and came toppling down towards him. He tried to struggle upright but couldn't and in a mesmerized trance he saw the whole thing in slow motion and lay helplessly, waiting for the blackness to engulf him. Hefty arms grabbed at him, dragging him away from the deadly hail of bricks and glass, but they weren't quick enough, and the beam pinned his right arm into a bed of plaster, close to the spot where only minutes before a small boy had lain, too frozen with terror to do more than whimper like a lost puppy.

CHAPTER 4

Carl Zeitler, the pilot of one of twelve Heinkel bombers of Bomber Squadron IKG3, rocked gleefully in his seat. He squinted down through the Plexiglass panels of the gun cupola to the pink glow where the incendiaries and the rapid flashes of the H.E. bombs had split enormous craters in the ground and turned the little burgh of Clydebank into a raging inferno.

The rest of the group were heading back to base; but Zeitler, in a gluttony of excitement, was taking the risk of making one more bombing run over the burning town. With skilled airmanship he steeply turned the lumbering bomber for a triumphant sweep above the murky clouds of smoke. The feeling of power was strong within him, and the rhythmic throb of the Junker's Jumo 211 twin engines seemed to beat right into his heart, giving him a confident sense of security. He was an excellent pilot and, though he was barely twenty-five, already had an exemplary career behind him. He had brought his plane safely over Scapa Flow, Narvik and Dunkirk, with little more than some superficial damage to show for it. True, on one occasion his navigator had been peppered with flak and he had flown back to base with the dying man's cries of agony filling the plane. Another time he had lost his rear gunner. No one had known he was dead till the ground crew had slid open the rear door and were bathed in the blood that gushed from the holes in the gunner's face. Dunkirk! The remembrance of it always made Zeitler smile. All those stupid bastards strung out on the beaches like flies on a wall! Just asking to be picked off! He must have wiped out dozens of them. The French had been beaten and the Allied British had taken to their heels with their tails well tucked between their legs.

Even as he turned to make the final sweep over Clydebank Zeitler felt echoes of the thrill Dunkirk had given him. His very bones shivered with delight and he threw back his wedge-shaped head in an arrogant smile. But anger mingled with his pleasure, anger at the British for still managing to remain on their toes despite the concentrated blitz. Europe had gone under like a drowning dog! All except the bulldog British. Despite the hammering they had taken those proud, clever bastards were still keeping their heads above water. For someone like Zeitler, tuned in to Hitler's wavelengths like a well-programmed robot, the pill was a bitter one to swallow. Deep in his heart he admired the cool-headed British for their fighting spirit and their admirable allegiance to the British Premier, Winston Churchill. There was a leader for you! A good soldier too, experienced in the fields of both war and politics. But Churchill was the enemy and

42

Zeitler's hot-headed fanatical devotion to his own leader, Adolf Hitler, soon blotted out his rare moment of level-headed thinking.

He stared through the Plexiglass. The moon was beautiful, a cold bluish disc hanging in the sky. But Zeitler didn't see it as an object to be admired. It was there in the sky to aid the success of these night attacks. This raid was strange, they had come quite some distance to reach this industrial complex in Scotland. The targets were the docks, shipyards and oil depots. Difficult. The target area was small over this point. The landscape showed a lot of dark patches that were fields. Spasmodic streaks of flak spattered up from the fringes of the town. It was all quite different from the big raids over London and Coventry. These night raids on England had caused terrible havoc, yet still she remained unconquered. The damned place had nearly been blown off the face of the earth but still Britain popped up smiling, each time with a new trick, a new defence, up her voluminous sleeve.

The pilot's thoughts made his pale blue eyes bulge with chagrin. Dark rings under his eyes made him look older than his twenty-five years, and normally the illusion was completed by premature balding, but with his head enveloped in his leather flying helmet the effect was lessened considerably. He removed a large, gloved hand from the control column to adjust his face mask. 'Die Späten answers well, eh, Anton?' Zeitler yelled through the intercom.

Anton Büttger, bomb-aimer and commander of the aircraft, lay belly-down on a foam rubber pad in the nose of the gun cupola. The muscles in his jaw tightened and his keen blue eyes snapped like fire-crackers. He guessed that the reason Zeitler was making the unnecessary fly-over was so that he could gloat. The destruction caused by the raid was pleasing him, exciting his cold, calculating emotions. Whenever bombs smashed into concrete, Zeitler showed his immense pleasure by sucking his breath and rocking his pelvis in a strangely sensual way. Though Anton couldn't see Zeitler from his position, he now heard the familiar sucking

43

sound. During a sortie Zeitler's favoured expression was, 'Don't shit! Hit!', a phrase Anton had heard through the intercom so many times in the last twenty minutes that the young commander couldn't keep back his seething feelings of dislike for the pilot. Zeitler was so completely cast in the mould of so many hot-headed Nazis that he seemed to have no individuality, no character of his own. His personality was about as pleasing as a chunk of cold metal.

'Go now, Zeitler,' Anton ordered. 'Make a mess of this one and your days in the air are numbered.'

Zeitler hunched his shoulders, sucked his breath, and straightened the rudder. Soon the Heinkel was ripping through the cold night sky.

Anton relaxed slightly. He tried not to think of the scene below but couldn't keep the pictures out of his brain: the spilled blood, the cries of terror . . . the moments of death for the women and children. The hearts of the living would be filled with anger, frustration, compassion. He shuddered. It was easy to press the bomb-release button. Too easy. There was no challenge, no feeling that you had achieved something the way you did during air combat. He had joined the Luftwaffe because he loved flying. He had never imagined his career would one day turn sour on him. Up here in the vulnerable position of the gun cupola he always felt a certain measure of unease, often long after a raid was over. The bomb-aimer, and the gunners, perhaps, always had more on their conscience than the pilot. But it might be that not everyone felt as he did. He would rather be at the controls, but Zeitler was the better pilot and was arrogantly aware of the fact, using any opportunity to display his prowess and undermine Anton's authority. In an odd kind of way Anton understood: he was younger than Zeitler, and had only recently taken over command of the plane. Zeitler had made umpteen bombing raids with the usual commander, Willi Schmitt, who had been grounded because of illness. Anton knew you had to fly with someone a long time to get in tune with him.

'We have managed to make a pretty little bonfire!' It was

44

Zeitler again, his lips stretched in a gloating leer which the other couldn't see but could feel. 'Look! Down there, the flames leap high. An oil depot perhaps! Drop the rest of the high Es, Anton. Might as well put them to good use instead of wasting them in the sea!'

Anton didn't answer. His fingers touched the bomb button but he didn't press it immediately. He knew he should. If he didn't lighten the load now he might have to later . . . perhaps in a field, or an open stretch of water . . . or on a little country farm with all the people in bed, unsuspecting, unprepared . . .

He felt very tired. The kind of dull, heavy tiredness that fills the veins with lead instead of blood. When this kind of exhaustion swept over him he remembered things he had thought forgotten: far-off days filled with happiness; small-boy days when his world was of green fields and golden corn; ambitions to be like his farmer father; the dreams of childhood. The grown-up Anton loved aeroplanes. When his father had spoken about cows or horses he had thought about aeroplanes, not so much about their operational functions as of their performance, engine power and attainable height. He thought about diving and banking, the sensation of zipping through lacy cloudbanks to the blue roof of the sky, and then looking down at the clouds drifting lazily over the world. His visions of flying hadn't included war and the personal tragedies it brought, the raids over Berlin in the late summer of 1940.

Late summer . . . his father out in the fields, working on after last light . . . his mother in the kitchen baking the bread for morning, the fragrant smell of it filling the room . . . his two little sisters, asleep upstairs. At least they'd had no time to know the terror his mother had known, buried in the rubble of the kitchen. She had lived for a short while after rescue, his father a few weeks, all because of one bomb, one stray British bomb that had missed the town and fallen on a little country farm . . .

A sob caught in his throat and for a moment he didn't care about the hail of flak that crackled in the air like sparks in the blackened chimney of a cosy farmhouse kitchen . . . 'Take her up, Zeitler!' he said in a slightly breathless voice. 'The searchlights are on us!'

'Did you drop the bombs?'

'Damn the bombs! Get her up!'

The searchlights were criss-crossing into the skies, violating the blue-black reaches. Zeitler throttled forward and the Heinkel responded by gaining height steadily. But still the beams were on them, clinging like leeches to a leg. Something inside the pilot's head, a built-in instinct of impending danger, warned him that this time his conceit had tempted Providence too far. His knuckles tightened on the throttles and he knew an unaccustomed rush of apprehension.

In his place in the gun turret, Ernst Foch, the wireless operator, watched the flak and the searchlights through the Plexiglass fairing. Their time over the target-area was up, and now they would be heading back to base. Every sense in him was alert but thoughts of his family back home in Germany strayed briefly into his head. It had been an eternity since he had last set eyes on his pretty wife, Helga, and his small sturdy son, Franz. He wondered why it was sometimes difficult to remember their faces. Little scraps of dear, familiar things came to mind but the memories did nothing to soothe him. He wondered how long the war would last. Like Zeitler he was devoted to his country. From the age of fourteen he had been a member of Hitler's youth movement, proud to wear his brown uniform and to carry a dagger like a man. His young mind had been very receptive to the Nazi regime, and he had felt part of a glorious system. But the softening influences of a wife and child had dulled his enthusiasm for mass regimentation. He didn't want his son to grow into a puppet with a master-mind controlling his life. It took more than a uniform and a dagger to make a man. There had to come a time when common sense and the need for individuality came to the fore. He wondered about Zeitler up front in the pilot's seat. The man was a brilliant pilot but a mindless fool otherwise. If the Führer ordered every Nazi to burn piss holes in the snow in the sign of the swastika then Zeitler would be the first to open his fly.

Far below, the gun crews on a Polish destroyer, docked in John Brown's for repairs, stood by their ack-ack guns and sent an almost constant barrage of shells tracing upwards to the aircraft caught in the beams of the probing searchlights. The smoke from the fires made visibility difficult though John Brown's shipyard was comparatively free of serious blaze.

Jon Jodl, the lower-rear gunner, lay on his belly near the ventral sliding door, in front of the machine-gun housing. 'Why is Zeitler hanging about?' he thought. 'Get out of it!' He watched the flak shells exploding about him. Down here it was cold but he felt a trickle of sweat running between his shoulder blades. One of those shells was going to pierce the Perspex door or the stressed skin and plating shell at any moment. A tremor passed through his body and somewhere inside his thin frame a tightly coiled knot of nerves made him feel sick.

At 1000 metres, Zeitler sought cover in a massive cumulus cloud, maintaining climb on his blind-flying instrument panel, and the searchlights and the tracers disappeared from view. Jon reached out to the tin can that was jammed between two metal plates and retched miserably into it. He was neither a coward nor a hero and he didn't give a damn about the Führer and his greedy dream to conquer the world. All his life Jon had been plagued by feelings of inadequacy even though he had shown great proficiency in his academic studies. His very appearance was stamped with a studious sagacity, from his thin clever face to his long, tapering musician's fingers. But he had never been 'one of the crowd' and he had always walked alone, though sometimes this introvert nature of his made him deeply unhappy. He had seen the German Luftwaffe as an escape to freedom, a chance to prove to the world he was as much of a man as the next. His big domineering mother had not approved. 'You were not made for such things, my Jon,' she had told him firmly. 'You must continue with your music, it is what you were born for.' But at the first opportunity Jon had taken himself off to an air crew training school. With his natural intellect and manual dexterity he had eventually passed out as an air gunner. The mathematics of airborne shooting had come easily to him, as had the required mastery of gun-assembly and fault-finding and an understanding of the intricate equipment inside an aircraft. All the other boys had wanted to be top pilots but not Jon. What he had chosen to do took courage enough. However, with the coming of war he quickly realized he didn't have the 'guts' to cope with the rigours it brought. His tightly strung nervous system simply couldn't take the strain. After all, his world was in Hamburg with his gentle little henpecked papa and his large, overpowering mamma who was like an indestructible mountain. All his life she had pampered him and he knew now that he wasn't strong enough to break away from her shadow. 'You were not made for such things, my Jon!' Her words echoed emptily inside his head. But it was too late now, there was no turning back. Jon was at breaking-point but tension was such a familiar thing in his life he wasn't aware that his crawling nerves were stretching tighter with every turn of the airscrews.

They flew out of the cloud and back into a criss-cross probe of searchlights. The flak was falling short. The crew breathed sighs of relief and Jon Jodl felt the sweat drying under his helmet. 'Thank you, my God in Heaven,' he prayed childishly and shut his eyes in gratitude. Another raid, another test of nerves was over for a while.

Then suddenly the flak from an ack-ack gun on the fringe of the town caught them unexpectedly and a hail of lead peppered the fuselage.

'I couldn't get her up high enough!' Zeitler roared in disbelief. 'You should have dropped those bombs, Anton!' The burst of incredulity momentarily suspended his reactions and the aircraft staggered along for a few seconds then terrifyingly dropped thirty metres. Zeitler felt his backside rammed down into his seat. The others hit the floor like stones. Shuddering gently, the Heinkel was suspended for a split second in the sky, and Zeitler, using his innate airmanship and the visibility that was left, levelled out and stabilized flight without recourse to instruments. 'Get up here, Anton, and check the damage!' Zeitler yelled through the intercom.

Anton lurched into the cockpit, head down to scan the instrument panels. The lights were gone, several of the needles were dead, others swinging senselessly.

Jon, detached from the intercom, saw Anton yelling at him and pulled aside his helmet to hear Anton shouting, 'Watch fuel and oil, take this torch.'

Zeitler waved a gloved hand at the blind-flying group of instruments in front of him and then squinted out through the windscreen. High above, cirrus blanketed off the moon, and below a bank of mist and low stratus obscured the earth.

Anton was rapidly checking the instruments and saw that the altimeter, airspeed indicator, artificial horizon and gyro compass were either destroyed or useless. 'Zeitler, set course 155 degrees!' he commanded sharply.

At that moment Zeitler sighted a cloud bank looming ahead and told Jon to shine his torch on the grid-ring of the magnetic compass beside his knee. Silently Jon did as told and squinting down, Zeitler set 155 on it.

Anton realized he would have to read off height and airspeed to Zeitler from the bomb-aimer's panel and began to crawl back up towards the cupola, but at that moment Zeitler was blinded by a searchlight's glare reflecting off the instrument panel. The aircraft entered cloud and Zeitler fiercely hauled the plane into a steep port turn, his eyes glued to the bank-indicator and engine revolution gauges, his sole remaining assurances against complete disorientation and a fatal fall.

They were still in cloud when the crump of a shell shook the Heinkel violently. Zeitler glanced downwards and saw that the compass light was now gone and that only the needle and grid were faintly visible. Panic gripped him just as they flew out of cloud and into clearer skies and he kicked viciously at the rudder bar. The rear part of the fuselage was being tugged from side to side in a crazy motion and though they all knew that the air was streaming over a damaged rudder, Zeitler continued to drum the useless pedal with his foot. For a long moment nothing happened but Zeitler persevered grimly and eventually managed to get the rudder under control with Anton assisting him to stabilize course and level by use of trim and servo. They flew on through the clouding night sky. Everyone was very quiet, even Zeitler, who could sense the others' resentment at his putting them all at risk for a few moments of greedy triumph.

'Go back to the bombsight, Jon,' Anton said quietly. 'Keep reading height and airspeed to Zeitler through the intercom.'

They were now down to 950 metres and Anton suspected that they were leaking fuel. 'Throttle back, Zeitler,' he ordered. 'Maintain cruising speed of 250 kilometres an hour.'

Zeitler didn't answer. He felt drained, so exhausted that he felt if he shut his eyes just then he would die.

'Ernst,' Anton said through the intercom, 'how are things up there with you? Radio intact?'

'Kaput!' Ernst answered shortly. 'The aerial! Tell Zeitler he's a bloody maniac, not fit even to ride a bicycle in a cemetery!'

But Anton, alarmed by the low readings on the still-intact gauges, made no comment. He checked his map and rapidly wrote up his log sheet. Wind speed and direction he could only estimate, and now one hour from target-area, he marked a reckoned position . . . well into the north of England. Through the intercom, at regular intervals, he heard Jon read to Zeitler. Both exchanged comments on the heavy cloud layer beneath them and simultaneously they spotted a breakaway. Visibility was clear below and the moon slanted its pale beam across the sea. Apprehension flooded Anton's brain and he checked his map again. He realized that they had crossed the English coast and were now over the North Sea. Alarm made him feel weak. Navigational conjectures flashed through his mind. A westerly gale? Zeitler's compass course? Compass deviation induced by airframe damage?

'Coastline ahead!' Jon called through the intercom.

All of them peered towards it. They were flying at less than 1000 metres and could see plainly the moon-flecked waves breaking surf on land. Anton saw that it curved away to port and starboard ... An island? But where? There were no such places in the North Sea! He examined the compass closely, shading his torch beam with his bare hand, for the luminous paint in the dial was old and long overdue for renewal.

That was it! Anton gave a muttered curse and cried, 'Red on blue, Zeitler! We are heading for the Atlantic ... been flying reciprocal last hour! No hope of reaching base now ... Circuit this island, everybody on recce lookout!' Anton had been briefed and mapped only for the operation over the Clyde and had little idea as to where they were. Zeitler had committed the cardinal error of setting the reciprocal course on his compass which meant he was 180 degrees wrong, and had headed north-westerly instead of south-easterly, but Anton bitterly blamed himself. He should have checked sooner. But there was no time now for self-recrimination.

The starboard wing was dropping. Anton had released the remaining bombs into the black depths of the sea but even so the Heinkel was losing altitude. The engine could burst into flames at any moment though there couldn't be much fuel left in either tank because the fuel change-over had been made some time ago.

'Get ready to jump!' he ordered his crew imperatively.

'On that postage stamp?' Zeitler squawked

'All right, we go in the sea then!'

'I prefer to swim in kinder waters,' Zeitler returned sarcastically.

Jon swallowed his rising gorge, the thought of the inevitable jump bringing him out in a cold sweat. Anton shoved a tin at him and said kindly, 'Don't keep it back, Jon. Airsickness is nothing to be ashamed of. What about Kommodore Vati Mölders? Look at the position he is in despite airsickness.'

'Unlike Mölders I have no ambition to be a pilot, ace or otherwise . . . but, thank you for understanding, Anton.'

Anton crouched by Zeitler. 'Take her round once more. The island is split by a range of high mountains but there is a good stretch of open ground just beyond. We must all try and land there.'

'I will stay with her,' Zeitler said.

'You will bail out, and that is an order!' Anton snapped. 'It would be madness to attempt a night landing. Look at those mountains . . .'

The aircraft gave a sudden downward lurch. When she steadied rather shakily, the starboard wing was dropping dramatically and the exhaust manifold was spitting a rush of bright red flame.

'Try to maintain height, Zeitler,' Anton said. 'Ready now! Jon, you go first, get it over with.'

He accompanied Jon to the hatch. The smell of the red-hot manifold made them splutter. Jon swayed dizzily, looking down to the sickening curve of the watery world below.

'Now, Jon!' Anton ordered and Jon jumped. The airstream grabbed him and hauled him away from the aircraft. Before he pulled his ripcord the speed of the drop churned his belly. He choked on his vomit and barely had time to get his wind before the pull of his released chute brought him up with a jerk. Now he was floating like a piece of thistledown to the dark little patch of moor. Ernst had followed close on his heels and was just above but behind him.

'Now you, Zeitler,' Anton said firmly. 'I will fly her now.' He was taking no chances with the dogmatic Nazi whose arrogance had led him to believe he was the master of any situation. Zeitler's eyes flashed but he unbuckled his straps and went without a word, leaving Anton at the controls.

PART III

RHANNA
March 13th 1941

CHAPTER 5

Angus McKinnon hurried along the shore path that skirted the harbour. The moon had ridden out from its curtain of cloud to shed a pale brilliant light over the now calm Sound of Rhanna. The horizon seemed a timeless distance away and the great stretches of the Atlantic Ocean lay placid and hauntingly beautiful. The River Fallan rushed down from the mountain corries in mercurial wanderings and the sound of it thundered in Angus's ears as he crossed the bridge. For a moment he stopped to lean on the rough stone parapet, bowing his head to watch the frothing flurry of river tumbling into the sea.

'Uisge-beatha,' he murmured softly and smiled benignly at the 'water of life'. The smell of it was like nectar to his senses. On its journeying it had gathered the crystal-clear air of high mountain places; on its flight across the moorlands it had claimed the tang and tinge of peaty heather roots, which gave it a clear, amber glow and made it an altogether soft, fragrant concoction. A light came into Angus's eyes and his smile was one of triumph. 'Lovely Uisge-beatha,' he addressed the river with approval. 'Tonight you will be proving you are more than just a pretty sight. I'm goin' now to be havin' a taste of you.'

He lumbered on over the bridge but a sound, other than that of the whispering sea, made him stop again and peer upwards into the sky. Was it his imagination or was that a plane he was hearing? It seemed to him he was always hearing planes these days, and without quite knowing why he felt uneasy. He hated the sound of aeroplanes. They sounded peaceful but he knew that was only an illusion. The war had changed everything. No matter how hard he tried he was haunted by an ever-present sense of guilt, which was made worse by the knowledge that two of his brothers had joined the navy. His supposedly bad back gave him no more than an occasional twinge; the heart murmur discovered during his medical examination did not detract from his easy, peaceful life, yet it and the backache had exempted him from active service. But the general opinion was that he was just lazy.

'The Uisga Hags will get you if the Germans don't,' Canty Tam had warned, grinning his aimless grin and staring out to sea as if willing all the water witches of myth and folklore to come leaping out to grab Angus in their evil clutches and carry him off to sea.

'It's a useless idiot like yourself they're more likely to be after,' Angus had answered with confidence. Nevertheless he hastened to pray to St Michael, the guardian of those on land or sea, and he was careful to wear his Celtic cross even if he was only mucking out the byre.

A little wind ruffled the sea and to one cursed with guilt it was easy to imagine that the sigh of Hag voices rode in on the breeze. Angus shivered, pulled his coat collar closer round his ears, and went quickly on his way. He was making for his father's wash-house, a place that had been grandly christened 'the Headquarters'. Here a number of men met once-weekly, widely broadcasting the fact that they were, for all intents and purposes, patriotically keeping fresh all the instruction they had received during the Home Guard training courses.

He knocked hurriedly on the stout door of the wash-house, and there was the sound of scuffling and loud whispering before the door creaked open. 'You're late,' came Tam McKinnon's muffled reproach. 'We have started long ago.'

'Ach, I'm sorry, Father. Wee Colin fell out o' bed and I had to go for Nurse Biddy. Then she was fetched to go over to Todd's. Was he here when he was taken bad?'

'Ay, and a terrible job we had carrying him outside, for he was drunk as a lord. In the end we just put him in the wheelbarrow and took him home while Ranald went up for the doctor. How is things with him now?'

'The doctor had him opened up when last I saw him.'
Angus gulped at the memory. 'He says he just caught the appendix in time.'

'Ach, poor Todd, a shame just,' Tam said sympathetically. 'But come away in now, son. It is even better than we thought. Like nectar it is, so easy it goes down.'

Angus had forgotten Todd. He stood in the doorway of the wash-hoosie like a child on the threshold of Wonderland. A suffocating heat rushed out to meet him coupled with the palpable, overpowering fumes of whisky. 'I could get drunk just standin' here,' he said happily, staring into the little room where flames from a peat oven gleamed warmly on a pot that was set into a corner of the room. A concoction of pipes and tubes sprouted from it in a glorified jumble that would have baffled the casual observer. But the sweating, glassy-eyed assembly in the wash-house had had plenty of time to acquaint themselves with the still and its intricate workings.

Tam McKinnon had acquired the antiquated machinery in a most unexpected manner. He had been fixing the thatch of a blackhouse at Nigg which was used by blind Annack Gow to keep peat and other fuel, though it wasn't unknown for her to live in the house during the winter months because she claimed it was cosier than the 'modern hoosie'. A rummage in the byre for a hammer had revealed the pot still, sitting like a nugget of gold amidst an assortment of farm implements and a pile of cow manure. Excitement choking him, Tam had hastened to Annack with an offer to clear out the accumulated junk in the byre.

'How much will you be wantin'?' she had barked, peering at him through her thickly-lensed specs. 'An old body like myself has no money to spare with my man gone and only myself to work the croft.'

'Not a farthing, Annack,' Tam had choked. 'Just the odd bit of junk you will never be using. Being a handyman I can make use of some of it.'

'Ay, well, don't be stealing my dung while you're about it,' she had returned suspiciously. 'I need all I can get for my vegetables . . . and a creel or two of seaweed wouldn't go wrong either,' she had ended cunningly.

Tam's face had fallen at the thought of gathering seaweed and humping it over the hill to Nigg, but the temptation of the still had been too much and the deal had been made. In the process of clearing the byre he had found all the bits and pieces relating to the still and happily had trundled the lot home on his cart.

Tam had been already adept at making beer and had enjoyed long years of solitary tippling, but the delicate art of making malt whisky needed several pairs of hands, and he had taken into his confidence those of his cronies whom he considered tight-lipped enough not to give his illicit little game away. With much patient devotion the men had carried out the various stages of the whisky-making process, working willingly, the sting of the task taken away by visions of ever-flowing golden whisky. The most critical stage of the business was fermentation and distillation and the men had taken it in shifts to make sure the temperature of the still was kept constant. Bewildered wives, wondering at their menfolk sneaking off in the middle of the night, had been fobbed off with a variety of excuses and long before Tam's still was ever to prove its worth many a Rhanna wife had harboured suspicions about the faithfulness of her espoused.

But that was all in the distant past. The first batch of malt, lying in cool wooden casks carefully prepared by Wullie the Carpenter, was ready to be sampled; perhaps a little too soon for proper maturation, but the men could wait no longer to reap the rewards of their labour. In defiance against superstition they had chosen the thirteenth night of the third month for the tasting ceremony. For weeks they had waited for 'the night of the Uisge-beatha'. Now it was here. Tam had gone into the cool little closet extension of the wash-hoosie and, with the delicacy normally reserved for the handling of the newborn, had brought forth the first cask of matured malt. Quite unconsciously, every man in the gathering had removed an assortment of headcoverings in a moment of homage to the Uisge-beatha, and now they lay about the floor, each in a different stage of inebriation.

In their midst, propped shoulder to shoulder, sat Kate McKinnon and Annack Gow, a long history of temperamental differences drowned in the happy delirium induced by the Uisge-beatha. Annack's arrival had caused quite a stir, for she had come on the arm of Tammy Brown, one of the confraternity. It had soon transpired that Annack was neither as senile nor as blind as her demeanour suggested.

'You silly bugger!' she had scolded Tam McKinnon. 'Did you really think I was not knowing it was my Jack's still you were after? Clean out my byre indeed! You that canny even keep your own grass cut! It's the sheeps that do it for you!' Here she and Kate had exchanged hostile glances. 'No, it's not daft I am, Tam McKinnon,' she had continued with asperity. 'My Jack was brewing the malt while you were still cutting milk teeths!' A dreamy look had come into her short-sighted eyes. 'My, the times we had in the blackhoosie . . . up there in the wee secret room . . . ay, they knew how to build hoosies in those days. My grandfather was the one to start the still and the secret of it was passed down to my Jack . . . ay, and much as I've missed him it's a wee taste o' his whisky I'm missing too. Yours will never match his but since you're a beginner to the art I will give you fair judgement.'

'But how did you know it was tonight, Annack?' Tam asked humbly.

'Hmph! Anybody with half a nostril could tell, so don't think I'm the only one to be knowing. Every time I am passsing your house my nose is telling me the malt gets riper. I have been keeping a sharp guard on Tammy here . . . all that snooping about at all hours. I knew there was something brewing all this time so I threatened Tammy with the Customs mannie and he couldn't get me along here fast enough.'

But Tammy and his ready treachery had been soon forgotten in the spree that followed. The whisky, its attraction doubly enhanced by its rich amber colouring, had soon transported everyone into an idyllic world where no enmity existed.

And so it was when Angus came into this gathering and the door of 'the Headquarters' was securely bolted. The uninhibited sounds of hilarity in the wash-hoosie very effectively shut away the sounds of the outside world and no one heard the drone of an aircraft circling low over the island.

Shona had gone up to bed early and lay looking at the moonbeams spread over the floor of her room. It was a habit of hers to keep the curtains open so that she could lie and look at the night sky before falling asleep, and also to see what sort of day it was as soon as she wakened. Even if it was a grey, wind-tossed day the bright yellow cloth always gave the room a sunshiny feel. She always insisted on yellow curtains because somehow they were a part of her childhood and gave her an odd feeling of security, something that didn't change when everything else did.

Just before New Year, Kirsteen had wanted to put new curtains into her room but she had refused the suggestion vehemently enough for Kirsteen to look hurt and slightly bewildered. Shona was sorry she occasionally showed her temper to Kirsteen, but it was something she couldn't help, that and the feeling of being on the defensive at a lot of the little changes that Kirsteen naturally enough wanted to make to Laigmhor. But the last two days had been wonderfully happy for her. It was so good to be back on Rhanna. Her separation from it had made her appreciate it all the more. Her outlook on life had broadened a good deal in the last few months, and coming home had let her see just how lucky she was to have Kirsteen and her father to come home to, and though she had been away from them she was somehow now closer to them than ever. Her father was so different from the proud, aloof creature who had mourned in his heart for many years, first for her mother, then for Kirsteen during their long period of separation. Finally, his deep, dark eyes had lost their look of sadness and now glowed with the joy of living. Then there was Grant Fergus, a manly, dimpled little boy with the looks of a cherub and the gruff façade of a child with a heart so soft he had to try hard to hide it all the time. He tried with Shona but never quite succeeded, and into her own heart crept a real tenderness for the small stranger who was her half-brother.

But if only Niall was home and they could get together again, be the way they were before the war, young and carefree with no heavy burdens of the heart to weigh it down and make it ache all the time. Shona felt about under her pillow and her fingers curled round the locket Niall had given her as an engagement present before he had gone away to France. His picture was in it, beside hers, and the only time she took it off was when she went to bed. She trembled suddenly and put up a slender finger to trace the outline of the little damp patch above her bed which was shaped like the head of Jesus. 'Oh my dear sweet Jesus,' she whispered, 'you are the only one who can help me now for I feel I can't help myself any more. You know what I did with Niall was wrong but somehow I know you've forgiven me for that. But it's myself that can't forgive myself, if that doesn't sound too daft, so please help me, dearest Lord, to overcome myself. Let Niall know in his heart that I love him more than anyone else in the world. He's so nice and dear and it worries me sometimes that someone else just might come along and take the feet from under him and I couldn't bear that. If Mirabelle is there beside you at this very moment let her know that I love her and still miss her so. I can still see her nice rosy face and her white hair shining out from under her mutch cap. Good night for now, Lord.'

Her prayers to God were always very simple, childlike affairs but were so satisfying for her that they never failed to bring her a certain measure of comfort. She stared through the window up into the velvet blue-black night where millions of stars glittered brightly. It was so beautiful she pulled herself up in bed to get a better view of the night world. The moon was peeping sullenly from behind a big silver-lined cloud, its pale halo making the heavens vast and coldly infinite. The ragged peaks of Sgurr nan Ruadh reared up to embrace the great emptiness of space with intimate approval, shutting out the tiny speck of Man from the secrets shared by the heavens and the highest places of Earth.

A light tap came on the door and Babbie whispered, 'Can I come in?'

'Yes, I'm not asleep.'

The door opened and Babbie flitted over to sit on the bed. 'Of course you're not asleep, you daft thing. If you had been you wouldn't have answered me, would you?'

'I might, I sometimes talk in my sleep,' Shona giggled. 'Will I light the lamp?'

'No, the moonlight's lovely. Just let me snuggle my feet under a bit of your blanket. Then we can have a cosy talk before bed.'

'Have you just come up?'

'Yes, I was helping Kirsteen fill the zinc tub. She's having a bath in front of the fire.'

'But, wasn't Father there to do that? He usually makes it his business to do such things for Kirsteen, for myself too for that matter.'

'He went up to bed early-ish so I stayed behind to have a chat with Kirsteen. She's a dear. Interesting and a lot of fun. She has a great sense of humour. Funny little things pop out when you least expect them. I knew you wouldn't be asleep, that's why I looked in. You were thinking of Niall, weren't you?'

'Ay, as a matter of fact I was.' Shona's tone was wary. 'Isn't it natural to think of someone you love? Bed I always find is the best place for such thoughts because during the day everyone about you prattles on about nothing that matters and you can't get a thought in edgeways. Don't *you* ever think about your most secret things when you're in bed?'

'Of course I do,' Babbie laughed lightly. 'That's why I always try to go to bed as late as possible so that I don't have the strength left to think.'

Shona put out her hand and clasped Babbie's firmly. 'You daft thing,' she said affectionately. 'Would you like me to get up and make you a nice big mug of hot cocoa? I know we've

62

already had some but a second cup won't do any harm . . .'
She smothered a laugh. 'Just as long as you know where to
find your chanty in the middle of the night.'

'How could I miss it?' choked Babbie. 'These country
chamber pots are so enormous you could have a bath in
them! I think we'll forget the cocoa though . . . After all,
Kirsteen is having her bath in the kitchen.'

'*She* won't mind. I often wash her back for her.'

'Maybe you'd best leave that to your father this time.'

'But he's in bed and likely asleep by now!'

'I wouldn't be too sure.'

Babbie sounded so mysterious that Shona burst out, 'Ach,
you talk in riddles, Babbie Cameron!'

'And you're so naïve at times I feel like giving you a good
spanking. You're often too old for your years but sometimes
you're like a little girl who can't see what's under her nose.
Your father and Kirsteen haven't been speaking to each
other since we came.'

'But . . . they've been talking their heads off! You're a
witch right enough, Babbie.'

'Oh, they've talked all right, but only for our benefit.
When she isn't looking he's making sheep's eyes at her
and when he isn't looking she looks as if she might eat him at
any moment. What better way to make up than over a bath
tub?'

'Oh.' Shona wasn't too sure she liked the idea of that and
easily betrayed her thoughts by her tone of voice.

'Listen,' Babbie laughed, 'if you were Kirsteen and your
father was Niall wouldn't *you* take advantage of a midnight
bath in the kitchen?'

'I don't know,' Shona said doubtfully.

'Ach, of course you would! Me too for that matter. We're
all human, Shona McKenzie, and like it or no, your father
and Kirsteen are so much in love at the moment they're like a
couple of bairns playing at houses. You and me are going to
have a nice long talk even if it's only a lot of rubbish. Stop
grabbing at the blankets and give me a nice big bit to wrap
round my legs. Hand me one of those rag dolls of yours to

cuddle then we can both be comfy. Fancy, rag dolls at your age! You're worse than me with my teddy bears!'

Babbie was right about Fergus and Kirsteen. For two days Kirsteen had been cool with him because of a tiff over a matter so trivial that both knew they were being foolish but neither would give in. Earlier that evening she had kept her fair head averted all through supper. He had watched the fine beauty of her slender body and had wanted to crush her to him because she was even more desirable when she was aloof. Covertly she had observed his strong rugged features with his stubborn set of chin and, as always, the sight of him, his sweet nearness, had turned her heart to jelly. Looking at the little white hairs in his raven sideburns always brought a strange choking feeling to her throat, and just to see the muscular hardness of his body thrilled her with its maleness, yet she had eluded his burning black eyes. It was childish of her, she knew, but somehow the little times of disagreement between them made the making-up doubly exciting. He had gone to bed early but she hadn't followed and he had tossed and turned, uable to sleep without her at his side. Now it was late, but he finally got up and went quietly down to the warm kitchen. She had just stepped out of the zinc tub and her glistening body was tawny in the glow of the firelight, her crisp hair a deep golden halo of ruffled wet curls. For a moment neither of them spoke then she said coolly, 'It seems I am afforded no privacy of my own, no matter how late the hour.'

He felt the laughter rising in his throat. 'My darling!' His lilting voice was deep with joy. 'Am I to spend the rest of my life finding you in dark corners wearing nothing but your birthday suit?' He was thinking of their first meeting in the fragrant woods above Loch Tenee when he had come upon her drying herself after a swim. It had been the start of a long and turbulent affair that had finally culminated in a promise of marriage. But that had been before he had lost his arm in the accident, before she had sailed away. Now she was his wife of nearly six months and he felt that all the years of unhappiness were just a bad dream. Everything in his life was now doubly precious, and Fergus strode tall and proud, paying no heed to the gossip that had begun in the first weeks of Kirsteen's return.

'His lordship will no longer be standing on his pedestal,' Behag Beag had sniffed to her cronies. 'First his brother Alick gets a girl in trouble and has to be sent away in disgrace. After that we are seeing the terrible shame of his daughter with child and the little hussy holding up that McKenzie head of hers like she was royalty. As if that wasn't bad enough our ex-schoolmistress comes back to Rhanna complete with McKenzie's son born out of wedlock. 'Tis a bad name they will be giving this good place and I hope the Lord will forgive them indeed.'

At that point Erchy the Post had sent everyone scuttling about their business by opening the door and saying in a loud voice, 'And it is yourself, Mr McKenzie! Just in time for a nice cosy gossip!'

But now, with the worst of the talk behind them, Kirsteen and Fergus lived a relaxed and happy life. Occasionally there was a clash of personalities because the dominant Fergus liked to get his own way. But Kirsteen had acquired a strong willpower of her own during her years of independence and he was quickly learning that his moody tempers held no threat for her. Also, there was the problem of getting to know the little stranger who was his son. On the whole Grant Fergus was a good-natured child, but he was possessed of a temperament that could change like quicksilver from one mood to another. Fergus didn't want to introduce the heavy hand too soon but he was a disciplinarian and unable to repress the urge to control the boy. This had brought a spell of resentment, but it was short-lived because the little boy's irrepressible sense of fun wouldn't allow him to stay sullen for long. His respect for Fergus was growing stronger with each passing day, as did his sturdy admiration for the big man who had so recently materialized into the father for whom he had always longed.

Overriding all was the warm, wonderful sense of Laigmhor, once more a family home. For too many years it had been a place with an atmosphere of waiting for an infusion of the life that Fergus's first wife, Helen, seemed to have taken with her on the night she had died giving birth to Shona. But all that was over now. Fergus was fulfilled and happy. The days were busy with the work of the farm, the evenings filled with the warmth of family togetherness. And the nights belonged to two people making up for their years apart.

At Fergus's reference to their first meeting at Loch Tenee Kirsteen's lips curved and she peeped at him from lowered lashes. Despite the power of his body he looked like a small boy eager to make up for being bad. Her breath caught in her throat and she felt the tears of her love for him pricking her eyelids. She was unable to retain her dignity any longer and a soft chuckle escaped her.

'Fergus.' She whispered his name enticingly and in moments he was crushing her against him, fierce in his passion, his lips hard on hers.

His heart was beating rapidly. The smell of her was like the sweet, fresh air on the top of a summer mountain; natural, unmasked by perfumes and cosmetics. She was that kind of woman: clean as a mountain burn and uncluttered by feminine trappings yet so utterly desirable in her own right that his senses reeled with her nearness. For a moment he remembered the first night of their marriage with the bed cool and remote-looking, spread with sheets of pure white linen. Unaccountably he had felt awkward and shy, like a young boy entering an unknown phase in his life. She had entered the room looking like a mythical goddess dressed in a white silken nightdress, her hair shining like the pale gold of a summer cornfield. They had been like young lovers, awkward and unsure, lost for words in those first breathless moments. The new white sheets had rustled in the quiet room, adding to their embarrassment; then their feet had touched an assortment of brushes and other bristly accoutrements, placed there by Shona in a moment of mischief. The incident had broken the ice and they had shrieked with stifled merriment, finally falling into each other's arms in a passion of untamed desire. The memory made him catch his breath with tenderness even while his mouth crushed her lips and his tongue played with hers. Her skin was like silk, parts of it still damp from the bath, the intimate parts that made him forget all else but his need for her.

Suddenly she pushed him away, her eyes going to the windows, which, though heavily curtained, were a distraction to her senses. 'Not here, Fergus,' she whispered. 'Let's go up to bed.'

'No, here, Kirsteen . . . by the fire . . . like the night at the schoolhouse.'

'But – we were alone then, my darling. Shona and Babbie are upstairs, they could come down . . . Grant might come into the bedroom looking for me – you know he does that sometimes and . . .'

'No, I'm not having that!' he laughed. 'All those excuses. The house is asleep . . . and I can't wait . . .' He kissed her again and her resolution left her, it always did when he was beside her, doing things to her body that made her forget all else. The hard strength of him excited her; the heat from the fire seemed to burn right into her, till every life force within cried out for release.

Anton Büttger had noticed little white dots of habitation below and he wanted to get the crippled plane away from them. The only uninhabited area appeared to be the dark stretch of land where the others had jumped. He was over it now and would have to try and come back. He looked at the starboard wing. The fire had fizzled out. It meant the fuel was almost gone. A series of shuddering spurts of speed brought him round the western curve of the island once more. At a dangerously low altitude he flew past humping black mountains and his heart pumped into his throat. He had to get the plane higher in order to jump safely. Relentless slopes rushed to meet him, and even while his pulses raced he thought, 'There are no houses on top of a mountain. It might be better if she crashed now . . .'

67

He tugged at the controls but there was no response. His face was awash with sweat. This was it! Miraculously the Heinkel then responded to his wild handling and lumbered upwards into the sky . . . high enough for him to make the jump. He wondered if he ought to try to climb out of the sliding hatch above the pilot's seat . . . No, there wasn't enough time to manipulate himself through the small opening. He ran aft and jumped out of the rear-gunner's door. The freezing night air whipped him cruelly, and the jagged edges of a massive peak reared up to greet the frail speck of life. Frantically he guided his chute away only to see the cold face of a tiny basin of water sparkling in the moonlight.

At Laigmhor, the kitchen drowsed on warmly: Snap and Ginger slept peacefully atop the oven; the clock tick-tocked on the mantelshelf; somewhere behind the skirting-boards a mouse scurried among the plaster. But the things Fergus was doing to Kirsteen were drowning out all her usual senses. All she heard was his harsh, quick breathing, his lilting endearments. She stroked his thick dark hair, her love for him meeting and whirling with her passions. He had pulled the zinc tub away from the fire and the rug was soft and warm. For a moment she saw the shadows leaping about the ceiling then he pulled her down and in towards him; and her eyes closed, driving another of her senses inwards. In his rough search for fulfilment he brought her both pleasure and pain, so deep inside that she could hardly distinguish one from the other. Somewhere, in the world outside, a plane pulsated, robbing the night of silence; then it was gone; and the island dreamt on undisturbed.

Kirsteen felt the mist of tears in her eyes and she held his head against her breasts. 'My Fergus,' she whispered, 'tonight we have made a child. At this very minute our baby is being conceived.'

He looked at her for a long moment, cupping her chin in his hand, his black eyes alight with his love for her. 'I had thought that Shona was the only one in the household with a

68

fancy to her imagination. I can see all that folklore you are hearing at the ceilidhs is getting at you too.'

But her smile was full of conviction. 'You wait and see . . . I'll give you the second of those five sons I promised . . .' She giggled. 'In fact – just to spite you I might have twins – if Alick and Mary can do it, then so can I.'

Somewhere in the distance the German bomber crashed, sending shock waves through the glen. The soft breath of the wind carried mere ghostly echoes of the sound, but they were unusual enough for Fergus to say uneasily, 'What the hell was that . . . ? I wonder . . . did you hear a plane a whily back?'

'Yes, but . . .'

A sudden high eerie wailing just outside the door made them both scramble quickly to their feet. Kirsteen wrapped herself into her woollen dressing-gown while Fergus, angry at the interruption, whatever it was, quickly made himself decent. He composed himself for a few moments, then wrenched open the door to find Dodie, the island eccentric, standing outside. Dodie lived a lonely spartan existence in his tiny isolated cottage on the slopes of Sgurr nan Ruadh and it wasn't unusual to see him on any part of the island, day or night. He was a simple soft-hearted creature, as much a part of Rhanna as the very soil itself. Childlike in his innocence he was unable to understand the complicated natures of those around him and was very easily hurt. He was so introverted that he would come to a house only if invited, and something momentous indeed must have happened to make him stand and wail for help outside Laigmhor's door. He was a sorry sight to see, weeping into his big calloused hands, his stooped shoulders shuddering with long drawn-out sobs. He was a bedraggled, unhappy spectacle, and Fergus, who had a soft spot for Dodie and who also admired the way he worked so hard to provide the simple necessities for himself, said kindly, 'Och, c'mon, now, man, what ails you?'

Dodie looked pathetically forlorn and so afraid it was a long moment before he said in a whisper of embarrassment, 'Ach, Mr McKenzie, it's feart I am! I was just out lookin' for

Ealasaid when one o' them airy-plane things swooped low over the moor like a damt great eagle and near took my head off. I started to run but it ran after me and . . . just as I was coming over the glen it came right round the hill so low I could hear the whistle of it in my eardrums. I'm not knowing a thing about airy-planes or the war and nobody is ever telling me anything . . . and . . . and Ealasaid's out there and I'm too feart to go and look for her. It's ashamed I am just!'

'Ealasaid can take care of herself,' Fergus soothed, knowing how much Dodie loved his wanderlust cow. 'Come you in now and Kirsteen will make you a bite to eat.'

Just then Shona and Babbie came piling down to the kitchen.

'I thought I heard thunder,' Babbie said breathlessly, 'but there's hardly a cloud in the sky. Is it always as quiet as this on Rhanna?' She was quietly pleased that Fergus was standing with his arm protectively round Kirsteen's slender shoulders. It was obvious the pair had made up their differences.

'I may be wrong but I'm sure I heard the roar of a plane just minutes ago,' Shona said, her blue eyes big in her pale face.

'I think we heard it too,' Kirsteen faltered, her face reddening.

They all jumped at the sudden appearance of Bob in the kitchen. His gnarled fingers were bunched on the bone handle of his shepherd's crook and he wasted no time with pretty words of apology. He had witnessed the spectacle of the bomber heading for almost certain destruction on Ben Machrie. 'Are you deaf, man?' he asked Fergus sarcastically. 'The damt thing must have come right over Laigmhor! It came down so low it rattled the dishes on my dresser!'

Before Fergus could answer, the sound of the kirk bell could be heard pealing over the countryside. It was pulled by Righ nan Dul who, from his elevated position on the windswept cliffs of Port Rum Point, had seen the bomber juddering round the village of Portcull.

For a long incredulous moment he had watched it

embracing the slopes of the mountains, heading for a crash on the quietly menacing slopes of Ben Machrie. 'Jesus – God – St Michael! Help us all!' he had muttered aloud to all those unseen guardians of life, and then taken off, limping hurriedly down the spiral stairs to emerge atop the smooth, cropped turf of the Point. To the left of it lay the needles of the Sgor Creags – grey, jostling pinnacles of treachery, the swish of the sea deceptively peaceful in its picturesque frothing round the slimy, barnacle-encrusted rocks. To the right of it lay the natural little harbour of Portcull, protected from the worst weather by the long finger of Port Rum Point. Righ had scuttled along the path to the kirk, which sat starkly aloof at the top of the peninsula. With its creaking elms and black, huddled headstones casting long moon-scattered shadows, it was an eerie place, but Righ had no time to let himself be haunted by monuments to the dead. His thoughts had been for the living and he had given the gate a mighty push that had set it creaking on its rusty hinges. The kirk was never locked. On Rhanna people seldom locked anything and to the Bible-thumping Reverend John Gray an ever-open kirk door meant an ever-available sanctum to repentant sinners wanting to unburden themselves to the Lord.

For several minutes Righ kept doggedly at the ropes, until finally, with aching arms, he withdrew from the kirk and hobbled away through the other old gate set into the wall atop the Hillock. He emerged to find little black blobs were scurrying from all quarters, hastily pulling outdoor clothes over night attire. The tall figure of John Gray came rushing from the Manse, followed closely by his small dumpy wife who was inserting her false teeth as she ran. No catastrophe on earth was worth the price of her dignity, to which she clung fiercely on an island where many of the older generation wore false teeth only on Sundays or at funerals.

Even while Righ was delivering his message to the community straggled out on the slopes of the Hillock, the bell he had recently rung was finding its echo all over the island. It was a pre-arranged signal to everyone that something connected with war had come to Rhanna.

At Portvoynachan, four miles to the east, Mrs Jemima Sugden, the elderly schoolmistress of the tiny school in that area, was vigorously ringing a huge handbell though she had no earthly idea what was happening. Elsewhere on the island general confusion followed, but after a few bewildering minutes a certain order began to emerge as the Home Guard assembled at their various posts to await orders. The efficiency of the Home Guard was hampered somewhat by those members who had come staggering out of the Headquarters in a merry drunken heap, but in the excitement of the moment, no one minded too much. Left behind was Annack Gow who sat with her arms lovingly entwined round the cask of malt, her head resting on the barrel in a manner that allowed her generous nose to inhale unhindered the strong sweet fumes of the Uisge-beatha.

CHAPTER 6

Tom and Mamie Johnston of Croynachan, who had been wakened rudely by the dreadful tearing of metal ripping through earth, were hardly able to believe their eyes when they rushed out to see bits of a German bomber strewn over their field.

'Don't panic, mo ghaoil,' Tom soothed his wife. 'It's only bits of an old aeroplane.'

'A *German* plane,' Mamie said faintly, quickly following her husband who had rushed into the kitchen to fetch his shotgun.

'You stay with the bairns,' he told Mamie. 'Lock all the doors and open them only to the neighbours or myself when I get back.'

Tom saddled his horse and galloped to Croft na Beinn, then on to the tiny clachan of Croy, quickly and efficiently gathering together every able-bodied man.

But the people of Nigg had no need of warning bells to let them know that something unusual had happened. Old Madam Balfour of Burnbreddie was standing on top of the high tower of her gloomy old house, lustily banging a dinner gong and shouting at the top of her high-pitched, hysterical voice. Her bedroom lay at the top of the big square tower and the German bomber on its third sweep round the island had flown at such a low altitude she had fully imagined it was coming in on top of her. With her only son, Scott, the young laird of Burnbreddie, fighting with the British Army somewhere in Greece, she felt vulnerable and abandoned despite the fact that she had the companionship of Rena, her very able daughter-in-law. Having screamed to Rena that the house was under air-attack she had made a very agile flight to the roof to bang her gong and shriek. Rena's two children, hearing their grandmother conducting herself in a manner that would have frightened the Uisga Hags themselves, began to scream also and Rena had her hands full trying to soothe everyone.

But Righ had dispatched several members of the bicycle brigade to places that were bereft of menfolk, and before long, frightened women and children were receiving welcome comfort. Meanwhile, other squads of bicycles and horses, gathering on their way the various little bands of men assembled at their posts, were moving up to the eastern end of the island, from where the sound of the crash was thought to have come.

The sight of the twisted wreckage of the plane near Croynachan brought gasps of incredulity from all who gazed upon it. The starboard wing lay in the Johnstons' field, and the stench of red-hot metal oozed from the exhaust manifold, mingling with the sharp air washing over the moors. Ragged ailerons, trim tabs, the tail wheel and tail gun littered the ground. The fin had snapped from the fuselage in a ragged fracture, and the rudder hung by mere scraps of material. The bold, sharp symbol of the swastika gaped mockingly, looking terrifyingly out of place in the wild, peaceful stretches of the Muir of Rhanna. There was no denying it: the Germans were actually on Rhanna and the evidence was there for all to see.

As the islanders bore down on the plane like a horde of ants, excitement made them revert to their native Gaelic, yet caution hushed their voices when the men spread out over the moors, their steps taking them warily through the snagging clumps of gorse. Out here in the open a keen little wind moaned in from the sea and wailed softly around the cloisters of the old Abbey ruins situated near Dunuaigh, the Hill of the Tomb. It was a lost, lonely place and in normal circumstances the islanders gave it a wide berth, even in daytime. Now, in the hushed shadows of night, it brought chilling fears to the more superstitious, magnified a thousandfold by the thought that Nazi Germans might be lurking among the time-worn stones.

A few minutes later Fergus and Bob arrived with Dodie, who had been so anxious about his cow that Fergus had allowed him to come. As Fergus and Bob wandered off to join the men, Dodie stared at the wrecked plane with joy, his tall ungainly figure a looming spectre at the feast. His fear of the Germans forgotten, he looked lovingly and longingly at the tail piece with its swastika plainly visible in the light of the moon peeping round the shoulders of Ben Madoch. ''Tis nice colours on it,' he whispered childishly. 'A nice pattern so it is.' But no one heard him, concentrating as they were on the search that was taking place somewhere in the darkness below.

It was Fergus who found Jon Jodl, sitting on the ground, huddled against a mossy boulder, staring dreamily out over the wild, dark moors.

'Up you get now, man,' Fergus said quietly. 'You will not be hurt if you do just as you are told.

Jon didn't understand a word, but he knew what was expected of him and slowly unwound himself from his parachute and got to his feet.

In the pale glimmering of the moon's light Fergus saw the strained white face of the youth and the German flying suit stained with vomit. 'You are just a laddie and ill by the look of you,' Fergus said, compassion making his voice soft. He hadn't been able to imagine what his feelings would be coming face to face with a German. He had expected to feel some sort of resentment, or anger, and had good reason to feel both because of the indirect sufferings that war had brought to his own family. But the slim boyish figure of Jon Jodl, stamped with the vulnerability of the young, brought only feelings of pity. Yet . . . this was the Enemy. God alone knew what lay in the mind behind the face of the boy!

Fergus's thoughts were interrupted by the others, arriving on the scene in a clamour of excited Gaelic. Jon swayed on his feet and Doctor Lachlan McLachlan strode over. 'Get away from him!' he ordered sharply. 'Can't you see the laddie is in a state of shock? He needs all the air he can get! Let me examine him!'

Some distance away the keen air of morning was bringing Tam quickly to his senses but he wasn't able to join the search for the Uisge-beatha that had filled his bladder, and, handing his shotgun to Jock the Ploughman, he stepped behind a bush – and tripped over Ernst Foch lying in the heather. A guttural roar of surprise split the morning asunder as Ernst sprang to his feet and a highly indignant Nazi and a white-faced terrified Gael faced each other.

'It's sorry I am indeed, just!' Tam gabbled, forgetting for a moment that he was addressing the Enemy. He stood transfixed, unable even to make the effort of doing up his fly.

A stream of islanders soon descended and Ernst was then bundled into a trap beside Jon Jodl. 'Jon!' Ernst cried, glad to see one of his own kind. 'You came down safely? I am glad.' His eyes raked the moors. He wondered where Zeitler and Anton had landed, there seemed to be no sign of them.

Everyone else was wondering the same thing. But as the various search parties drifted back to the scene of the crash, in the midst of one group was the bull-headed Zeitler, dragging his feet and scowling when he was shoved unceremoniously into the trap beside his companions.

The islanders stood around talking in subdued tones while they observed the captives with dismay. They had been so intent on the search that no one had given a thought about a place suitable enough in which to keep German prisoners.

'It would be fine if we could just chain them up in the Abbey·ruins till help arrives from the mainland,' Ranald suggested hopefully, his ideas influenced by the adventure stories he read so avidly. 'I was reading a war book about prisoners put in shackles in a cellar and fed on only bread and water.'

Tom Johnston snorted and said sarcastically, 'Ay, and that was maybe taking place away back in the Dark Ages. They are human beings though they are Jerries and must be treated with respect.'

Doctor Lachlan McLachlan stamped impatiently, his compassionate brown eyes fixed on the wearily crumpled figure of Jon Jodl. 'I want to see to that lad and I don't care if I have to take him back to my house to do it! I have a spare room . . . Phebie always has it ready,' he added quietly, and Fergus looked at him admiringly.

'Hold on! I'm coming! I will take them into *my* house!' the Reverend John Gray yelled as he burst on to the scene. He was dishevelled and dirty and a little stubble of beard made his face look haggard, even in moonlight. Rhanna, used to a neatly-turned-out minister with never a hair out of place, stared as one man. 'I was helping with the search,' he explained with dignity. 'And I got rather off the beaten track. I am not used to the moors, but the Lord guided me.' He looked at his flock sternly. 'We should *all* have faith in him. He is our comfort and stay.'

The men muttered and one or two bowed their heads but old Bob said something in Gaelic and the minister glared at him. He had never troubled to learn the native tongue and was continually frustrated by the dour Gaels who took every opportunity to make him feel an interloper, though he had been preaching on the island for many years.

'These men will be safe in my house,' he continued. 'God will guide us all to His way. Their stay will be brief but I would not be doing my duty if I didn't try to nourish their thoughts with the love of God . . . take their minds off war

. . . I can speak a little German, we will understand each other.'

A gleam came into the eyes of the gathering. What could be better for the enemy than a day or two of bible-thumping under the minister's roof? He would be in his glory trying to save the German's souls, and they would be only too anxious to save their sanity by getting off the island the minute they could.

'Ach, it's a good man you are just,' Angus said solicitously.

Bob's weathered face broke into a mocking smile. 'Ay, good to be learning the German but never a word o' the Gaelic.'

The full implication of his words hit home. Everyone looked at each other quizzically and Fergus rapped out impatiently, 'Why don't you put your knowledge to good use, Mr Gray, and ask these men a few questions? There's a lot we would like to be knowing.'

'Hmm, yes, you're quite right of course,' the Reverend Gray muttered immediately, 'but I don't think we will find out very much. Nevertheless, I'll lend my hand to it, with God's guidance, of course.'

Ernst gave surly replies to 'the interrogation', repeating his name, rank and serial number so many times that even the minister's patience began to wane.

'It's as I told you,' he said to Fergus finally. 'He will tell me nothing of his mission but I gather he is concerned about his Commander.'

Fergus nodded. 'One more to be found, but I think we should leave him to the Military. If Mistress Beag got her message through, help should be arriving quite soon. If not, we will continue the search in daylight.' Wearily the men agreed and everyone began to move away from the scene of the crash.

Little Grant Fergus was marching up and down the drying green of Laigmhor with a meal basin on his head and a stout tree branch hoisted against his shoulder. He was practising 'being a soldier' and Kirsteen, watching him from the window, was angry at the influence of war reaching out to her son.

'Ach, don't worry yourself, Kirsteen,' Shona assured her. 'All wee boys play at soldiers – girls too – I did it myself when Niall and me were bairns.'

She folded the dish towel and turned to pick up a basket from the table. 'I'm away over to Tina's with a bite of dinner, and I'll do some wee odd jobs while I'm there. Matthew says she can hobble about the house but can't get out much to see to the beasts.'

Kirsteen looked at Shona's white face and felt a great surge of affection as, unbidden, a memory came of a slender little girl starting her first day at school; a child with glorious auburn hair tied back with a blue ribbon and skinny legs clad in black woollen stockings. Little had Kirsteen thought in those far-off days that one day she would marry Shona's father and become the mistress of Laigmhor . . . She had always got on well with Shona but her time of separation from Fergus had also separated her from his daughter, the only female in the household after the death of dear old Mirabelle. She could sense Shona's well-hidden resentment of the situation but understood her feelings on the matter. Impulsively she reached out to grasp Shona's hand and looked into her incredibly deep blue eyes.

'Shona,' she sighed, 'you're so sad inside – I can feel it even though you try so hard to hide it. I know what it's like – to love someone and be apart from them. What's wrong between you and Niall?'

For a moment a veil of hostility hooded Shona's eyes. She was growing more like Fergus every day, jealously guarding her most private feelings. But then she saw the genuine concern on Kirsteen's face. 'It's not Niall . . . it's me, Kirsteen. I need time to sort out my feelings. I love Niall, I think I've loved him since we were children. It was like a fairy story . . . the way we grew up together then discovered how much we cared . . . but . . .' she hesitated then went on in a rush, 'it never ended like a fairy story – that's the trouble with

78

real life. I blame myself for that, everything that happened to make it all go wrong. It's like a dream now ... the cave ... me bringing that little life into the world ...' She stared at Kirsteen with huge eyes then went on in a whisper, 'I didn't give him life – I gave him death. The only time he lived was when he was ... in here.' She touched the flatness of her belly with trembling hands. 'When I knew Niall was coming back from France I thought I had forgotten that time in the cave with that poor little dead baby but I hadn't. It seems to get worse and worse all the time. I go over it and over it in my mind ... it's like a nightmare without an end!'

Kirsteen put her arms round the girl's slender shoulders and said tenderly, 'Shona, we're all guilty of something. Your father and I could spend the rest of our lives feeling guilt, but our time is too precious to waste on useless self-reproach. A lot of our years were wasted because we were both foolish. Don't make our mistake, Shona.'

Shona forced a smile. 'You're right, of course, but it's easy to be wise after the event – I don't mean that to sound cheeky, it's just the truth. Och, it's lovely to be back on Rhanna, yet it won't be the same till Niall is here too.' She paused to look out the window to the misty blue of the mountains. 'This is where we both belong – no matter where I go my heart is always on Rhanna.'

'If you really love Niall, you would follow him to the moon. He won't be studying forever, you know.'

Shona went towards the door where the hens were cocking beady eyes into the kitchen. 'I'll have to go now,' she smiled. 'Thanks for listening to all my worries.'

'Be careful out there,' Kirsteen warned. 'Your father was making quite a fuss about that missing German. He doesn't think it safe for us defenceless females to be wandering about unescorted. Shouldn't Babbie go with you?'

'Ach, the lazy wittrock is sleeping late after the excitement of last night. I took her up a cup of tea but she just turned over and went back to sleep.'

At that moment a yell came from the garden where Grant had missed his soldierly footing and fallen into the thorns of the rose bed. Kirsteen rushed to the rescue while Shona grabbed a broom and chased the hens from the kitchen.

A crestfallen Grant came over the cobbled yard. 'Can I come with you, Shona?' he called. 'Mother's out of temper and there is still a while to go before school.' Mr Murdoch, the balding, fussy master of Portcull school, had gone to assist the Home Guard in their search for the Commander of the German bomber, giving all the children an unexpected morning off.

'Aren't you wanting to go down to the harbour?' Shona asked. 'If old Joe's there he might tell you a story.' The little boy loved the harbour with its collection of boats and old men always ready to recount an adventure of the sea. Already he knew a lot about fishing, jumping at any chance to dabble about in a boat. Whenever he could he went to help with the lobster creels and accompanied some of the older boys when they clubbed together to hire one of Ranald's boats for a day of sea fishing.

Grant hesitated at Shona's words, but seeing her basket of food, decided that a cosy strupak would better pass what remained of the morning. 'Old Joe has a bad head,' he told Shona in his precocious manner, his cultured English already showing traces of the lilting island tongue. 'I think, too, he is weary from chasing Germans all night and he told me earlier he was going to sleep off the effects of some meeting to do with the war.'

'The war was it?' Shona smiled. She had already heard about the 'disgraceful drunken behaviour' of the Home Guard. 'On you go and ask your mother then,' she conceded, 'but mind, you mustny bother Tina with your blethers.'

He ran to tell Kirsteen that he was going with his big sister to 'protect her' and a few moments later his grubby little hand was curled trustingly in hers. The misted fields were frosted with white which scrunched crisply underfoot as they walked, and the child's normally pink cheeks were soon like red apples in the stinging air. He was a picture with his black curls, snapping black eyes and dimpled chin. Tunelessly he

80

began singing a sea shanty taught to him by the fishermen and after a minute Shona joined in, feeling something of his exuberance and youthful buoyancy.

Soon they were in the field that sloped upwards to a tiny cottage huddled under the brown heather slopes of Ben Machrie. Here Matthew, grieve of Laigmhor, lived with Tina, his ample, easy-going young wife and his two children, Donald and Eve.

Little Donald, a big-eyed dreaming child, was quietly pleased to see Grant and took him off to view a golden plover's nest he had chanced upon.

'Don't be going far,' Shona warned. 'Remember what Father told you this morning.

Grant gave her a cherubic smile. 'I'm minding, Shona, don't worry . . . anyway . . .' he pulled a roughly-fashioned wooden dirk from his pocket, 'I'll kill any Germans with this! I'll not let them touch Donald or myself.'

Tina came limping from the byre, clutching a bucketful of manure mixed liberally with hen's feathers which drifted like snowflakes from the brimming container. At sight of Shona she put up a languid hand to tuck away strands of fine hair into two kirbys that were meant to be supporting a lop-sided bun. The grips were totally inadequate for the purpose and loops of hair descended in fly-away abandon.

'Ach, bugger it,' she swore mildly, her good-natured face showing not a trace of dismay. The boys scampered off and she told Shona consolingly, 'Don't you be worrying your head about wee Grant. Donald might be looking like his head was up on the moon but he is all there and knows every inch of the moor. I was hearing anyways it was only one airy-plane that came down though there were rumours of there bein' three. It's all a bitty mixed up. Matthew says he caught two of the Huns last night an' the soldiers will find the other later.'

Shona had to hide a quick smile. Tina's simple, devoted faith in her husband was such that she believed everything he told her. Her vision of an all-conquering hero was limited entirely to her spouse. It was perhaps her acceptance of his

81

manly boasting that made the marriage one of rare, uncomplicated happiness.

'Ay, you'll likely be right, Tina,' Shona said. 'Though I hear tell that some of the men have gone out to guard the plane. Father was a bit worried about Grant and myself coming out of the house at all this morning.'

'Ach, you'll be fine wi' me. If there is one smell o' a Jerry I'll set my dogs on the buggers!'

They had wandered into the house by now and Shona, looking at the jumbled assortment of canine and feline bodies that were heaped contentedly on hearth and sofa, wondered if even a whisker would have twitched if a dozen Germans had come marching into the room.

Little Eve, who had been having her morning nap in the commodious bottom drawer of the dresser, tottered through from the bedroom, rubbing the sleep from her huge bright eyes. The drawer had been her bed from babyhood and she simply popped into it when the mood took her. She was a rosy, intelligent child, delivered by Shona the Christmas Eve before last. The very timing of her birth seemed to have bestowed on her everything that was reminiscent of Christmas: roly-poly legs supporting a plump little body; stars shining in velvet eyes; a halo of flaxen hair that was a startlingly beautiful feature in a child otherwise so dark. At sight of Shona she giggled with glee then, turning very solemn, lifted her dress and stretched the top of her knickers till it seemed the elastic must surely snap. Peering over her pot belly she pointed between her legs. 'Wet!' she announced and collapsed on the rug in an ecstasy of baby chuckles.

'I've been training her to sit on the po,' Tina explained, 'but I'm no' able to bend much just now.' She collapsed into the depths of a huge armchair, pinning the tail of a skinny white cat against the springs. With a terrified squeal it struggled with the ensnaring layers of flesh till Tina was forced to ease herself up an inch and in doing so upset the brimming pail she had carried in from the byre. Dung and feathers littered floor, furniture and animals.

'Fevver!' Eve squealed, crawling amongst the mess to stick fluffy bits of down into her hair.

'Ach, my,' Tina clucked in slight anxiety. 'This damt ankle is keeping me back right enough. Matthew will be in for his dinner an' me that's so quick with everything will never have it ready, just.'

Shona's spirits were rising rapidly. Tina, with her effortless air of unruffled peace and uproarious over-statements, was a breath of spring sunshine. 'Don't upset yourself, Tina,' she instructed laughingly. 'I didn't just come over to blether, you know. I've brought some nice things for a strupak, then I'll get Matthew's dinner going.' She eyed the dangling pail in Tina's hand. 'Where were you going with that when I came along?'

'Just over to the midden. I'm saving it for the vegetable patch but I'm not wanting Matthew to know. I'd like fine to surprise him with a fine crop this year. Last year the tatties were like bools and the turnip so dry no' even the sheeps would eat it. Matthew hasny the time for it, the soul works that hard. I was having a mind to gather seaweed as well but this damt ankle has slowed me down with everything.'

In a few minutes Shona had swept the floor clean and the kettle was puffing gaily among the peats. Then she settled Tina and Eve with tea and scones and went to get the hens' pot from the jumbled array of cooking containers in the little stone-flagged outhouse Tina grandly called a kitchen.

The hens were gobbling greedily when Grant and Donald burst out from the windbreak of firs that sheltered the house from the windswept moors. They were arguing the way children do when greatly excited. It soon transpired that they had wandered up to the shores of Loch Sliach to look for rabbit burrows but had been frightened away when they saw a 'monster' floating on the loch.

'It was all spread out with humps on it!' said a round-eyed Grant. 'And it was moving about and making noises!'

'Ach no!' Donald's protest was faintly scornful of an incomer's inability to relate a properly embroidered tale. 'It was a Ullabheist right enough but it was dead because it was all white and limp. It was not making one sound but a water kelpie on the wee island was greetin' an' moanin'. Maybe it was crying for the Ullabheist though I don't know why 'cos they are feart o' them as a rule and should be glad it was dead!'

'We ran away,' Grant put in rather feebly, his pale face showing he had suffered quite a scare.

Shona was about to dismiss the childish ravings as of little import but her quick mind suddenly recalled Righ's saying that he thought the German bomber was surely bound to crash on the slopes of Ben Machrie and that instead it had careered round the mountains to come down on the open moor. Everyone had assumed the pilot would have bailed out on to open ground . . . but supposing there hadn't been time? Donald's Ullabheist sounded very much like a parachute.

Making a quick decision she bundled the protesting children into the cottage just as Matthew arrived for his dinner. Taking him into the kitchen on some pretext she hastily imparted the news to him. 'Get away now!' exclaimed the youthful grieve of Laigmhor, good-natured and easy-going like his wife, but, unlike her, possessed of an energetic taste for adventure.

'Can you get some men together?' Shona whispered.

'Ach, it would take too long. The last I am hearing they are all up at the airy-plane. Anyways . . .' he puffed out his well-developed rib cage. 'I'm here! I'll get my gun and I'll be goin' . . . you will maybe stay here and send some help after me.'

But Shona was not a McKenzie for nothing. 'Havers! I'm coming with you. I'm a nurse, remember, and the pilot of that plane might be badly injured. It's not a silly wee girl you are talking to, Matthew.'

'But Tina has that bad leg and will no' be able to send for reinforcements. I'm no' mindin' going to look for this Jerry so long as I know the lads will be up at my back. The island is crawling wi' strange men. Totie Little of Portvoynachan saw them early this mornin' rowing away from a big boat out on the Sound. They came over in rubber dinghies and hid them in the caves at Aosdana Bay. It's surprised I am you havny heard!'

But Shona's brilliant blue eyes were smiling. 'Ach, that's just a lot of rumour. Father thinks Behag sent a wrong message and it is soldiers – *our* soldiers who have come to Rhanna. There will be ructions and no mistake.'

Matthew's eyes were bulging and he hissed, 'I am hearing it was Robbie took the message to Behag!'

Shona nodded sympathetically. 'Poor old Robbie. Behag will never forgive him, his life will be worse than ever. But c'mon now, it's time Grant went down the road to school. I'll get him to stop off at Laigmhor and ask Father to come with Bob and the others.'

Grant was given instructions and, fairly bristling with importance, scampered off with Donald at his heels, leaving Tina to mourn gently about 'poor Matthew's empty belly'.

The path through the woods was a thick carpet of russet pine needles which muffled their hurrying footsteps. There, in the cathedral of tall trees, it was dim and mysterious, a world apart from the surrounding open spaces. Matthew's steps were a little less jaunty now and he took frequent peeps over his shoulder.

'Did the bairns say something about a Ullabheist?' he asked nervously, the threat of the ethereal appearing to worry him far more than the possible presence of Germans.

'Ach, don't be daft, Matthew!' Shona scolded. 'The boys were exaggerating and fine you know it! Look, we'll go over the burn here and come out of the woods quicker.'

They wobbled their way over slippery stepping stones and, skirting a rise, saw Loch Sliach below. It was a dark, umber pool with the steep crags of the mountains on one side and the amber stretches of the moor on the other. A tiny tree-clad island rose in the centre, separated from dry land by a wide area of water. Billowing out from the island was a long length of translucent white material, humped into odd shapes where pockets of air lay locked in the folds. And plainly, on the cool breath of the calm, frosted air, there came an unintelligible thread of sound . . . human, yet, there in the shadow of the sleeping Ben, with the ever-present sigh of moor and sea, frighteningly uncanny and unreal.

'It's a spook or a Uisga Hag wandered inland,' Matthew gulped. 'I think we'd better be wise and wait for the lads, Shona.'

'Nonsense! You have a boat tied up here, Matthew, for I know you go fishing on the loch with Robbie. Where is it?'

Unwillingly he pulled aside clumps of bracken to reveal the boat in a hollow of sand, and with a distinct lack of enthusiasm helped Shona drag it into the water. As she sat in it, gently bobbing in a scurry of wavelets, she looked at him with quizzical eyes, and a few moments elapsed while he stood on the shore, embarrassed but unmoving. She grabbed the oars and began to pull away.

'Wait! I was just coming!' he said peevishly. 'I will not be having a lassie doing a man's work.'

They reached the islet in minutes. Matthew made a great fuss about tying the boat but Shona climbed quickly ashore and in a very short time found the delirious figure of Anton Büttger lying on a bed of frantically gathered heather and bracken. His eyes were closed but his head was moving from side to side in the madness of his inward nightmares. His uniform was a cold, sodden mess. Of the trousers only tatters remained, and blood seeped from a jagged gash in his leg. But it wasn't that which made Shona's hand fly to her mouth. She was staring at his stomach where a cruel finger of rock had ripped it open, allowing part of his intestines to escape in a red congealing mass. The skin of his legs was blue with exposure, but worse, the fingers of both hands were waxen white with frostbite – the ragged fragments of his flying gloves having afforded him little protection from the elements. The pathetic vulnerability of him lying there, his partially covered genitals giving him the innocence of a small boy, made the tears of pity well into Shona's eyes, and she forgot that this was the Enemy, a young man trained to take life. She forgot that long months of worry over Niall and the subsequent loss of her tiny son had been brought about by the Nazis and their greedy war. She saw only a critically injured human being, lying as Niall had lain, in a foreign land without consciousness to aid the instincts of self-preservation.

'My God, what way did he survive?' a wildly staring Matthew muttered before he rushed behind a bush to vomit.

CHAPTER 7

Babbie, rising soon after Shona's departure, had taken herself off on a walk to Portcull to fetch some groceries for Kirsteen, and when she entered Merry Mary's shop the atmosphere was charged with excitement.

Little Merry Mary was an Englishwoman who had for many years been labelled as an 'old incomer' which she regarded as an honour. But now, after more than forty years she was regarded as a native, and with her quaint tongue and equally whimsical ways she might indeed have sprung from Hebridean soil. Limp ginger hair hung over a bright, inquisitive face from which protruded a square nose, dubiously decorated with a large brown wart. Unknown to its host it had been an object of great interest to the island children over the years: the first child to notice its demise being promised a monetary reward from every other youngster on the island. Like everywhere else Rhanna suffered from inflation and likewise did the value of Merry Mary's wart. Happily she was as unaware of her wart as she was to the mischievous attentions paid to it, and in her delightfully jumbled shop that morning her tongue was wagging busily, entirely oblivious to all but the latest events on the island.

The tiny shop was crowded, tongues clicked, heads nodded, and curious looks were directed frequently towards the Post Office. The news about the ludicrous situation that had arisen on the island because of Behag's misleading message had reached every corner of Rhanna and it was a near-certainty that the subject was being analysed with thorough enjoyment over dinner-tables everywhere.

Soon Erchy the Post came strolling out of the Post Office, a nonchalant whistle on his lips. He walked very casually over to Merry Mary's but his composure failed him at the last moment and he almost fell in the door.

'Well! And what is she saying for herself?' came the inevitable cry of unconcealed curiosity. Under normal circumstances the islanders gave the impression of being disinterested in gossip even while they listened avidly. If a stranger was in their midst a gently malicious tale would cease and the interest would quietly be transferred to something mundane. But as events that morning were of a great magnitude and kettles had been singing over peat fires all night, no one paid the slightest attention to Babbie, who was gazing at the array of glass sweet jars with what seemed to be undivided curiosity. During her childhood in the Argyllshire orphanage Babbie had picked up a fair Gaelic vocabulary from an ancient gardener and, although it was a vastly different Gaelic to that of the Hebrides, she nevertheless got the gist of the conversation. Furthermore, one or two of the younger islanders lapsed frequently from Gaelic to English, which was a great advantage.

Erchy ran a hand through his sparse sandy hair and looked faintly bemused. 'She is not saying a word! Not a single word. It is like the shock has taken her tongue. Poor auld Robbie is begging her to speak but the bitch is just standin' at the counter with her lips tighter than the backside of a day-old chick. 'Tis lucky she is human enough to have calls o' nature like the rest of us, giving Robbie a chance to tell me the news . . .' He paused importantly while sounds of encouragement echoed round him then went on. 'Well, Robbie was thinkin' there were three German airy-planes over the island last night. Righ said it was a Heinkel three and Robbie thought he said three Heinkels and told Behag so. Well, you see, she reported that parachutes were droppin' everywhere and help was to be sent urgently. It was Totie

88

Little saw men landing over at Aosdana Bay before dawn this morning and she told that writer, Dugie Donaldson, who told the Home Guard. For a whily everyone was running round in circles dodgin' the lads from the boat till they found out they were Commandos come to rescue the island. A lot o' them have gone away again but a few have stayed to help wi' the Jerries. Just as well, too, I'm thinkin', for Robbie was after tellin' me that one o' the Jerries has escaped from the Manse . . . that big bull-headed one wi' the bulging eyes. He ate a slap-up breakfast given him by Mrs Gray then just buggered off. He knows he won't get off the island but being the type he is just wants to make things more difficult for the soldiers. Time is precious to these lads and there's goin' to be a fine stramash over the whole affair.'

There was a gasp of surprise over this last piece of news and everyone looked at each other rather fearfully.

'They will take the contraption away from Behag!' said someone in awe.

'Totie will be gettin' it in her Post Office,' put in Morag Ruadh, the nimble-fingered spinner who also played the ancient church organ which Totie had itched to play for years. 'Totie always has her eye on other people's occupations,' she finished with a toss of her red hair.

'Ach well, she is having a clever head on her shoulders,' hazarded Mairi McKinnon, Morag's cousin.

Morag's eyes blazed. 'And what are you insinuating, Mairi? There is *some* brains in the family!' Morag had a spiteful tongue, more pronounced since her dithering, simple younger cousin had, by means more innocent than calculating, got herself pregnant which in turn had got her swiftly to the altar, a fact not easily borne by Morag, who was at a loss to understand why she had never arrived at that revered spot herself.

Tears sprang to Mairi's guileless brown eyes. Her happy life had been shattered since her adored William had gone marching away to join the navy and she was more easily hurt than she had ever been. Kate McKinnon, fresh-faced and full of her usual energy despite her nocturnal activities, rushed to defend her daughter-in-law to whom she had grown close after an initial spell of resentment. 'Ach, leave her be!' she scolded Morag Ruadh. 'Can the cratur no' make a simple remark without you jumpin' down her throat?'

'Simple right enough,' Morag muttered, but Kate's boisterous voice drowned out all else as she addressed Mairi earnestly.

'And how is your poor father, mo ghaoil? It was a bad state he was in when I was last seein' him.'

'Ay, well, he's right enough now,' Mairi faltered, recalling to mind the picture of Todd being trundled past her window in a wheelbarrow before midnight. She had merely thought he was being delivered home by his crapulous friends and no one had told her otherwise till the operation was over because she was useless in an emergency. 'The doctor made a fine job of him but we were thinkin' that someone would be over to see was he better this morning but neither the doctor or Biddy has come.'

At that moment, Elspeth Morrison, the gaunt, sharp-tongued housekeeper of Slochmhor, pushed into the shop. Her life had been embittered by her childless marriage to a fisherman who had met his end through drink. Her saving grace was her dour devotion to the doctor and his family and she jealously guarded her position in the household.

'The poor doctor is exhausted being up all night,' she imparted haughtily. 'He is in no fit state to be gallivanting after people who bring illness upon themselves! A fine thing indeed to be operating on a man pickled in drink and the stuff so scarce it is a mystery how he managed to get so much of it inside himself!' Here she looked meaningfully at Kate who was looking at bobbins of thread with great interest. 'Biddy is the one should be seeing to Todd,' Elspeth went on. 'Knowing her she will have had her fill o' sleep. The doctor was sayin' she must have decided to bide the night at Todd's because she was feart to go back over the glen with the Germans about, but she should have checked in at Slochmhor to see was she needed this morning . . .'. She snorted disdainfully. 'The doctor wanted her to call in at the

Manse to see how was the Germans. I wouldny blame Biddy if that was maybe why she is makin' herself scarce!'

Mairi, looking uncertain of her facts, murmured, 'Ay well, she was not near the place this early morning and Father worrying a bit about his stitches too tight.'

Elspeth put her sharp nose in the air. 'And tight they would have to be to keep all that liquid from oozing out . . . he will be uncomfortable for quite a whily,' she ended unsympathetically.

The subject of Todd's health having been exhausted the shop then turned eagerly to fresh speculation over the fate of Behag Beag and the two Germans who were still wandering loose on the island.

Babbie, having made her purchases, hurried back to Laigmhor, and mischievously imparted all the gossip she had heard. To Fergus, who had been at dinner with Bob when Grant burst into the kitchen with the garbled message, it only confirmed what he already suspected, for by the time he had heard his son's tales of 'monsters and ghosts' on Sliach he was in no mood to believe in further ridiculous rumours. Nevertheless there was still the question of the two missing Germans and, though they would soon be found by the efficient Commandos, he felt he couldn't take any risks till the whole affair was sorted out.

As Fergus pushed away his half-eaten food and began to struggle into his jacket, Bob wiped his mouth with a horny hand and said gruffly, 'The bairns are havering, man! We have no time to be chasing fairy tales!' Old Bob was annoyed at the disruption the German bomber had wreaked in his normal working routine. At sixty-eight he was gnarled and tough from a lifetime of working in every kind of weather the winds brought to Rhanna. He revelled in the hard work his job as shepherd brought him, but it was a time-consuming task which left little room for interruption.

Fergus looked at his black-eyed son and solemn-faced Donald standing with his hands folded behind his back, but before Fergus could speak Kirsteen intervened.

'I know when Grant is lying,' she said quietly. 'And I

don't think Shona would have sent him to tell a fairy tale.'

Grant looked up at his father. 'Shona said the monster was a parachute . . .'

'And the kelpie on the wee island was likely a German,' Donald added breathlessly.

It was enough for Fergus. 'You get on with your work, Bob, I'll go over to Sliach and see what all the fuss is about!'

But Bob suddenly felt ashamed. He knew Fergus wouldn't ask help of any man unwilling to give it and if it wasn't for Kirsteen's kindness his midday meal would be nothing more than bread and cheese washed down with milk. He scraped his chair back and strode to the door to push his feet into muddy wellingtons. 'I'll get along with him, lass,' he told Kirsteen. 'Thankin' you for my dinner.'

She gripped his knotted brown hand briefly. 'Thank you, Bob,' she said simply, but he knew what she meant. He made to follow Fergus but she stopped him by calling in rather awed tones, 'Shouldn't you take a gun? It – might be dangerous.'

'Ach, no, Matthew will have his! If the German has come down on Sliach it's more likely prayers he'll be needin'.'

'Can I come with you, Bob?' Grant asked anxiously, the idea of chasing Germans far more appealing to him than an afternoon with school books. 'I have a fine gun I made myself.'

Seeing Kirsteen's rather harassed look Babbie put down the dish cloth and began to peel off her apron. 'I'll take you to school . . . the pair of you,' she said firmly. 'But we'll go to the harbour for a wee while first and chase the seagulls.'

Grant snorted, feeling himself far too manly for the pastimes he had revelled in only recently, but Bob was already hurrying away, calling on Dot, his sheepdog, who had rounded up a dismayed squadron of hens.

When Bob saw the young German airman he knew it was well that he had come because Fergus with his one arm and a visibly shaken Matthew would never have managed Anton into the boat.

But at first Fergus had no intention of doing such a thing.

His dark eyes had snapped and the muscle of his jaw had tightened. It was one thing for the men of the island to deal with the Enemy, but it was entirely another to see his daughter tenderly ministering to one of them. And as he watched her frantically tearing strips from the hem of her white petticoat to make them into bandages, he was consumed with rage. A German lay on Rhanna soil and his daughter was behaving as if his life was a precious thing that had to be preserved.

His hand flashed out to grip her roughly by the shoulders and haul her to her feet. 'Get away from him!' he ordered harshly. 'Bob and myself will see to him!'

Tears of anger glinted in her eyes. 'Will you, Father – will you see – to this?' She pulled back the blood-saturated cloak to reveal the terrible wounds.

'Dear God, help him!' Bob muttered, swallowing hard.

'God – and Lachlan!' she cried passionately. 'He needs attention quickly or he'll die . . . if he doesn't anyway,' she added so sadly that Fergus put his arm round her and whispered huskily, 'I'm – sorry, mo ghaoil – it was just – things that bother me sometimes.'

He raised his voice. 'Matthew, row like the devil then get along over for Lachlan! Tell him to bring his trap as far as your house!'

Matthew, glad of something to do, almost fell into the boat and splashed away hurriedly.

Fergus looked down at Anton. 'Is . . . there anything you can do for him, Shona?'

Wordlessly she laid a broad strip of petticoat over the gaping viscera. Bob and Fergus gently lifted Anton's body till a thick wad of material was fixed in place. It was immediately soaked in blood and Shona stepped out of what remained of her petticoat and bound it over the bloodstained pad.

'My, but you're a bright lass,' Bob said admiringly. 'There's more in your head than was put there by a spoon.'

'But I can't do any more.' Her voice was filled with frustration. Her experience of nursing was of a limited

93

nature though her few months' training had equipped her with an efficiency that was at times even a surprise to herself. Her legs were shaking and she felt sick with reaction. Silently she sent up a prayer that the doctor hadn't been called to another part of the island. She looked at Anton's face. It was drained of colour and the congealed blood on his forehead leapt out from the whiteness in a vicious riot of purple and red.

It was very quiet. The cold green water lapped the little island. A lone Red-throated Diver paddled hurriedly by, uttering its melancholy mewing wail, annoyed that its chosen nesting territory had been violated by humans. Over the crags of Ben Machrie a great bird soared majestically.

Bob's hand rasped over the stubble on his chin, his eyes raking the misted azure of the sky. 'Damt eagle,' he muttered uneasily. 'It's roamin' up there like it's waitin' for the lambs comin'.' But his unease wasn't incurred by the sight of the eagle whose home lay in the remote mountain ledges. His eyes kept straying to Anton lying like one already dead and his grip tightened on the bone handle of his shepherd's crook.

Fergus leaned against the bole of a tree and lit his pipe with a show of calm but his mind was racing. He tried to keep from looking at Anton but couldn't, the anger in his heart now replaced by a pathos he could barely understand. It wasn't right to feel like this about a German. He struggled with his thoughts. What was right? To hate because it was the proper thing to do in war? The night before he had looked at Jon Jodl and had felt only pity. They were all the victims of circumstance. This dying youngster was just another victim in a world created by the greed of his so-called leaders; another pawn in the deadly, intricate game of war. There was something else, too, that leapt into Fergus's mind, that reared up from the depths of the past: his terrible battle with the deadly waters round the Sgor Creags. The frail speck of his life had struggled with a sea that had wanted to crush his body to pulp and that had mangled his left arm beyond repair. Lachlan had amputated it while he lay in a world of hellish delirium; when he'd been without his senses he'd had to depend on the help of the people who loved him most. And now the wounded German was unconscious and dependent. But if he wakened at that moment who would be familiar and beloved enough for *him* to ask, 'Will you help me?'

Fergus blew a mouthful of smoke into the hazy blue air. For a moment it hung suspended, and when it gradually dispersed all the prejudices that had swathed his thinking went with it. Shona twisted round in a gesture of impatience and caught the look of tenderness in his black eyes. 'You're a fine nurse,' he told her quietly. 'You did a grand job. I'm sure he'll be grateful to you.'

'I don't want his thanks, Father, just a chance of life for him, that's all. I wish Lachlan would hurry.'

Dot was barking impatiently from the shore. She had followed Matthew through the woods but realizing that her master wasn't coming behind she had come back to look for him. The sound of her yelps echoed into the corries of the Ben, then rebounded back over the loch to be lost over the shaggy moors.

'I'll kill that damt dog!' Bob cursed as the eerie ghost bark bounced again and again off the face of the mountain. In normal circumstances he would have roared at Dot to be quiet but hard and tough as he was he felt himself to be in the very presence of Death and his watery eyes gazed broodingly at the unrestrained antics of the lively dog.

Time is an eternity when filled with urgency, but barely thirty minutes had passed when the tall, slim figure of Lachlan finally burst through the thicket of pines on the opposite shore and jumped quickly into the waiting boat. As he pushed it off and came gliding through the calm green water, the men let out sighs of relief and Shona gave a welcoming cry, for the sight of his black bag and the air of reassurance that seemed to enshroud him brought both peace and hope to everyone there. As everyone on Rhanna knew just to look at Lachlan McLachlan was to know love: his tanned face was finely drawn, his mouth firm and sensitive. But it was in his eyes that anxious souls found peace, where they beheld the compassion of his heart. It was the last thing that many of his patients saw before letting go of life.

When Lachlan reached the island he looked at the neat bandage Shona had made and patted her arm. 'You've done well, mo ghaoil,' he approved quietly before starting on a swift examination of Anton's broken body.

Fergus stood against the tree and watched Lachlan's long, sensitive fingers. The doctor had removed his coat to cover Anton and his shoulder blades showed through his pullover. He was thin and still boyish with his dark curling hair that always strayed over his forehead when he bent over. So Fergus remembered the doctor Lachlan who had tended him so devotedly, and for a moment Fergus held his breath. How he loved the man who was both doctor and companion to him. But it hadn't always been so. Fergus's first wife, Helen, had died giving birth to Shona and in his grief Fergus had blamed Lachlan, and it was only many years later, at the time of Fergus's accident, that the two men had healed the rift between them. Something caught in Fergus's throat. How bitterly he regretted those lost years. He had wasted so much precious time that could have been richly spent with the man who healed with skill and unstinting devotion.

As Lachlan began slowly to remove Anton's helmet Fergus knocked his pipe out against the tree and went to kneel by the doctor. 'Does he have a chance, Lachlan?' he asked softly.

'It's difficult to say till I get him back to the house. I've sent Matthew over to fetch Biddy, and Phebie is getting the surgery ready. He ought to be in hospital,' he continued. 'With complete asepsis and every modern surgical technique . . . but I'll do my best.' He passed a hand over his brow. He was always doubtful about his abilities as a surgeon. Working on an island with limited facilities, he'd had to deal with many emergencies over the years – and the patients who had come healthily through surgery carried out in crude, makeshift conditions were a testimonial to his capabilities.

But he was completely without ego and it was perhaps the lack of it which endeared him to so many.

He paused as he lifted the helmet off the wounded man's head. The young man had already reminded him of Niall with his youthful features and firm chin, but now, the crop of fair curling hair completed the illusion. He gently ran his fingers through the thick blond thatch. 'He's got concussion, but the helmet saved him from more serious damage. It's the shock I'm worried about . . . he's lost so much blood.' He looked at the little boat rocking peacefully. 'In my haste I brought only my bag – could you – all of you – take off any clothing you don't need and pad out those planks a bit?'

Wiry old Bob was coatless but he pulled off a tattered cardigan and stood in his shirt sleeves without the hint of a shiver. Fergus removed his jacket and felt the goose pimples rising, but he moved to the boat and began to lay the pitifully inadequate coverings on the bottom. Bob came at his back armed with a bundle of dead bracken which he pushed under the clothing.

'You have a head on you, Bob,' Fergus commented and he too began to gather moss and bracken. In minutes a soft bed was made and the arduous task began of getting Anton into the boat, which was no easy job, for, though slim, he was tall and muscular. Bob and Lachlan grasped his shoulders, Shona supported his middle in an effort to keep the wound from opening further, and Fergus took his ankles in the strong grasp of his right arm. Fergus got into the boat first and his stomach lurched as the frail little craft tilted alarmingly. For a moment he hesitated and looked down. There was no gradual shoreline from the tiny, rocky islet – the land dropped down immediately into deep black depths – and the sight of it made him shudder. Water had frightened him from boyhood. The land was his backbone, water something to be admired so long as his two feet were firmly on the ground. He stumbled against a thwart and the little boat responded by bucking alarmingly.

'Steady, man,' Lachlan said quietly, and the moment was

over. Soon Anton was lying on his bed of mossy bracken but taking up most of the confined space.

'Only two of us will get in wi' him,' Bob muttered, blowing his nose into a grimy hanky with a nonchalant air. 'It's how we'll be managing on the other side that worries me.'

No one looked at Fergus, for never by a word or glance had any man suggested that the loss of his arm was an inconvenience to him. But he was always quick to sense unspoken thoughts and he said roughly, 'Get along over, I'll wait here.'

Shona slid a thin arm round his waist. 'I'll wait with you, we can keep each other warm.'

He looked at her anxiously. She had divested herself of most of her warm clothing to cover Anton, and Fergus felt a rush of protectiveness. He pulled her close and she felt the warmth of his body burning into her, the very nearness of it dispelling the chilly tremors that were bringing her out in goose pimples.

Bob pulled swiftly at the oars. In his days of tending sheep and cows he had seen many a sickening sight, but they were of things within his experience. The sight he had just witnessed was without those bounds, and his tough old stomach churned, making him row the harder. Dot saw him coming and her barks grew in volume, but her sense of devotion was lost on her disgruntled master. He lunged at her with his boot the minute he jumped ashore, whereupon she tucked her tail well between her haunches and slunk into the bushes.

'Come back till I toe your arse, you bugger!' Bob cried in frustration, and then turned his attention to helping Lachlan. Both men were grimly aware of Anton's open wound and were able to ease him over the planks only a few inches at a time, a task made no easier by the swaying of the boat. Bob stopped to wipe watery mucous from his nose. 'It's no damt use, Doctor!' he spat. 'We'll never manage the lad between us! I'd best go back for McKenzie! We need another pair o' hands!' Which last remark was proof of

Bob's invincible faith in Fergus. But before they could move, Dot began making a nuisance of herself again, whimpering in the bushes and making excited half-yelps. The distraction was too much for Bob and he roared, 'Shut up, you brute, or I'll skin your hide – '

He wasn't able to finish the threat. The dog suddenly shot out of the undergrowth, followed by the muzzle of a murderous-looking Tommy gun held by a man attired in khaki battledress and a tin helmet from which sprouted sprays of fir branches.

'Your dog was causing a bit of a nuisance,' he pleasantly told a surprised-looking Bob. The soldier then turned to Lachlan. 'You look like you could be doing with a bit of help?' but before Lachlan could answer he called into the trees, 'Out of it, lads. We need some muscle here.' Magically there appeared from bush and tree half a dozen young men all sporting a variety of natural camouflage. Without a word they went straight to the boat and lifted Anton out as if he were thistledown. Bob immediately climbed back into the boat to row to the island for Fergus and Shona, leaving Lachlan to introduce himself.

'Pleased to meet you, Doctor,' said the thick-set, heavy-jawed young man whose gun had sent Dot yelping. 'I'm Dunn, the officer in charge of this charade.' His teeth showed in a flash of amusement before his eyes travelled to Anton. 'I see you have found another of the bomber crew?'

Lachlan nodded slowly. 'Yes, he's very badly wounded and needs immediate attention. My house is a fair distance from here but I've brought my trap to the clearing at the edge of the wood. We'll have to carry him to it . . .' He spread his fine hands in a gesture of despair. 'I'm worried about the bumping he'll get on the way down. The track is a rough one.'

Dunn grinned reassuringly. 'Don't worry, Doctor, we'll get him back to your house.' He turned to the others and there was a swift exchange. Before Bob was half-way over the loch the men had removed their battle-jackets, fashioning them into a strong, pliable stretcher into which they placed Anton. There was no regimental dividing line between officer and men. They worked together as an efficient team and Lachlan looked on admiringly. Soon they were all making their way through the dark, silent wood with a subdued Dot slinking at Bob's heels. Fergus had wrapped his jacket around Shona who was carrying her bloodstained cloak over her arm.

Dunn looked at it and his professional mask fell for a moment. 'He's lost a lot of blood. Do you know how he came to injure himself?'

'Probably on the mountain – coming down,' she said quietly. 'There's a lot of jagged rocks on this side of the mountain.'

'And you've just found him?'

'Ay, the children heard moans from the island.'

'So he's spent most of the night in the open?'

'And most of the morning. He's suffering badly from exposure.'

'A real tough-skinned Jerry!' Dunn's words were harsh but Shona knew they were only a cover.

When they reached the clearing Dunn nodded towards the trap. 'You get in, Doctor, and lead the way. It's better that we should carry him, lessen the risk of rattling him around.'

Fergus fell into step with Dunn who was at the head of the stretcher party. 'It's been a wild-goose chase for you,' Fergus said in his deep melodious voice. It wasn't a question, but a blunt statement of fact.

The officer appreciated it, and laughed. 'Wild geese would be a bloody sight easier to catch than the ghosts we've been chasing. We were told the island was invaded by German paratroops and were sent over to investigate – can't be too careful – never know what the bastards will be up to . . .' He checked himself and went on pleasantly, 'We've got on to Naval Patrol to let them know it's a bit of a false alarm . . . some of us are staying though . . . there's still the pig-headed one of the crew to locate and it seems your Home Guard are having a bit of trouble running him to ground. We met some

100

of them over on the north side of the island but they didn't seem too keen to hang around there.'

Fergus smiled at this but Bob's weatherbeaten countenance creased into a frown. 'No one in their right senses will be staying round that damt place for long!' It was a cryptic remark, one typical of the superstitious older generation, and Bob, being one of the best Seanachaidhs (story tellers), was renowned for his ability to arouse curiosity in the least imaginative beings, but the officer merely smiled politely and said nothing.

Bob's gnarled fingers curled tighter round his crook. 'The De'il deals wi' his own,' he snarled, defensive yet assertive about his beliefs. 'It is a consecrated place yonder at Dunuaigh. The monks will no' be likin' the intrusion that is goin' on wi' folks of all nationalities trampin' over their restin' places!'

Shona smiled impishly. 'But Bob, there is only one German likely to be wandering – and no doubt wishing he hadn't been so hasty in escaping from the Manse this morning.'

' 'Tis enough! 'Tis enough!' Bob barked and he stamped away to begin his belated work, calling impatiently on Dot who went scampering after him gladly enough.

Tina was standing at the door of her cottage. She raised a languid arm in the manner of one acknowledging a carnival procession, her only betrayal of surprise manifested by the slightly breathless utterance, 'You have caught the German laddie then?' Which singular observation rendered the sturdy presence of the Commandos as of little import. 'If any o' you are seeing Matthew, send him home for his dinner,' she added in slightly accusing tones, then turned to scoop Eve from the water barrel into which she was gleefully climbing.

Shona ran ahead and climbed into the trap beside Lachlan who immediately tucked a rug round her legs. 'You take care, mo ghaoil,' he told her. 'We must have a nice rosy lass waiting for Niall when he gets home.'

She laughed, tucking her arm through his. 'Don't worry,

Kirsteen has stuffed so much food into me since I came home Niall will think I'm a prize turkey when he sees me. A good excuse for him to thraw my neck!'

Their laughter drifted back to Fergus who had just heard from the officer about the raids over Clydebank the previous night. First-hand news could be had from the accumulator-powered wireless sets owned by those interested and affluent enough to possess one. Fergus had one in his parlour but the morning had been too rushed for anyone in the household to think about switching on. The officer went on to say that it was believed the bomber that had crashed on Rhanna was one of a group which had taken part in the raids, and then, having been hit, had lost all sense of direction.

'Oh God, no!' Fergus breathed. 'The doctor's son stays in Clydebank. He and my daughter are sweethearts! Good God! Is there no end to it?' It was a cry from the heart and Dunn looked at him in sympathetic enquiry. 'Niall was injured at Dunkirk,' Fergus explained. 'Lachlan, his wife, Shona – all were wild with grief because they believed him to be dead – but he came back with a wound that meant no more fighting for him . . .' He smiled wryly. 'It would seem the war has caught up with him anyway. How am I to tell his parents that?'

Dunn cleared his throat. 'Would – you like me to do it?'

Fergus hesitated as he watched the stretcher party marching carefully down the grass-rutted track. It was very peaceful there among the fields, with the crushed grasses releasing an almost forgotten scent of summer. The dairy cows, released from winter byres, let out soft little half-bellows which they blew into each other's ears. The frost of the morning had disappeared and there was a gentle heat in the haze of the sun, a delicate promise of the green, Hebridean spring to come. Banners of blue smoke curled from croft and farm, rising to hang in tattered shrouds against the misted purple of the mountains.

Down below Lachlan and Shona turned, curious as to why Fergus and the officer had stopped.

Fergus wondered wildly what to do. How would Shona

feel having an echo of the past brought back? Phebie would react typically, with a quiet display of normality hiding her deepest fears . . . And Lachlan, the doctor in him rising up out of his despair to try and save the life of a German . . . But how would Lachlan the man feel afterwards? How would they all feel till news of Niall filtered out of the confusion of an air raid? Shona . . . Again Fergus hesitated. She had come back to Rhanna for a holiday, to rest that tightly-strung little body which Fergus was still inclined to think of as belonging to a child. But even though she had been home such a short time he was seeing a change in her. She had gained a lot of poise, her emotions were under a tighter rein. Once, Rhanna and all it meant had been her only horizon, but now there were others which seemed to have broadened her whole outlook on life . . .

Fergus straightened his shoulders. 'I'll tell them,' he said abruptly to Dunn and ran down the rutted track to catch up with the trap.

Lachlan heard him out in silence, a faint flush high on his cheekbones the only sign of his inner fears. Shona, her deep blue eyes wide, stared at her father as his firm lips formed halting words into some kind of meaning. She wanted to put her hands over her ears, to scream at her father to be quiet, to shut her mind to the facts. It had been easier in childhood when little fantasies had helped her over the many hurdles of her young life. But she wasn't a child any more, there were no little illusions to help her now. In a dream she heard herself saying, 'No one will be knowing the facts yet. It – will be some time before we hear any news?'

'I'm afraid so,' Dunn murmured, coming up behind Fergus. 'Everyone is too shattered and harassed to make much sense of anything. I believe it all started last night and the all-clear didn't come till just before dawn this morning. Everything will be in a turmoil but I'll get some enquiries through if I can . . .' He smiled kindly and went on, 'Mr McKenzie tells me the young man has had experience of battle and is at present with Civil Defence so I'm sure he knows how to look after himself.' What he didn't add was

103

that there was a strong likelihood the German bombers would return to Glasgow and Clydebank that night but he felt he had already said enough on the subject.

The stretcher party had halted some distance ahead, and Lachlan turned to Shona. 'Go home, mo ghaoil. I'll understand.'

She put her small hand over his and shook her head vehemently, tears welling up in her eyes. 'No! You'll need all the help you can get! If I sit at home I'll just dwell on all the things that might never happen. It would be useless to try and contact Niall, all the usual communications will be down but . . .' she turned appealingly to Dunn, 'if you hear anything further or can get any sort of enquiries through would you let me know immediately?'

'Count on it,' Dunn nodded.

Fergus took her other hand and crushed it tightly. 'You take care, Ni-Cridhe,' he told her softly.

Shona caught her breath. 'Ni-Cridhe' was the Gaelic endearment for 'my dear lassie'. It wasn't often he expressed himself so freely in public and she knew that he was feeling something of her pain. It was his way of telling her how much he cared. 'I'll take care, Father,' she whispered.

'We'll expect you in for tea,' he said, and then turned abruptly on his heel and strode away.

CHAPTER 8

A curious crowd had gathered outside Lachlan's, ample proof that Matthew's tongue had been busy. When the stretcher party hove into view everyone began to talk among themselves as if by doing so they were proving that their presence in that remote spot of Glen Fallan had no bearing whatsoever on the latest events. So absorbed did they appear that it seemed an impossibility their interest could lie in anything that was happening outside their own little circle.

As Lachlan came by in the trap, heads lifted one by one in a great display of surprise.

'It is yourself, Doctor,' acknowledged Kate McKinnon innocently. 'We were just thinkin' over the things o' last night and wondering where the other two German lads were hidin' but I see you have another one there.' With one accord they all turned to look upon the deathly pale face of Anton being marched past their vision.

Lachlan got down from the trap and said with a deceptively charming smile, 'And you have all left Portcull to have a little chin-wag in the middle of Glen Fallan?'

Old Joe's sea-green eyes betrayed nothing. 'Ach no, not at all, Doctor,' he rebuked gently. 'We are waiting for the lads to come over the glen to see will they have news for us.'

'Ay,' put in Erchy the Post who, with his satchel slung over his shoulder and one foot on the pedal of his bike, had the air of someone who had been rudely interrupted in the middle of a busy day. 'That is a fact, Doctor. Also Matthew was asking us to wait and tell you that Biddy is not at home.'

'But I know that!' Lachlan cried. 'She spent the night at the Smiddy!'

Fingal McLeod, a tall lanky young crofter who had lost his leg to a fox snare, nodded wisely. 'Well, well now, that is likely why she is no' at home.'

'But I told Matthew she would be at Todd's,' Lachlan said.

'Ach well, that's where she'll be right enough,' Erchy murmured.

Lachlan was growing exasperated. The islanders could be trying and unhelpful when they had a mind, and it was obvious they were in no mood to be helpful now.

Shona felt her temper rising. It was a trait over which she had to exercise control but just then it erupted in a mixture of anxiety and grief. 'Well!' she cried hotly, 'one of you get along over to Todd's and fetch Biddy!'

'Matthew will be over there now,' Fingal said soothingly.

Shona tossed her auburn head and her eyes sparkled with rage. 'You are just like a bunch of old women! The laddie you are gaping at so eagerly may die! Lachlan can't do everything himself and I'm not fully trained to help properly! For God's sake! He's a German, I know, but he's also a human being!'

Lachlan had disappeared into the house leaving Elspeth listening at the door. Her strangely immobile face was gaunt with outrage at the very idea of a German, wounded or otherwise, being allowed to cross the doctor's threshold. In Elspeth's mind, Slochmhor and everyone therein owed all to her efficiency as a housekeeper and she felt it was her right to exercise her opinion as to what went on there. When Phebie had asked her to help prepare the surgery for an emergency case she had agreed willingly enough, scrubbing and cleaning till the air reeked of antiseptic. But not until the Commandos crossed the doorstep with Anton did she realize that for the past hour she had been preparing the way for a German airman, and she was speechless with indignation. Now, though, at Shona's words she found her tongue quickly. 'Wait you there, Erchy McKay!' she said to Erchy, who, shamefaced, was straddling his bike ready to push off. 'It is the King's business you should be about! You have no right to be gallivanting off when you are on duty!'

Elspeth was coming down the path into the crowd and Erchy stopped in mid-flight, his kindly face bewildered and angry. He was about to tell her that the 'King's business' was only a part-time job on an island that received mail only three times a week, but before he could speak another figure came flying past on a bike, pedalling swiftly along the bumpy glen road. It soon proved to be Babbie Cameron, her wind-tossed hair a fiery beacon, her pale, freckled skin whipped to a delicate rose. The bike had been left in the ditch by Murdy the night before and Babbie had simply borrowed it. It was a rusted heap with a wobbling front wheel and Babbie now discovered it had no brakes. Babbie's feet rasped along the stony road in an effort to stop the machine, but she catapulted into the crowd, sending everyone scattering. Gallantly the menfolk rushed to her aid, having

106

to make no excuses for hands that grabbed at forbidden fruits in order to avert a catastrophe.

Babbie was an attractive sight standing against the backcloth of the mountains. Her red hair, which breathed of sunshine and all the bright fire of autumn, made the slopes of Sgurr nan Ruadh look dull in comparison. The pallor of her skin was startling in its glowing frame yet oddly in keeping; her mouth was too generous for her to be beautiful, but her smile was so radiant that to observe it was to know enchantment. She was slim to the point of being skinny but though her sweater was in itself shapeless it couldn't entirely hide the curving swell of her breasts. Rhanna men liked their women 'well padded', and no matter how beautiful the face or figure of a slim woman she rarely merited a second glance after the first swift appraisal. But it was a different matter if the slimness was enhanced by properly placed padding, and Babbie fitted this category. While she panted for breath the men fussed and Elspeth glowered.

'Sorry everyone . . . and thanks,' Babbie smiled, adroitly removing Fingal's hand from her left thigh. She turned to look at Shona. 'Your father popped in to tell us about – things . . . I thought I might be needed.'

Shona felt like hugging her there and then in the middle of the glen. Instead she put out her hand. 'You're just in time, Babbie – the doctor will be waiting.' And with her head held high she marched with Babbie up the path to Slochmhor, an outraged Elspeth forced to make way for them at the gate.

'I'll be telling Biddy to look in on her way home,' called a rather subdued Kate. 'She will not be liking it if she feels left out.'

'As you like,' Shona said from the door. 'Though 'tis a pity you were not thinking about it sooner.'

The villagers ambled back to Portcull in a somewhat embarrassed silence, Fingal and Erchy breaking away from the others at the hill track leading to Nigg. Erchy's satchel already contained two rabbits which he had collected from his snares half an hour earlier. He pushed his bike into a clump of bushes and grinned at Fingal. 'Let us go about the

King's business then,' he said in a hideous falsetto. Both men roared with laughter, made all the merrier at the prospect of an afternoon poaching Burnbreddie.

'We might find the other Jerry waiting to ravish her ladyship,' Fingal snorted ecstatically. He halted for a moment to sit down on a mossy stone. 'Wait you, Erchy, I will have a wee look to see have I got everything we need.' Carefully, he unscrewed the bottom half of his peg leg, peered inside, and then, satisfied as to its contents, fixed it back in place. 'Old Peggy is fully equipped,' he grinned. 'I have an extra flask of Tam's whisky in there too. We will no' go thirsty.'

In the surgery at Slochmhor, Lachlan, too, was finding every reason to be grateful to Tam. Earlier in the day he had pressed a generous bottle of whisky into Lachlan's hands, and nodding and winking he had warned, 'Don't be telling a soul, Doctor. 'Tis for your nerves when you have to be doing these awful things like Todd's appendix.' Lachlan had put the bottle to the back of the cupboard thinking it unlikely that it would be needed in the near future, and now he smiled wryly at the small glass in his hand. Todd's appendix was nothing to what waited for his immediate attention. Anton lay scrubbed and ready . . . Ready for what? Life or death? The responsibility lay with Lachlan and the thought made his hands shake.

'Ready, Doctor?' One of the Commandos, a sturdy young man with a strong stomach, who had volunteered to stay behind and help, popped his head round the door.

Lachlan gulped down the whisky and spluttered, 'Yes, I'm ready.' He smiled. 'I don't make a habit of this, Private Anderson.' Anderson looked at the whisky bottle with interest. 'Would you like a drop?' Lachlan asked, amused despite himself.

'I don't mind, sir, I really don't mind.' He gulped down a generous mouthful, straightened his shoulders and followed Lachlan briskly into the surgery.

Phebie was just coming out. Inside, her stomach was churning with misery, and all she could think about was

Niall, her son, her beloved eldest child, once again bringing anxiety and deepest despair to all those who loved him most. Her bonny plump face was strained and pale but she managed to smile at Lachlan and whisper 'Good luck, Lachy. Shout if you need me.'

He gripped her shoulders tightly and bent to kiss her cheek. 'It's you I should be with just now,' he said huskily. 'You're always such a tower of strength, yet I know . . . even the strongest of towers need a bit of propping up now and then. Our son will be all right, my darling. The young rascal has come through worse. I'll be in there operating on a mortally wounded German laddic but my prayers will be with Niall.'

'Mine too,' she said shakily and stood back to let him pass, hardly able to see for the tears drowning her eyes.

Babbie, masked and gowned, stood looking down at Anton. He was wrapped in wind-bleached folds of gleaming white linen which seemed to match the deathly pallor of his face. His forehead was patterned with bruises whose livid colour leapt out from the white skin. He looked very young and completely helpless and Babbie thought, 'So, this is a German. If you had been ugly . . . perhaps just a little bit evil-looking, Anton Büttger, I might have hated you . . . but you're not, you're not! If you had been then I might not feel so obliged to help try and save your life. Damn you, Anton Büttger,' her heart cried. 'Damn you for looking so young and innocent. I hate you for making me feel that I must do all the right things to give you a chance of life!' Her thoughts made her feel sick and her hands trembled.

Shona saw the hesitation and though her own legs were shaking, she said reassuringly, 'You're doing fine, Babbie. The beginning's always the difficult part.'

'Are you all right, Babbie?' Lachlan asked a trifle sharply, all the old doubts about his own abilities piling into his head at sight of the young German's ghastly wounds.

'Yes . . . I just skipped eating most of my dinner with all the upsets,' Babbie said faintly, her green eyes full of an odd apprehension. 'It's just hunger pains.'

'Would you like me to get you something?' Anderson asked. He had not batted one eyelid at the sight of Anton's stomach piling out from the surrounding flesh.

'No – no, I'm fine now.'

Lachlan gave her a worried look. 'You have had experience of surgery, Babbie?'

'Oh yes, yes of course . . . it's just . . . never with a German.'

'You must put that out of your head,' Lachlan said gently. 'Just think of him as a patient who deserves all our skill to pull him through.' Then Lachlan turned to begin the operation, and as he worked he forgot all about his doubts and concentrated solely on the task at hand. His long, sensitive fingers worked with a faultless skill that made everyone in the room glow with admiration. His aura of confidence seemed to reach out and embrace them all and after the first few minutes they were working together as an efficient team.

Biddy grumbled long and loudly as she struggled awake. With a dry mouth and an aching head spinning alarmingly, she hastily closed her eyes again. She felt sick and for a moment couldn't sort out one thought from another. Then the smells of the Smiddy came to her: horse manure, leather, fragrant hay and rusting bits of iron. For a few seconds she lay unable to believe it was daylight and that she must have spent the night in Todd the Shod's barn. Bits of hay had worked their way into her clothing and were making her very uncomfortable. Carefully she moved an arm in an experimental gesture. Well, one limb was still intact anyway. Slowly she shifted the position of her cold, cramped body and immediately a searing pain shot through her ankle. 'Damt bugger!' she swore through gritted teeth, the pain bringing her sharply to her senses. Wincing, she raised herself on an elbow to grope for her glasses, but they eluded her searching fingers. Screwing up her eyes she peered round the big shed but there was no sign of life. The visiting horses had probably been collected earlier by their owners, and as she was ensconced in a pile of hay which was almost smothered by a jumbled heap of ironmongery, she must have escaped notice.

Biddy's first feelings of surprise soon turned to extreme indignation. What kind of place was it where people went about everyday affairs without a thought to the nurse who had tended them so devotedly for years? The cold of the night had played havoc with her circulation. Her extremities were like lumps of lead, especially her feet which were nearest the side door. 'Damt Germans!' Biddy muttered under her breath. 'I'll kill the buggers if I catch them!' Then she raised her voice, uttering appeals for help which flowed with such lusty frequency that the pigeons in the loft fluttered up in a cloud of dust and made a hasty exit. Then Mollie McDonald came running in, a red-faced bustle of amazement.

As Mollie stood in the doorway, taking in the sight of the old nurse, toothless and without spectacles, lying among the junk and hay, her mouth fell open. It was well known that Biddy was fond of 'a wee tipple'. She carried a hip flask wherever she went and fortified herself whenever she felt the need. It was purely for 'medicinal purposes only' she told anyone who questioned her, but few did. Hers was a job that called her out at all times and in all weathers and so devoted was she that no one blamed her for 'having a wee snifter to warm her auld blood'. Indeed, the islanders saw to it that her flask was never dry and frequently topped up her 'firkin for the fireplace'. But Mollie was in a mood that morning to blame the 'Uisge-beatha' for a great many things. Her good nature allowed her to overlook many of her husband's little misdemeanours, but the manner of his arrival home the night before had caused her some embarrassment. And now Biddy was lying in their barn hideously glassy-eyed and stupefied, her wiry grey hair hanging in limp strands over her lined, yellow face. She was obviously suffering from a massive hangover. Mollie folded her arms and moved forward into the shed.

'Well now, Biddy McMillan!' she said, her voice taut with disapproval. 'A fine thing this is indeed, and you with your reputation to uphold. It's a reputation for an alcoholic cailleach you'll be earning and no mistake. I knew last night there was something funny goin' on wi' Todd and his cronies but never – never – did I imagine that yourself of all people would be in on a thing like that. You're worse than auld Annack Gow and that's sayin' something for she was never sober when Jock was alive if I'm mindin' right!'

Biddy was speechless. She had found her specs and had hastened to put them on in order that she might hear better the words of sympathy that would surely follow her discovery, for it was a belief of hers that glasses aided not only the sight but also the hearing. Small inarticulate grunts escaped her toothless mouth.

Mollie snorted and continued softly. 'Ach, but it is terrible just. The world is goin' to ruin! Germans and soldiers all over the island an' our very own nurse lyin' drunk in my Todd's place o' business. 'Tis no wonder you were not over seeing to him this morning,' she clucked reproachfully. 'Biddy, mo ghaoil, if you had to sleep it off could you not just have stayed in the house to be decent-like?'

Biddy removed her specs because she could hardly believe her ears. Her ankle was throbbing, she was frozen to the marrow, and instead of sympathy she was receiving abuse. 'Is it blind you are, Mollie McDonald?' she gasped through tears of exhaustion and self-pity. 'It is the doctor I am needin' this very meenit! I feel like I am dyin' wi' exposure and my ankle is broken! Get help quickly, you silly woman – and put the kettle on for a cuppy.'

But before Mollie could hasten away Kate McKinnon appeared, and she too stared at Biddy. 'What way are you lyin' there for, you daft cailleach?' she twinkled. 'It's no wonder Matthew couldny find you! They are needin' you over at Slochmhor.'

Biddy's howl of derisive indignation split the air asunder. 'Needin' me! God! It's the doctor I am needin' and quick! Go and get Matthew and get me in that house before I die!'

Matthew came running at Kate's boisterous call, and between them they carried Biddy into the house amid a shower of abuse, instructions and complaints.

'Go you and fetch the doctor, Matthew,' Kate ordered. 'And don't be longer than two minutes.'

An astonished Todd, wallowing in self-pity over his post-operative discomforts, found his martyrdom seriously undermined by the advent of Biddy who was placed near him on an adjoining sofa. Mollie hastened to swing the kettle over the fire while Kate went upstairs to look for spare blankets.

The operation was well underway when Matthew's voice, loud and excited, drifted through from the hall, mingling with Phebie's soft and pleasant tones. Moments later she tapped on the surgery door and put her head round. 'Biddy had an accident last night,' she explained in some harassment. 'She was asleep in Todd's kitchen when she thought she heard noises in the Smiddy. She went out to look, thinking it might be Germans and she tripped on some junk and knocked herself unconscious. Mollie found her just a short time ago and it seems as well as everything else she has hurt her ankle rather badly.'

'Damn!' Lachlan cried, exasperated. 'I can't possibly leave this.'

'I'll go,' Shona said rather gladly, her first experience of surgery rendering her so nauseated she had been wondering how long she could go on without fainting. 'It sounds like something I can deal with.'

'Biddy says she wants the doctor!' Matthew's voice echoed from the hall.

'Well, she'll just have to make do with me!' Shona said firmly. 'I'm better at the Jack-and-Jill stuff anyway . . .' She took a last look at Anton on the table. 'A lot better than anything I can be doing for him. Is it all right, Lachlan?'

'Run along, lass,' Lachlan said kindly. 'You've done a grand job here. If Biddy starts grumbling at you just you tell her I'll be along later to sort her out.'

On the sofa Biddy groaned loudly with pain in between gulps of hot tea laced with brandy. 'It's broken, I know the bugger

113

has broken itself!' she proclaimed loudly, addressing her swollen ankle.

Kate helped herself to tea from the huge pot, then sat down on the edge of Todd's sofa to eye Biddy thoughtfully. 'It's an assistant you should be having, Biddy,' she began sternly, pausing to let the inevitable barrage of protest subside before going on. 'I was just thinkin' the thing last night when I heard you had to sprachle out your warm bed to see to Todd here. It's too much to ask o' an auld chookie and now you are having this accident and maybe endin' up wi' piles and piddle trouble wi' the cold gettin' up your passages all night.'

Biddy wrapped a patchwork quilt round her knees and glowered into her tea. She knew Kate was right but she wasn't going to admit it because to do so, even to herself, was a signal that she really was getting beyond nursing the island single-handed. There had been an assistant several years before but she hadn't stuck the post for more than a month, and this fact she sourly pointed out to Kate, who made a gesture of impatience with her big, capable hands.

'Ach, c'mon now, mo ghaoil! Is it any wonder the poor soul skedaddled like a fart in front of a turd? You never gave her a chance! Criticized everything she did . . . in front o' her patients too. I mind her saying to me, "I am not able even to give an enema but that old bitch is peering over my shoulder to see am I putting the tube in the right passage". Near to tears she was telling me that, and myself knowing she was good at it, too, for she gave me one thon time I was laid up wi' my back.'

Todd had been mending the handle of a goffering iron with what appeared to be single-minded intent but when he looked up, the smile on his craggy face showed otherwise. 'It will not be a man causing a mistake like that,' he observed with an avidness that was out of keeping with his supposedly delicate condition. The profundity of the statement seemed to surprise even himself and thoughtfully he spat on the peats from the conveniently placed sofa, and then watched the results with every sign of enjoyment.

114

For a few moments the sizzling of roasting saliva filled the kitchen until Biddy said with slow deliberation, 'It is well you are not yet knowing what we had to sew up last night, Todd McDonald. Ay me, the Lord giveth and the nurse taketh away . . .'

Kate spluttered into her tea, Todd's guileless blue eyes glazed over and Mollie, coming back with a bowl of cold water from the rain barrel for Biddy's ankle, stood in the doorway, her loosely-hinged jaw once more falling to its lowest extent.

'Ay, ay,' Biddy continued wisely. 'It can happen! These scalpels is sharp things and your belly that round a wee slip's no' an easy thing to avoid – but, ach – don't worry, Todd, at your age it won't be mattering too much and it will never be noticed! Lachlan is a great hand wi' the embroidery and I am having a fine wee keepsake o' yourself to be remembering you by. It's fine for an old body like myself that never was having a man to occupy me, as you have told me yourself on more than one occasion.' She sighed regretfully. 'I can be lookin' at it and thinkin' "Ay, poor auld Todd, he was aye generous wi' himself right enough".' She fixed him with a fond gaze. 'Just think, you will go down in posterior like that other chiel . . . Napoleon I think it was. There was always a rumour they preserved his in a wee boxie.' She stirred her third cup of tea with a great show of calculated sorrow. Todd's face had grown bright red and he was glaring at Biddy with malevolence.

'It is no' an assistant you are needin', Biddy McMillan! It is a replacement! I am going to write to the Medical Board and ask for one to be sent right away!'

Kate threw herself back on the sofa in a fit of laughter and Todd yelled in pain as her weight pinned his legs. 'Ach, but you should see your face, Todd,' she screeched. 'It is yourself will be needin' the replacement and maybe Mollie another husband, for who would be wantin' a man that's nothing more than a castrated ram!'

Mollie's mouth quivered but she managed to scold sternly, 'It's your tongue should be cut out, Kate McKinnon! Todd is all the man I need. Poor soul, he is no' able to take any more shocks, he had enough last night to last him for a whily.' She turned to Biddy. 'Now then, Biddy, Kate and myself will see to that ankle o' yours.'

'It's broke I tell you,' Biddy protested, but Mollie quelled her with a stern eye and Biddie allowed her shoe and one of her black woollen stockings to be removed.

Mollie's lifetime of administering to a slightly hypo-chondriac husband had hardened her sympathies and she was inclined to think that everyone exaggerated their ills. 'Ay, you've only twisted it,' she asserted with a nod.

'I tell you it's broke,' Biddy said faintly although she knew by experience that her ankle was only badly strained.

Todd's post-operative pallor took on a distinctly rosy glow during the removal of Biddy's stocking. It was one thing for a Gael to make jokes about the female form but quite another to have a feminine leg exposed to his vision, even though the limb in question resembled a badly warped spurtle. 'Here,' he protested, 'this is no place for a woman to be doing such things.'

Kate got to her feet with a mischievous grin. 'Ach, the poor bodach is right enough! Him bein' a virgin mannie now won't be having the thrill of a woman's leg any more. He'll be celebrite like thon monks in the monkeries!'

'Damt women!' Todd exploded, while Kate, with a great show of solemnity, fixed a blanket between the sofas so that it formed a screen.

Into this unexpectedly merry gathering came Shona who looked at the scene with some surprise. 'I was told to expect a house full of invalids and here you all are looking as though you are having some sort of concert party.'

'Ach, it was poor auld Todd,' Kate said placidly. 'He was feart the sight of Biddy's ankle would set his passions leapin' so I fixed up the blanket to keep him from doin' himself a mischief!'

'Well, I've been sent over to see to the pair of them. Lachlan is busy operating on the bomber commander but he will be over to see to you both later,' Shona imparted, hiding a smile at sight of Biddy's outraged expression.

'Hmph!' Biddy snorted. 'No doubt I'll keep yet for a whily. I've survived this long after lyin' half-dead all night while the doctor attends to Germans,' she ended with an air of blatant martyrdom.

'Ach, c'mon you silly cailleach, let me see your ankle,' Shona said affectionately. The swelling had subsided slightly, thanks to Mollie's administrations and Shona praised the act.

'Just as well she did something,' Biddy grunted, 'for when her and that Kate found me they just stood looking at me like a couple of spare farts! It's a wonder I didn't die before they got me in the damt house!'

Shona began to strap up the ankle and Biddy noticed the dark circles under the girl's eyes and the dispirited droop of her shoulders. 'My bonny wee lassie,' she murmured tenderly. 'Here is me rampin' on like a bull wi' the skitters and your poor hert breakin'. I can tell something is ailing you.'

'Niall is ailing me that's what, Biddy. The Germans bombed Clydebank last night – and – and I have no way of knowing if he's dead or alive.'

'Ach, my bairnie,' the old midwife drew Shona's head down to her scraggy old bosom. 'Greet now my wee one, it will help the pain.' And cry Shona did, softly and helplessly, while Biddy stroked her hair and crooned loving words. Behind the curtain Todd gave a small forlorn sigh.

'What ails you now, Todd? Is it a hangover you are having?' Kate dimpled mischievously.

'Indeed I am not!' he protested with dignity. 'It's my stitches too tight and myself wishing the doctor could be here to see am I all right.'

'They'll be tight for a whily,' Biddy told him, 'but no tighter than you were yourself last night so it serves you right if you are uncomfortable. The disgrace of it! But never mind, Shona won't mind taking a wee look at them I'm sure.'

Todd was aghast at the idea of a young girl 'looking at his condition'. 'Indeed, she will not!' he asserted quickly. 'I will not have a bairn like Shona looking at my belly and if I have to die waiting for the doctor to do it . . . then die I will.'

In spite of herself Shona smiled. 'Ach, away, Todd. My friend, Babbie, is a trained nurse. I'm sure she won't mind helping Lachlan for a wee while.'

'Oh, but it will have to be done through the authorities,' Biddy imparted dourly. 'They'll have to send a spare nurse . . . just till I'm back on my feets,' she added hastily.

'We'll see.' Shona wiped her tears away impatiently and went back to her ministrations on Biddy's ankle.

CHAPTER 9

In the little guest room at Slochmhor, Anton Büttger lay like one who had already passed through the Valley of the Shadow. It was now evening and the soft lamplight shone on his fair curls crisping out from the layer of bandages encasing his head; his thick eyelashes lay on high cheekbones; and a fine little stubble of hair shadowed the hollows of his cheeks, making his face look thinner than it was. A faint dew of sweat gleamed on his upper lip and Babbie stooped to wipe it gently away. Despite his fever his hands were still clammily cold and again she put them under the blankets, stopping for a moment to check the bandages that swathed his middle. Shona plumped the pillows on the shake-down bed set in a corner of the room, and tried to dispel the numbness that surrounded her thoughts like a cloying shroud. She had listened to the tea-time news about the raids over Clydebank and Glasgow. It was a depressing account of devastation, of a chaos from which no order could yet emerge. A lot of people had died, a lot more had been injured, and there was simply no way of knowing if Niall was among the living or the dead. More raids were expected that night – tonight . . .

Shona shuddered and looked from the window to the moon breaking through the mist. It was 10.30. At that very moment the German bombers might be sweeping over Glasgow, crushing out the lives of innocent people, wrecking the lives of those that were left. She imagined Niall then: tall and handsome with his sun-tanned limbs and boyish smile, his corn-coloured curls glinting in the sun, his firm lips close to her own . . . She could feel them brushing her face . . .

She started and pulled away the net curtain that had blown softly against her cheek. The keen air from the moor whispered in through the slightly opened sash, laden with the sharp clean smell of the frost-rimed bracken on the hill. She turned and looked back at the room – at the bed occupied by the young German airman – and her memory took her back over the years to when, as a little girl, she had lain in the same bed. It was during the time that Mirabelle had died, and Hamish, too, the big laughing Highlander who had been grieve at Laigmhor, and whom she had loved. He had given her Tot, her dear little spaniel. The pup had been a present for her fifth birthday. Hamish had died on the treacherous rocks of the Sgor Creags in the same sea that had crushed her father's arm to pulp. It had all happened at once and she had spent her nights at Slochmhor, a frightened little girl unable to sleep. Niall had come to her then, an awkward boy of twelve, his thin arms enclosing her with his boyish comfort. 'I'm just through the wall from you – we can tap out messages to each other.' His words tossed back at her over the years and a sob caught in her throat.

Babbie looked up quickly. 'Are you alright, Shona?'

'Yes, I'm fine.' She composed herself quickly and added, 'How is he? Will he pull through, do you think?'

Babbie shook her bright head. 'Only time will tell that. He's young – strong – the doctor did a wonderful job. You're lucky to have such a man on the island.'

'Yes, I know, he puts up with a lot but seldom complains.'

'Some would say he was wasted here.'

'Wasted!'He probably does more healing in this wee island than many doctors do with all the modern aids of the big hospitals.' She looked at Babbie quizzically. 'Can you really see Lachlan swallowed up in a big city practice? Here he is somebody, he stands out . . . do you think that's as daft as it sounds?'

'I know what you mean,' Babbie said softly. 'He's special. I watched him today, Phebie too, working like Trojans to save a German even though they are worried to death about their son.'

'You worked pretty well yourself – though – I got the strangest feeling it went against your grain – working to try and save the life of a German.'

Babbie glanced at Anton but her face betrayed nothing. She gave a small shrug. 'It's as Lachlan says; he is a patient like the hundreds of other patients I've had to see to in my time.'

'Ay, but this one is a German and the idea of it affected you, Babbie, deny it how you will. You helped to undress him, you saw the Iron Cross. Young he may be, but he has killed, Babbie, and somehow you can't forgive him for it . . . Och, I hate this war! It does things to nice people, makes them all bitter – and – and horribly irrational in their thinking!'

Babbie left the bed and went over to Shona, her eyes dark with sympathy. 'You have a soft heart, Shona McKenzie. Despite all your tempers you're softer than butter. I wish I was a bit like you – you get it all out of your system and things heal up quicker inside you. I keep it all inside and it's as well folks can't see what's in my heart at times, times like today when I looked at Anton Büttger and for quite a few sick moments I wanted him to die! But you! You worked like a wee fury though you had just heard that Germans . . . like him . . .' she inclined her head towards the bed, 'had just killed and injured a lot of people and your Niall was right in the thick of it all. I admire you, Shona . . . but I don't understand you!'

Shona took a deep breath. 'I didn't want to think. I've discovered that's the worst punishment of all. It's the not knowing that's worst. It's like being in a dark tunnel, never knowing whether you're crawling towards the light – or going back into the darkness.'

'Yes, I know, it's the most terrifying feeling on earth . . . yet – somehow – in some strange way, one gets used to the dark.' Babbie spoke almost to herself. She sounded so strange that Shona looked at her sharply.

'What a queer thing to say, Babbie.' She forced a laugh. 'If the old islanders could hear you they'd be getting the shivers and saying you were a spook wandered from the tombs at Dunuaigh.'

'Sorry, I have a habit of saying silly things. The nurses at the home told me I gave them the creeps and now I'm doing it to you.' She was herself again, apologizing in character-istic fashion, the radiance of her smile lighting her weary face.

'It's bed you need,' Shona said firmly. 'I hope you manage to get some sleep, you look exhausted.'

'Don't we all? It's been a long day. Don't worry about me, you know what I'm like once I get into bed.'

Shona laughed. 'I'll be sorry for the man you marry, you'll never get up on time to see him off in the morning.'

A shadow flitted over Babbie's face but she forced a rueful smile. 'Ach well, I'd better stay the way I am, I'm heading for the shelf now – twenty-three and no man to warm the sheets of my bed.'

'A real grannie,' Shona giggled, feeling oddly cheered by the older girl's careless good humour, too careless in that moment for it to be really genuine, but Shona sensed the barriers were up once more and didn't pursue the conversation.

Babbie turned to her small suitcase and began to look out nightwear. She had been adamant about moving over to Slochmhor to be immediately at hand. Lachlan had protested even while he had desperately wanted to accept help. He had been exhausted after a night with little sleep and a day spent battling to keep the Angel of Death from taking the young German. With Biddy laid up, things were even more complicated, so after a lot of persuasion on Babbie's part he had given in and Shona had helped her move her things from Laigmhor.

'You don't know what you're letting yourself in for,' Lachlan had warned. 'Even though the lad can barely lift a finger the island will have you labelled as a lassie with loose morals. Ay, and a hundred times looser because the lad is a German.'

Babbie had laughed gaily. 'But Biddy would have done the same thing surely?'

'Ay, but there's a queer difference between you and Biddy! At her age she's not likely to do much damage, now is she?' They had both laughed, Babbie indifferently because in her compassion for the sick she cared little for the wagging tongues of the healthy.

Lifting a green nightdress from her case she looked at it in disgust. 'I suppose I'll have to wear it under the circumstances. I like to sleep in the raw but I can hardly do that here. The gossips would set their tongues afire if they heard about it.'

Footsteps crunched on the path under the window, plainly heard because the rest of the household slept and everything was very quiet. Shona looked from the window and saw a dark figure coming through the gate. 'It's one of the Commandos,' she reported. 'The one who helped in surgery today.'

'Yes, he was good, wasn't he? I suppose he feels personally involved. Go down, Shona, before he wakens the house. I can't be bothered with anyone just now. Tell him the usual things . . . Mr Büttger is holding his own, etcetera.'

Shona was back in a few minutes. 'He wanted to come up and see Anton but I told you were getting ready for bed. They were hoping to be off tomorrow but it seems they haven't found the escaped German yet and I have the oddest feeling that Anderson at any rate isn't too worried. I gather he just happened to pass Tam's house on the way over here and I think our young surgeon is a little bit merry. He put his arm round me and tried to kiss me . . . the cheeky bugger! He's waiting now to escort me up the glen just in case I come face to face with the wandering German!' With a weary little laugh she turned again to the door. 'I'd better away now or Father will be out looking for me. It's daft, I suppose, but he still thinks I'm a wee girl yet.'

'At eighteen – you are,' Babbie murmured.

Shona's blue eyes widened in surprise. 'How *old* you sound, Babbie, and how can I still be a bairn after all the things I told you about myself?'

'Because at eighteen you haven't really grown up. You think you've had all the experiences but there's so much more for you, Shona. You still have a bit of growing up to do.'

'You sound as if you've known me all my days.' Shona tried to sound light-hearted but the look in Babbie's eyes made her shiver, a look in which she glimpsed the wisdom that lurked in the faraway eyes of the very old.

'You're a witch,' she said lightly. 'Niall would call you Caillich Ruadh which means red witch. It's what he calls me to get me angry. Maybe there's a bit of the witch in us all. With Father I often know what he's thinking, and he seems always to know what I'm feeling. We're tuned in I suppose. Maybe that's why he likes to keep me in sight, though often he hardly says a word when I'm with him. I can just *feel* him caring.'

'You're lucky.' Babbie sounded wistful. 'It must be a good warm feeling to have a father – or a mother – or both. You have one, I have none, yet most people have both and never appreciate the fact.'

'Och, c'mon, Babbie.' Shona's voice was gentle. 'You must have someone . . . surely everyone has someone.'

'No, not everyone. I was lucky, I had an older sister – we were in the orphanage together. She left before me and though she married we always kept in touch. We were always fighting in the orphanage – you know what sisters are – oh, but of course, you don't – so sorry.' She paused for a moment then continued slowly. 'They say that sisters who fight a lot as kids are really very close even while they're pulling lumps from each other. Well, it's true, the closeness I mean. We had wonderful times when we grew up, even after

Jan got married – then – she died, three years ago now – she was twenty-six. I still miss her so.'

Shona caught her breath. 'Oh, dear God, how sad you must be, to have someone you love die so young. How can you bear not having anyone in the world you can call your own?'

A little smile hovered round Babbie's lips, and her eyes were very faraway. 'But I'm not alone, Shona. I have friends. I have you here, I have others scattered everywhere and . . .' She laughed suddenly. 'Underneath all my heathen ways I'm really very close to my Maker. I'll see Jan one day, I know that for sure. It's quite exciting when you stop to think about it.'

A little groan from the bed made them both jump. 'Our young hero is still in the land of the living anyway,' Babbie said. In seconds she was a cool, efficient little nurse again, whose devotion to her patient seemed to divorce her from everything that went on in the world outside the sickroom, and Shona slipped quietly out of the house to meet Anderson and walk with him up the lonely moon-washed glen to Laigmhor and the people she loved.

Anton's brain was swimming. He felt as if he was in a vortex which was spinning him round and round, carrying him in a sickening whirl of motion towards the face of the mountain. He struggled to get away from it, to rise upwards and outwards from the gyrating force that held him, but he hadn't the strength to struggle, or even to cry out. All he could do was pray silently, 'Please my God, do not let me die now. I am sorry, I am sorry – for everything.'

A river was rushing down the face of the mountain. He could see it glinting in a strange heavenly light, some of it was splashing on to his cheeks, but it wasn't cold like he thought it would be. It was warm, warm and salty . . .

Salt water did not run down the face of a mountain. He put out his tongue slowly and licked the water . . . only it wasn't water – it was tears, his tears! Commander Anton Büttger was crying like a baby. 'Don't let me die a coward.

Oh God! Please don't let me die a coward!' he sobbed in a demented torture of mind and body. His head was throbbing and something deep in his belly was burning like the fires of hell. Was that it? Was he dead and already in hell? Was this his punishment for killing all those people he had killed when he was alive?' A bubble of sheer terror rose in his throat. 'Please God not this!' The thoughts clamoured into his aching head. 'Let me live a little while longer to let me prove I am worth somewhere better than hell'.

'*Please, God!*' he cried aloud, opening his eyes suddenly. But everything was in a mist. The mists of hell! Smoke from the fires? The fires of hell or the fires of burning towns? The haze was lifting a little, his eyes were beginning to focus and he saw that he was in a little room with rose-sprinkled wallpaper, canted ceilings, and a tiny deep window looking out to bronzed hills basking dreamily in the sun. He was back home, in Berlin, in his own bedroom; his mother was downstairs cooking breakfast. The fragrant smell of sizzling bacon drifted up to his nostrils. The door opened and someone came in. He struggled to sit up. 'Mother! Mother, is that you?' But it wasn't his mother, it was a young woman with eyes the colour of emeralds and a halo of hair which made him think of the setting sun. She put out a cool little hand and touched his forehead.

'Are you – an angel?' he said in some bemusement. 'Am I in heaven?'

Babbie smiled and said dryly, 'An angel? With hair this colour? More a devil I'd say, Mr Büttger?'

'I was never lucky with women,' he said with a little smile, his eyes still drowsily half-shut. 'But I can tell . . . you are Scottisch. A Scottisch devil might not be so bad. My mother, she spent a holiday in Scotland once and she tells me, when I am a little boy, the Scottisch, they are kind. Are you kind – Fräulein?'

'You speak English well, Mr Büttger.' Babbie was struggling to remain aloof. She was looking at the tears glistening through his lashes, at the pale handsome face lying on the pillow. It was a fine face, sharply chiselled, boyish,

125

very delicate in the morning light with faint purple shadows under his eyes. He had come through a night of hell. She had bathed him, talked to him soothingly in the delirium of his nightmares, touched him and all the time she had had to keep reminding herself he was a German, a young man who flew planes and committed himself to killing other young men, young men with boyhood still stamped on their features . . .

'You do not like Germans, Fräulein.'

The statement caught her unawares. 'Nonsense', she said brusquely. 'Come now, enough chatter. I want to examine you . . . Oh, it's all right, Mr Büttger, I am a fully-trained nurse. To me you are just another patient.'

At that moment he opened his eyes wide and the blue brilliance of them in his white tear-stained face made her catch her breath. They were luminous eyes, and even though he was ill, keen and sharp and clear. She felt as though he could see right into her very soul. Already the sight of his frost-blackened fingers had brought a lump to her throat, and now – those eyes, looking at her with unwavering perceptiveness . . .

'How are you feeling, Mr Büttger?' she said briskly, trying to hide her confusion.

'A short time ago I thought I was dead – dead in hell . . . When I saw you coming through the door I thought I must be mistaken . . . and I was instead . . . in heaven.'

'I'll get the doctor to come up and have a look at you,' she said, tucking his hands back under the blankets.

'Can you tell me first – what happened, where am I . . . and what day it is, Fräulein?' His voice was cultured, his broken English utterly charming, like little notes of sweet music occasionally touching the wrong chord.

'You hurt yourself when you baled out of your plane and Doctor McLachlan operated on you yesterday. You are in Scotland, on an island in the Hebrides – and today is March the 15th . . . two days after the first attack by German bombers in Clydebank and Glasgow.'

Babbie was immediately sorry for her last words. Anton had turned his head away from her and was looking unseeingly at the rugged slopes of Sgurr nan Ruadh. One hand came out of the blankets to grip the white counterpane but only two fingers moved, the rest lying immobile, rendered useless by the ravages of frostbite.

She bit her lip. 'Are you hungry, Mr Büttger? If you managed to eat something it would do you good.'

'I was, Fräulein,' he whispered through white lips. 'When I smelt breakfast frying I felt very hungry. I thought, you see, that I was home in Berlin and my mother was up already preparing the morning meal . . . But I was dreaming – my mother is dead, and so too are the rest of my family. No, Fräulein, I don't think that I am very hungry any more.'

'I'll – I'll see if I can bring you something to tempt your appetite . . .' She faltered and ran downstairs and into the kitchen where Phebie was at the stove and the rest of the family seated at the table.

'Mr Büttger is awake,' Babbie reported tonelessly. 'I think he might eat something if coaxed enough – but his fingers are in a bad way. I fear he may have to lose them after all.'

'I'll go up and have a look,' Lachlan said, rising at once and going to the door where Elspeth was hovering, having arrived just in time to hear Babbie's words.

'Hmph! A fine thing indeed,' she snorted, outraged, 'when a German comes into this good home and uses up the rations that are scarce enough as it is!'

'He can have my rations,' eight-year-old Fiona piped up, her bright eyes flashing in her rosy face. 'I like Mr Büttger, he's a very interesting-looking German with all those bandages all over him and eyelashes like butterflies' wings.'

'And who asked your opinion, Madam?' Elspeth flashed. Behind her back Fiona made a hideous face. The unlovable old lady was as attached to her as she was to the other McLachlans, but Fiona, being the youngest member of the family, received most of the brunt of her razor-sharp tongue and was forever trying to get her own back. From time to time she played terrible tricks, sometimes contenting herself by just casting spells over Elspeth from the safety of her bedroom, but none of them had ever worked, and in the end the little girl had decided that a toad was a far nicer creature to look at than Elspeth and didn't deserve the fate of inhabiting Elspeth's bony frame for the rest of its life.

'I'm saving my butter ration for Mr Büttger,' Fiona persisted, 'and for Niall, too, when he gets home. I wish he'd hurry up. I want to show him my frog spawn.'

At her words Phebie's eyes filled with tears and the pan of frying bacon wavered before her eyes. Babbie went to her and put an arm round her shoulders. 'Please, don't – don't worry yourself so. It will be all right. He wasn't spared the war for nothing. There's a better plan for your son's life.'

'But – there's been no news – nothing, and I don't know how long I can go on,' Phebie said brokenly, dabbing her eyes with the corner of her apron. A sob of despair broke from her and she rushed out of the kitchen and into the parlour. The picture of the boy Niall was there, on top of the dresser, smiling his beautiful, cherubic smile while the sparkles of mischief exploded from his eyes and brought smiles to the lips of all who looked into them. Phebie ran a tender finger over the glass, tracing the handsome young features she knew so well.

'So that's Niall,' Babbie said softly, coming up behind her.

Phebie nodded, her plump sweet face pink with pride and grief. 'Ay, my laddie, at fourteen. He's bigger now but he still does daft things, like pinching buttered scones behind my back and chasing me round the kitchen table . . . and sweeping me up in his arms when he comes home . . . and . . . and . . .' Her voice faltered and she couldn't go on.

Babbie took her into her arms and let her cry against her shoulder. She looked at the picture of fourteen-year-old Niall. Something about the boyish face tugged at her memory but the abrupt arrival of Lachlan in the room startled her back to reality.

'No breakfast for Anton, I'm afraid. Those fingers will have to come off. Today, this morning.' He strode over and took Phebie from Babbie and into his arms. He stroked her hair tenderly, and over her head his eyes met Babbie's. 'You've had an exhausting night, Babbie, and could be doing with a good whily to yourself. I canny ask you for any more help. I'll manage the operation myself . . '

Babbie was aghast. 'And do you think I would stand back twiddling my thumbs and let you carry on, on your own? Oh, no, Lachlan, you're not getting away with that . . . !' She paused and gave a little laugh. 'Just promise me one thing – when this is all over – will you call me Florence Nightingale?'

His brown eyes flashed for a moment and he put out his free arm. 'Come into the bosom of the family – Miss Nightingale.'

Her green eyes smiled, hiding the turmoil of doubts, fears and apprehensions that slid through her mind in a crazily jumbled procession.

PART IV

RHANNA

March 16th 1941

CHAPTER 10

As Niall watched Portcull coming nearer, specks in the bay resolved into the warm-hearted, familiar folk who had filled his thoughts constantly in the last few days. It was very early on Sunday morning and the scene was even more peaceful than usual because, as Niall knew, most folk were indoors donning Sunday best as they prepared for kirk.

No ferries travelled to Rhanna on Sundays but he had been lucky to arrive at Oban to find one of the Rhanna fishing trawlers ready to leave with the tide. He had managed to get some sleep in a cramped little cabin below decks but still felt heavy and weary. He hadn't been able to get word through to his folks that he was on his way home, and his thoughts were full of anxiety as to how they must be feeling. The picture of the Clydebank holocaust was keen on his mind. He couldn't forget the first night of the raids when his duties as an Air Raid Warden had taken him from horror to horror, and finally into hell on seeing that the place he called 'home' in Glasgow was no more. Despite a broken right arm and multiple bruises he had stayed on in the devastated areas of Clydebank to assist the rescue parties and help with the evacuation of the homeless thousands.

He stood on the deck of the boat and with hungry eyes devoured the serenity of the Hebridean island of his birth. After the chaos of Clydebank it was strange to look at a place where people ambled rather than walked, and never ran if they could possibly avoid it. The morning sparkled in a palette of breathtaking colours: the purple of the mountains thrusting stark peaks into the soft blue sky; on the hill slopes a faint fuzz of light green showing through the tawny patches of winter bracken, contrasting with the darker spires of the tall pines. Skirting the harbour, the cottages stood out like dazzling white sugar lumps, each one sending out fluffy banners of variegated smoke, and below it, a tranquil blue sea lapped the silvered white sands. Niall watched it all come closer, and he sniffed the well-remembered scent of peat fires. Closing his eyes he let the babble of the gulls and the slop of the waves wash over his senses till his heart surged with joy. And in the ecstasy of the moment he imagined Shona would be there to meet him as in days gone by . . . But that was all in the past. He wondered if she was thinking of him now in Aberdeen, wondered if she had heard about the raids and the destruction of his 'home' . . .

As the trawler puffed into the bay, pushing and slapping against the pier, a row of pipe-smoking old men sat on the harbour wall, watching the proceedings with languid interest. Old Joe, perched on a lobster pot, and looking like a snowy-haired gnome with his pipe sending busy little blue-grey clouds into the face of a sea-stained crony, suddenly let out a cry. 'St Michael be blessed!' He had spotted Niall coming down the gangplank. 'It's young McLachlan back from the bombs!' he yelled, rushing forward. At old Joe's signal, Ranald, who divided his time between tarring his boats and reassembling a collection of ancient black bicycles with the intention of hiring them out to unwary summer tourists, threw his tar-clogged brush into a sticky tin and rose quickly to run to the pier. Others followed in a hurry, and soon Niall was surrounded by the men, who greeted him eagerly, eyeing his plaster-encased arm with sympathetic interest.

'My, my, you've been in the wars right enough, lad,' old Andrew observed gently.

A smile lit Niall's weary face. 'Ay, but I'm home now for a while. My studies will have to wait for a bit.'

'True enough, son, you wouldny get much on paper wi' that arm,' Jim nodded wisely. 'No' unless you are amphibious. Some folks are – it means you can do things with both hands the same.'

Niall laughed and looked round the harbour with hungry eyes. 'It's as peaceful as ever. And wonderful to be back. I don't suppose much has been happening on Rhanna.'

A clamour of protest followed. At that moment the crew of the trawler, who had been away from Rhanna for several days, joined the gathering and everyone vied with each other to regale the audience with greatly embroidered tales about the crashed German bomber. Canty Tam, always to be had wherever there was a crowd, gazed vacantly but smiled with satisfaction at the goriest details. Old Andrew prodded his pipe into the sky, making exaggerated circles to demonstrate to a young fisherman how the bomber had thundered over the village before its final wild flight to the mountains. There were a few moments of pipe-sucking, thoughtful silence with all eyes fixed on the upper corries of Ben Machrie where trailing wisps of vapour drifted in and out of high secret places.

'It must have been quite a sight,' was the eventual general verdict.

Tam McKinnon nodded seriously. 'Terrible just,' he stated lugubriously. His cronies then nodded in sad agreement though, with the exception of Righ, not one of them had witnessed the event. But Righ was fast asleep in the lighthouse cottage and Tam was able to embroider his tale, helped by the bobbing heads and sympathetic 'Ays' of the others.

Canty Tam smiled secretively at the sky, addressing it with a grimace of conviction. 'And was my mother not after telling me you was all drunk that night?' he accused the lacy cloudbanks pleasantly. 'She said to me only that morning while I was supping my porridge, "You keep out o' Tam McKinnon's house, my lad, for he is after doin' things that will bring the Peat Hags on him."' He brought his gaze from the sky to grin at a vexed Tam. 'She told me lots more but there was no need for when the bells were ringin' I saw you all comin' out o' your Headquarters an' you was drunk! That German airy-plane was already on the island then!'

There was a howl of derision from the fisherman that brought blushes to the faces of the Home Guard.

'Och, c'mon now, lads,' Tam soothed earnestly. 'Surely you are no' believing that foolish cratur. We might have had one or two wee drinks but needin' them indeed for we were out all night lookin' for the Huns!'

But young Graeme Donald, a grand-nephew of old Annack, smiled with quiet radiance into the salt-washed faces of the other fishermen. 'Are you hearing that now, lads? Everywhere else whisky is scarcer than virgins and here is our Tam bathing in the stuff. Great-aunt Annack might be a cailleach but, by God! she has some nose on her face for sniffing out the hard stuff! She told me the time was near ripe for Tam's whisky an' it's here, lads! We just arrived in time!' His words were met with a great whoop of approval that sent the gulls screaming from the harbour walls.

'I was goin' to tell you, lads,' Tam assured them plausibly. 'What way would I be wantin' all that whisky to myself? There's more than enough and I was just thinkin' comin' over the track that a shilling a pint wouldny be too much to ask – '

'Sixpence!' cried a hard-bitten old sailor. Tam looked sad but he was already leading the way to his house followed by an eager, thirsty mob.

'The minister will be down on your heads!' Ranald called piously.

'Ach, him, is he no' after sayin' he is holdin' a ceilidh tonight for the Germans . . . and on the Sabbath too!' Tam returned placidly.

'A ceilidh . . . for Germans?' Niall asked incredulously.

'Ay, to give them a taste o' Scottish hospitality afore they leave,' Ranald imparted, scratching his head absentmindedly with his tar-stained fingers. 'The Commandos have still to find one big Jerry who got away from the Manse on Friday morning but they have narrowed the search down enough to think they'll get him today. The German officer o' the plane was torn to ribbons on the mountain comin' down an' damt near dead when we found him. Your father had to sew his stomach back in but some o' his fingers were rotting away wi' frostbite an' had to be cut off. The lads are guardin' him day an' night for you never know wi' Jerries . . . stayin' at your house he is.'

'My house?'

'Ay, he couldny be moved for fear he would die,' Ranald nodded eagerly, poking his fingers further into his thatch of brown hair.

'The airy-plane came over from blitzed places near Glasgow,' Canty Tam beamed. 'Everyone was sayin' they likely killed a lot o' people before endin' up here!'

'Be quiet, you glaikit bugger!' Erchy warned, coming from the boat with a creel of enormous crabs.

Niall had turned white at the news. The memory of his landlady with the teapot clutched in her hands and her dead eyes staring was extremely vivid. And Iain Brodie, smoke-grimed and red-eyed after endless hours battling with endless fires, his face empty and hopeless on learning the news. Niall felt the bitterness surging through him again, taking away some of the joy he'd felt at coming home. It seemed after all that the scourge of war had touched Rhanna. The thought of a German under the roof of Slochmhor made him feel sick with anger. How could his father calmly have taken the enemy into his home? Hot tears of rage pricked his eyes and he turned quickly away, his blurred gaze coming to rest at the Smiddy where a much-recovered Todd the Shod was sitting outside enjoying the spring sunshine. Beside him Biddy reclined on a wooden bench padded with cushions. They were both waving at him frantically and he raised his arm to wave back.

'Dear old Biddy,' he breathed thankfully. 'It will be good to have her moaning and fussing around me.'

Erchy shook his sandy head ruefully. 'Ach, not yet for a whily. The cailleach hurt her ankle and is stayin' at the McDonalds' till she is better. Todd had his appendix out and the pair o' them are driving each other daft.' A gleam of mischief came into his eyes. 'We had a fine young nurse lookin' after us for a whily. A right nice bum and bosoms she has too. We were all thinkin' up ways to see will she come and cure us . . . My ulcer has been bad this last day or two,' he finished, suddenly rubbing at his middle.

'But it's better you are now.' Jim Jim removed his pipe and

137

spat malevolently on to the cobbled pier. 'They are after sendin' over a spare nurse . . . came on the boat yesterday afternoon . . . like a gallopin' hairpin she is wi' a face like a forgotten prune! There she is now, goin' up to the Smiddy. Todd has not moved since his operation, though Mollie has been givin' him enough liquorice powder to shift a horse. He will be gettin' soapy water through a tube now – I forget what they calls it but I am hearing it does queer things to the bowels – makes them squeal like the bagpipes tunin' up.'

Todd watched the lanky figure of the 'spare' nurse coming towards his house and he squirmed with apprehension. Biddy watched also and her lips folded into a thin line of disapproval. Babbie had been to see her twice, and like everyone else she had fallen under the girl's infectious charm, but now she wished she hadn't been so persistent about a spare nurse . . .

'My God!' Todd gulped, his round face crimson. 'She is comin' this way!'

'Ach, never mind,' Biddy consoled. 'If it's an enema she's come to give I'll see she does it right. She has hands like frogs' feets and will not be gentle wi' the tubes like myself.'

'Hell no!' Todd couldn't stop the protest. 'Not *two* of you! I canny take any more o' this! That wee Nurse Babbie would have done fine for a whily!'

The nurse came through the gate, burying her long nose in the depths of a large hanky. 'I have had nothing but sneezes since I came yesterday,' she complained. 'How are you today, Nurse McMillan?'

'Fine – oh ay – much better, thankin' you! It won't be long till I am up on my feets!'

'Good, then we will all be happy! How are you today, Mr McDonald?'

'Never better, indeed no! I will be back at the Smiddy much sooner than I thought!' Todd gabbled in agitated confusion.

Biddy straightened her specs. 'Where is the young nurse? She said she would be over to see how was I keeping.'

The nurse sniffed disdainfully. 'Too busy with that young

138

German! Said something about changing his dressings. Well, she's welcome. I wouldn't touch him with a ten-foot pole. The child from the big farm was there too, the one with the long hair and innocent eyes.' She sniffed again. 'Looks like that are so deceiving. She and the nurse are fawning over him like sick kittens. Now . . .' she became suddenly brisk, 'will you come inside, Nurse McMillan – I'll do your enema first.' She smiled sourly. 'Ladies before gentlemen.'

'*Me!*' Biddy's yell of indignation sent a clutter of crows into the sky where they flapped angrily.

'Yes, indeed, Nurse McMillan. I met Mrs McDonald last night and she told me that for days you haven't been near the – er – toilet. She said you had only been passing water into the – hm – chamber pot.'

'That Mollie!' Biddy roared while Todd shook with delighted glee. 'I'll – I'll never bandage her varicose veins again!'

Niall managed a smile as Biddy's indignant yells filled the harbour. 'Well, *she* hasn't changed anyway! Still the same grumbling Biddy!' He began to move away and called back, 'I'll see you later, lads.'

'Ay, come to the ceilidh tonight at the Manse. The minister said it was a praise meeting for teetotallers only but he'll no' find many of these around here!' Ranald grinned. 'You will likely get a try of Tam's Uisge-beatha. Like nectar it is.'

Niall nodded appreciatively, and walked towards Glen Fallan, lifting his face to breathe the wild, sweet scent of sun-warmed heather. In the high fields above Laigmhor, Fergus and Bob strode among the flocks of sheep; a few tiny early lambs wobbled unsteadily near their mothers, and the sheepdogs ran purposefully about their business, answering to the different whistles with an eager obedience that reflected Bob's training. Fergus rarely went to kirk and shocked the minister and many of his neighbours by doing work on a Sunday, which normally was taboo. Bob was a regular kirkgoer but his work came first with him, especially at lambing time, so today he wore his best suit under baggy plus-fours and a roomy tweed jacket, ready to take off as soon as the kirk bell tolled over the island. Niall looked with delight at the familiar scene and he raised his arm. The men were engrossed in their work but a moment later they waved in response and Fergus's voice drifted faintly but joyfully, 'Hello there, Niall! We'll see you later!'

When Niall reached Slochmhor he found it quiet and deserted. For a moment he thought there was no one at home. He knew that Fiona would be outdoors, making the most of her time before getting ready for kirk, and that his father would be out on a call somewhere but, though he wasn't expected, he had anticipated his mother's welcome and felt unreasonably cheated. He had pictured her face on seeing him, the surprise, then the gladness bringing the roses to her cheeks. If it hadn't been for his arm he would have swept her up high and she would have giggled and spilled a tear or two, but as he couldn't do that he had planned to chase her round the kitchen table till she clouted him with the dishcloth . . . Niall looked round the kitchen which was warm and homely with two cats sprawled by the fire, one of them using Lachlan's slippers as a pillow. On the window ledge a vase of pussy willows managed to look graceful alongside a jar of frog spawn floating in obnoxious green water. Niall chuckled. Fiona was still pursuing her keen interest in all forms of insect and amphibious life. It was her favourite hobby. She was a child who kept pet spiders in jars and studied minute creatures with the aid of one of Lachlan's old microscopes. After eight years of struggling to keep her tom-boy daughter's room as feminine as possible, Phebie had gradually given up the fight and had ceased to be disgusted by the odd assortment of creepy pets she encountered while cleaning.

A little laugh came from upstairs and Niall stiffened. The laugh was so familiar to him yet the unexpected sound of it made his heart race madly. 'Shona . . . what the hell – ' he whispered and bounded upstairs. Even while he burst into the little guest room Niall realized this was where the wounded German lay, but on entering Niall got the impression that he had intruded into an intimate little world. Anton, pale but handsome, was laughing up at Shona whose hand was clasped in his, her blue eyes alight in her animated face.

'Shona!' Niall shouted her name in surprise.

'Niall!' She turned from the bed, to stare at him in joyous disbelief. 'Oh, thank God!' she said, rising to meet him. 'I prayed and prayed you would come back to me soon! We could get no news of you! I didn't know when you would be coming or I would have met you! You're hurt, my darling, what have you done to your arm?' She put out a hand to touch him but he pulled away.

'I didn't know you were back on Rhanna.' His voice held a note of suspicion.

'But – I wrote to you when I left Aberdeen! I told you I was coming to see you in Glasgow the minute I could. I'm home for a rest – I haven't been too well.'

He saw then her pale little face and her incredible eyes, smudged with a delicate blue-black under the lower lashes. He had forgotten how blue her eyes were, how beautifully shaped her small sensitive mouth. Her auburn hair was swept up from her face but gave it no maturity, instead it emphasized her cameo features and pointed chin. She looked like a little girl trying to appear grown up and the nearness of her overwhelmed him for a moment. He longed to crush her to him, to pour words of love into her ears but the picture of her with Anton had roused a stab of jealousy in his breast.

'I didn't get your letter,' he said briefly and bitterly. 'Mrs Brodie no longer has a letter box – it may still be attached to the door buried beneath the rubble of what was her home! Not that Mrs Brodie will worry about that now . . . she's out of it all . . .' He glanced at Anton accusingly. 'Mrs Brodie doesn't need her home now, but Iain Brodie needs it – and thousands more like him who lost everything in the raids last week!' His voice rose menacingly. 'Ask your German friend how he would go about helping the people he helped to kill . . . you might not find so much to laugh at then – *Fräulein!*'

'Niall!' She stared at him, shocked. 'Stop that! You're raving like a madman!'

'Maybe I am mad – mad enough for a bit of revenge! I keep seeing corpses, they're in my head and I can't get rid of them! I go to bed at night and see my landlady – a tiny wee body who never harmed a soul – lying among the bloody tons of rubble that buried her alive!'

'Niall.' Her voice was gentle because she saw the terrible tension in him. 'You'll have to try and forget. The raids were horrible, we all know that . . .'

'Do you! Were you there? Pray God you'll be spared anything like it . . .' He nodded towards Anton. 'He'll know, he was over the place! He must have seen the hell of it all. After all, he must have dropped some of the incendiaries that lit up Clydebank like a Christmas tree. Maybe his was one of the bombers that strafed the streets, spattering bullets about just for the fun of it! Ask him if he knows what it's like to be holed up like a terrified rabbit waiting for a bomb to drop!'

'Ask him yourself.' Shona's voice was barely audible. 'He can speak English quite well.'

'The intellectual type!' Niall answered scathingly.

Anton had struggled up in bed, his eyes meeting Niall's angry gaze. 'Niall.' He spoke the name with respect. 'Fräulein Shona tells me about you all day. We laugh just now about your times together as children.'

To Niall the words were flippant, designed to get him off the subject of the raids. 'So you know my name,' he said sarcastically. 'And you laugh. I wonder if we'll laugh when we know the names of all the people killed in Clydebank and Glasgow – and all the other cities bombed by the Luftwaffe!'

'Anton's mother, father and sisters were killed by the British in an air raid over Berlin.' Shona said the words quietly, her mouth frozen with dismay.

Anton had fallen back on the pillows, his eyes gazing unseeingly at the wall and he raised his bandaged right hand to pass it over his brow in a defeated, strangely touching little gesture. 'I hate the war as much as you do,' he said wearily. He reached to the dresser and picked up an Iron Cross which

142

he dangled idly in his fingers. 'This little decoration is meant to signify bravery – all it means is I have killed a lot of people. I am not really proud of it – but I wear it – in the same way the British wear their medals.' He laughed without humour. 'I am very relieved that I do not have to pin it to my pyjamas – I can forget it for a while.'

Niall suddenly felt deflated and uneasy. He hadn't expected to come face to face with an entirely whole German, and on the other hand he hadn't been prepared for one so obviously badly injured. Restricted though Anton's recent efforts at mobility had been, they had left him sweating and exhausted, and his rapid breathing filled the room.

A shower of sparks exploded from the coals in the grate and the clear, fluted call of a curlew came sweetly from the glen. Shona felt her heart beating swiftly. She could feel the tension spewing from Niall. It showed in his white young face, the clenching of his fist. He looked so forlorn, so unlike the loving, carefree Niall of her memories, that for a moment she was afraid. He'd come through the horrific experiences of Dunkirk, scarred but still buoyant of spirit. The war had wounded him yet again but she knew it wasn't that which had so crushed him: the first time he had gone to war expecting to meet death and destruction, but the second time war had come to him and she realized he hadn't been prepared for it.

'Niall . . .' she began huskily just as footsteps clattered and Babbie arrived breathlessly into the room.

'Oh – sorry.' She drew back at the sight of Niall. He turned and her hand flew to her mouth. '*Niall!*' The cry was one of disbelief.

He stared at her. '*Babbie!* What on earth – how did *you* get here?' They gaped at each other till Babbie finally stuttered, 'Shona brought me – at least she asked me to come back with her to Rhanna for a holiday . . . I'm in Aberdeenshire now . . . you know me, always jumping around! Pastures new all the time. Your name has been mentioned here constantly but I never dreamt – I never connected . . . I saw the picture of you downstairs and I thought the resemblance to you was uncanny though of course you've changed since then – amazing the difference a few years and a little moustache can make to a boy. It's such a coincidence . . .' She was unable to go on.

Shona looked from one to the other. 'It would be silly to ask if you know one another.' She laughed as lightly as she could. 'It seems you certainly do!'

Niall pulled himself together with an effort. 'Only vaguely,' he said briefly. 'Isn't that right, Babbie?'

'Oh yes, hardly at all. I didn't even know your surname – till now.'

From the collar of her dress, Shona pulled out the little locket that Niall had given to her as an engagement present. She snapped it open and said to Babbie. 'I should have shown you this sooner, Babbie, then you might not have been surprised to see Niall here on Rhanna.'

Babbie looked in some confusion at the little heart-shaped photos of Niall and Shona fitted into the locket and forced a smile. 'I wish you had, Shona. It would certainly have put me in the picture, as it were.'

Despite the careless words, Shona sensed unspoken questions bouncing between the two. They were trying too hard to be casual, Babbie fussing with Anton's bedclothes, Niall paying a great deal of attention to a loose thread on his sling. He looked up and caught Babbie's eye. She seemed flustered, with a pink tinge staining her pale face and her green eyes unnaturally bright.

'Your walk has given the roses to your cheeks,' Anton commented carefully, sensing that a situation had arisen which needed some delicate handling. 'It gives the sparkle to your eyes.'

'Yes, I went over by the cliffs at Aosdana Bay – the Bay of the Poet,' Babbie said. 'It was lovely there – peaceful – a good place to think. I didn't mean to go so far but I forgot time. I am finding that this island does that to one – time begins to mean nothing.'

She was chattering too much, too nervously. Shona held

her breath but no matter how hard she tried she couldn't stop the suspicions crowding into her mind. Niall and Babbie! There was something between them, something they were trying very hard to hide. Her heart beat swiftly in her throat. She felt weak with emotion but she forced her head high. 'I'll have to go now. Father will be in soon from the fields and I promised Kirsteen to lay the table before kirk. I'll see you – Niall.'

'Wait!' Niall stayed her hasty flight. 'When will I see you – Ni-Cridhe?'

He said the endearment softly and a sob rose in her throat. 'Ni-Cridhe!' My dear lassie. How long she had waited to hear the caress of his dear, lilting voice but her reply was non-committal. 'Whenever you want – though not this afternoon. I'm going over to help Tina – she has a bad ankle.'

'I could come with you. I'd like fine to see Tina and the bairns.'

'Och, but I'm just going to wash and set her hair. You would feel in the way.'

A flush of anger stained his fair skin. 'I'm having a taste of that already! Tonight then? There's a ceilidh at the Manse – for the Germans, would you believe! But we don't have to speak to them. As far as I can gather the islanders are going to make a bonny night of it with Tam's Uisge-beatha.'

'You and Babbie go. She hasn't been to an island ceilidh yet. I'll sit with Anton.'

'Please, Fräulein Shona, do not deny yourself for me!' Anton cried anxiously. 'My little friend, Fiona, will tell me some of her fairy stories and show me some of her pets,' he laughed. 'She reminds me of my small sister with her caterpillars and her frogs.'

'Count your blessings then!' Niall gritted so harshly that even Babbie glanced at him in some dismay.

'Well, are you coming tonight or not?' he demanded of Shona.

Her head went up again at his tone. 'I'll sit with Anton,' she persisted.

'Oh, grand! Just grand! I'm sure you and he will have a lot to talk about! You can always tell him about the baby you lost because you thought I was dead in Dunkirk! Away you go then! A lot of folk are waiting on you it would seem!'

Shona flew downstairs and hardly saw where she was going for tears, and later, at Laigmhor, she flounced about, clattering things on the table.

'I see Niall's home,' Fergus said carefully as he and Kirsteen exchanged looks.

'Ay, that he is! With a broken arm too! Niall always seems to be in the wars.' She kept her tone on a conversational level.

'And now you and he are at war with each other,' Kirsteen said deliberately.

Shona looked up quickly. 'If it's anybody's business, then you are right enough, Kirsteen!' she cried hotly. 'Niall would fight in an empty house . . . his temper is even worse than mine now!'

Fergus smiled faintly though a muscle was working in his cheek. 'That would take a bit of doing, mo ghaoil. I won't stand for it in this house – and I'll thank you not to talk to Kirsteen in such a disrespectful manner.'

Shona dumped a pile of plates on to the table with such a clatter that Ginger, a big placid tom, shot out of the door in fright. 'And who have I to thank for *my* temper?' she demanded wildly and stamped out of the kitchen in high dudgeon.

CHAPTER 11

The Rev. John Gray had never in all his years on Rhanna felt quite so fulfilled or so important as he had done since the captured Germans were delivered into his care. He had always felt uncomfortably out of his depth when carrying out his pastoral duties among a people who sensed his lack of

146

confidence and also his slightly superior attitude towards them. He had always given them the impression that he regarded them as heathens whose only salvation lay in a conscientious kirk attendance coupled with a selfless devotion to 'The Book' and its teachings. But his methods of trying to bring God to the people were hopelessly out of keeping with the simple faith of the Hebridean people. His theological sermons were away above the heads of the majority of parishioners and matters weren't helped by his stern refusal to learn the Gaelic which was the only language that many of the older inhabitants understood. He had of course picked up the odd Gaelic word, and an intelligent man such as he could easily have learned it all. But he felt to do so would be to encourage the easy-going islanders to take a step back in time. What he had failed to see was a proud little community of Gaels struggling to hold on to a culture that was their inheritance. In the name of progress too much had already been taken away but no one could rob them of their individuality. They had met the so-called civilized world half-way, but had no intention of stepping over the border to be swallowed into anonymity for ever more. And so the Rev. Gray laboured on under his delusions and the barriers between him and the people of Rhanna remained firmly erect.

Hannah Gray was a much less overpowering personality than her overbearing husband. Her years with him had taught her that silence was the best form of defence against his forceful outlook on life.

When her husband had first suggested a ceilidh for the Germans the idea at first dumbfounded her, but the more she thought about it the more excited she became. She had often longed to throw a ceilidh in keeping with tradition, but her husband wouldn't hear of it, telling her sternly that such events were only excuses for uninhibited drinking bouts and an invitation to the Devil to wreak havoc in drink-weakened minds. Over the years Mrs Gray made do with giving strupaks; but her visitors were stiffly formal and always looked poised ready for flight. By contrast, whenever she dropped into a neighbour's croft, a strupak was a gaily informal affair. She had never ceilidhed in the long, dark nights of winter, and when passing a cottage gay with laughter and song, she had often longed to join the merrymakers but knew that her presence would only embarrass them. But now she would have a ceilidh of her very own! The very thought sped her steps to the kitchen which was soon fragrant with the smell of baking. Normally such activities in the kitchen were banned on the Sabbath but in this instance such restrictions were dropped.

'It must be referred to as more of a praise meeting,' the minister had warned righteously, but when Torquil Andrew, a strapping figure of a man whose Norse colouring and piercing blue eyes, which made him a great favourite with the women, had appeared at the kitchen door with the sack of potatoes she had asked to buy from him, she gaily told him the news.

'A ceilidh, Torquil,' she had beamed happily. 'Here in the Manse tonight. Tell your friends about it . . . but . . .' she had put a warning finger to her lips and screwed her face into a conspiratorial grimace, 'you know Mr Gray doesn't like the drink . . . so only those who don't.'

Torquil's handsome face had broken into a wide grin at the idea of a whiskyless ceilidh. Laughing aloud he had pulled the small dumpy Mrs Gray into his bronzed arms and waltzed her round the kitchen. 'A ceilidh, Mrs Gray! Just what we could be doing with. Mind though – some might no' like the idea o' drinkin' tea, wi' the Jerries. But I'll be gettin' a few folks together, never you fear, mo ghaoil,' he had said, and went off to spread the news.

Mrs Gray peered with pleasure into the oven where a batch of scones were rising in fluffy puffs. 'It will be a fine ceilidh,' she whispered into the depths of the oven. 'And even though John will make everyone sing hymns I'm sure it will be a success just the same.'

But not even Mrs Gray was quite prepared for the unprecedented triumph of her first ceilidh. It started quietly with only a handful of islanders shuffling through the door to look in uncomfortable silence at Jon and Ernst sitting meekly together on a huge wooden settle.

'My, it's a terrible night, just!'

'Cia mar a Tha!' (How are you?)

The first arrivals muttered embarrassed exchanges in a mixture of English and Gaelic, then arranged themselves in silence around the big cosy room.

'A dreich night,' Merry Mary observed sadly, unwilling to relinquish the safe topic of the weather conditions.

'Ay, ay, right enough,' came the sage agreements, but after one or two similar observations the company grew unnaturally quiet and the focal point for all eyes became the crackling coal fire which everyone stared at with undivided attention

Mrs Gray looked round in dismay. But for the two Germans, old Andrew and Mr McDonald, better known as Jim Jim, the company was made up entirely of elderly women, and Mrs Gray knew that a good ceilidh needed a fair number of each sex to liven proceedings. She looked at old Andrew who sat with his fiddle cuddled on his knee. He appeared faintly out of his depth among such an odd company, fidgeting first with his bow, then with a pipe-cleaner which he poked into the depths of an ancient briar, extracting a great amount of an obnoxious tarry substance, and then depositing it carefully on the bars of the fire. Jim Jim was sitting about three feet from the hearth, a distance that was no deterrent to the well-aimed flow of spit which he shot across the intervening space at regular intervals. The sound of it roasting on the coals filled the room and the gathering stared at the popping bubbles with what appeared to be an avid interest.

Mrs Gray leaned over to Isabel McDonald and said in an anxious whisper, 'I wonder what has happened to Torquil and the other men. He seemed delighted when I told him about my ceilidh. What if no one else comes?'

Isabel McDonald looked at her in wonderment. 'Ach, mo ghaoil! It's the way o' things. The younger ones will ceilidh at each other's houses first! They always do. When they gather up enough o' a crowd they will be comin' round here sure enough – or maybe staggering more like!'

Mrs Gray looked at her in horror. 'Oh, but John will never . . .' At that moment the Rev. Gray came running downstairs and into the room. 'What . . . nobody singing yet?' he bellowed lustily. 'Where is Morag Ruadh? She should be at the piano by now!'

Isabel McDonald knew that her red-haired, quick-tempered daughter was passing the time at the door with two Commando guards. For long, Morag had been a source of worry to her elderly parents because though past forty she had, as yet, failed to find herself a suitable marriage partner. Morag, with her red hair and nimble body was not an unattractive woman but she laboured under the delusion that she alone was responsible for the welfare of her ageing parents. This had embittered her outlook on life to some extent and her scathing tongue quickly scared off any would-be suitors. Contrary to Morag's beliefs, her parents were longing to be free of her spicy tongue and they were quick to encourage the attentions of any men who chanced their daughter's way.

'Morag has been kept back tonight, she will be along later, Mr Gray,' Isabel said glibly.

The minister's voice thundered out imperatively. 'Where is everybody? We must have more men for the singing. Bring in the guards! There's no need for them to be out there now!'

'There I must disagree wi' you,' Jim Jim said in tones of slight reproof. 'You mustny be forgettin' there is still another Hun to be caught. You wouldn't like a big German charging in here to us defenceless people and shootin' us all down like dogs. Would you now?'

'Pray God, of course not, but – '

'Then leave the sojers be the now. You can be bringin' them in when the other lads bring in the Hun, we'll be needin' guards then wi' three Jerries in the place.'

'Well, all right . . . yes, surely, you're right, Mr McDonald.'

Jim Jim sat back amid nods of righteous approval from

the gathering while outside Morag Ruadh was carrying on in an unusually abandoned mood.

Earlier in the evening she had complained to Kate McKinnon of feeling 'a cold coming down' and Kate had made her drink a generous amount of the Uisge-beatha. After the first mouthful and the first indignant spate of outrage at what she told Kate was 'an evil trick, just', she had thirsted after more of the water of life, whereupon a liberal Kate had sold her a pint for just ninepence. Arriving home Morag had informed her parents she was going into the scullery to 'steam her head'. With a great show of preparation she had put Friar's Balsam into a bowl of hot water and then repaired to the privacy of the scullery where she spent a solitary hour alternately 'steaming her head' and tippling from the cough bottle that she had carefully filled with whisky.

Now she was ready to throw caution to the winds. She was neither drunk nor sober but had arrived at that happy state where no obstacles loomed in the horizons of life and all things were possible, even for a forty-two-year-old spinster. Her gay mood showed in a softening of her ruddy features. She looked almost pretty with her green homespun shawl reflecting the green of her eyes and showing to advantage the bright gleam of her fiery hair. It mattered not to her that the Commandos were years younger than herself. They were men, exciting men at that, so different from the withdrawn, easy-going males of the island. She giggled and gave the guards sips of whisky from the innocent-looking brown cough bottle. The men were glad of the diversion. The superb-tasting whisky was a welcome change from the endless cups of tea provided by the kindly Mrs Gray and the surprising heat of the home-brewed malt quickly melted any doubts they might otherwise have felt at being obviously seduced by a middle-aged spinster.

Morag looked at the black tracery of the elm branches lurking in the chilly mist. With an exaggerated shudder she drew the folds of her shawl closer round her neck. 'Look you, it's a bitty cold out here,' she said softly, her legs beginning to tremble in a mixture of anticipation and surprise at her audacity. She lowered her voice to a hoarse whisper. 'It's – it's warm in the fuel shed over yonder. A nice bundle of hay there too . . . just to be resting in for a whily.'

She drifted away into the mist and the older of the two men handed his gun to his companion. 'Me first, Thomson,' he said with a chuckle. 'She's asking for it and I've got it. By God, I'll put a smile on her face that will stay there for the rest of her days.'

While Morag was arranging herself enticingly in the hay, the minister was loudly bemoaning her delay in arriving. 'We must have Morag Ruadh for the piano!' he cried, running an impatient hand through his thick mop of grey hair. 'I asked her to come early! What can have happened to her? Morag has never let me down yet.' He swung round to Isabel who was gazing sleepily into the fire. 'Can something have happened to her?' he demanded.

'All things are possible,' the old lady murmured, hastening to add loudly, 'Do not be worrying yourself, Mr Gray. Morag was feeling a cold coming and you know she is always feart of gettin' stiff hands and feets, her a spinner needin' all her fingers – and there is the organ, too, of course. Morag would never forgive herself if she was never fit for the organ on the Sabbath. She has already steamed her head, now she will likely be rubbing herself with liniment to keep supple. She'll be along right enough in her own time.'

'Well, we'll have to do without the piano!' The minister frowned round at the motley company. He felt very disappointed. His big idea of showing the Germans a real display of Scottish hospitality wasn't getting off to a good start. He had visualized a devoted Morag Ruadh stolidly accompanying an enthusiastic crowd singing rousing songs of praise all evening. Instead there was only a handful of dejected-looking islanders who were being unnaturally polite to each other. They were also inclined to murmur to one another in Gaelic, which made the minister even more frustrated.

Suddenly Jon Jodl startled everyone by getting swiftly to

his feet. His thin, boyish face was alight as he addressed the minister in excited German. The exchange brought a smile of delight to the Rev. Gray's face.

'The boy's a musician!' he boomed joyfully. 'And he has offered to play for us. Be upstanding everyone and give thanks to the Lord. Then we will start with the 23rd Psalm – and I want to hear every voice raised to the Almighty . . . in English.'

'Balls,' Old Jim Jim muttered but his wife nudged him and hissed a warning 'Weesht, weesht!' but he paid no heed, standing up to sing, defiantly, the 23rd Psalm in Gaelic. The well-known strains drifted out into the frosty night where the solitary Commando guard began to hum under his breath while he strained his eyes into the ghostly darkness surrounding the Manse and awaited his turn with Morag.

Shona didn't see Niall till well after tea when he came walking down Glen Fallan with Babbie. She was securing the hen-houses and heard their laughter long before they reached the gate in the dyke.

'We're away over to the Manse!' Niall called. 'Are you coming along, mo ghaoil? Mother is going to keep your German friend amused so he doesn't need you to hold his hand!'

The sarcasm of his words and the sight of them together brought fresh anger and a swift rush of jealousy to her heart. She felt hurt and cheated. When she spoke her voice was high with a mixture of rage and tears. 'No, you two get along! I'm – I'm busy and I'm in no mood to go ceilidhing.'

'Shona, *please* come,' Babbie pleaded. 'I – can't bear to see the two of you like this . . . after all the waiting.'

'Ach, go away, go away and leave me alone!'

Niall said nothing. He just stood looking at her for a long moment and then linked his arm in Babbie's and pulled her swiftly away. Shona stood looking after them, unable to believe the turn of events. She couldn't believe that Niall and Babbie were nothing more than casual acquaintances. Was it possible that Babbie, whom she loved like the sister she'd never had, could have engineered her stay on Rhanna in the hope that she would be near Niall? Their surprise on seeing each other had seemed genuine enough . . . yet they certainly appeared to know one another quite well, there was no denying that – or the looks they had exchanged in Anton's room. She felt sick with misery and shivered uneasily.

She looked back at the big farmhouse with its soft lights glowing from the windows. It was warm and inviting but in her present mood she felt it wasn't inviting her. Kirsteen's light laugh rang out followed by Fergus's deep happy voice. For a moment she wished it was just herself and her father again. She could have talked to him in the intimate way they had adopted through the years. Sometimes just a word from him made her world seem right again; he had a knack of making her worries seem trivial . . . Then she remembered the years of his loneliness and she hated herself for grudging him one moment with Kirsteen. If it was difficult for her adjusting to the new way of things, then how much more difficult it was for them, starting off together in married life and her throwing tantrums like a baby . . .

When she went back inside Fergus turned from the table. He was enveloped in a large pink apron that was liberally coated with flour. 'This daft woman is showing me how to bake bread!' he said, his black eyes snapping with delight. 'Me who knows better how to plant grain! But I'll show her the McKenzies aren't to be so easily beaten, eh, mo ghaoil?' There was a message in the laughing words and their eyes met in a moment of understanding.

'Hey, I thought I was now a member of this mad clan,' Kirsteen said, rubbing her nose with a floury hand.

Shona giggled. 'You both look members of a ghost clan . . . and I'm sorry to the pair of you for this afternoon . . . Now . . .' she rolled up her sleeves to wash her hands then went merrily into the fray.

'I thought you were getting ready for this mad Manse ceilidh that's the talk of the place,' Fergus objected. 'You and Niall . . .'

'He's taking Babbie. She hasn't been to an island ceilidh

yet. They know each other, you know – Niall and Babbie – met in Glasgow. I'm going over later to sit with Anton.'

'But . . .' Kirsteen began, but Shona held up a floury hand. 'No more talk about me. I'm sure you're both heartily sick of me and my bothers.'

Fergus was about to reply when Shona interrupted with a shriek.

'I can smell burning! I think your bread is on fire, Father!'

'Bugger it!' He rushed to the oven. Kirsteen glanced at Shona and they both collapsed into helpless laughter as Fergus glowered at his burnt loaves and the three of them spent a light-hearted hour together before Shona went upstairs to tidy herself.

When she arrived at Slochmhor, Phebie was hauling a protesting Fiona from Anton's room. 'The little devil simply won't leave poor Anton alone!' Phebie panted. 'A grass snake this time – that after a frog, a newt and – '

'But he wanted to see them!' Fiona wailed petulantly.

'Well, it's bed for you now, Madam, and no nonsense or I'll give you a skelpit leathering!' She looked at Shona enquiringly. 'I thought you would be at this praise meeting-cum-ceilidh. I told Niall I would stay with Anton, though I fancy he would prefer you to an auld wife like me.' She put her hand on Shona's arm. 'Isn't it grand our Niall's come home to us, mo ghaoil? I feel ten years younger already!' She looked ten years younger with her bonny round face flushed and her eyes shining.

'Ay, it's wonderful, Phebie,' Shona agreed while her heart turned over. 'I told him to take Babbie out tonight. She's worked so hard here and she – the two of them – deserve a break. I don't mind keeping Anton company for a while.'

'You're a good lassie,' Phebie said while inwardly she wondered what had gone wrong between her son and his sweetheart. 'I'll go down and make Lachy some supper to come home to. He went away over to see Todd and Biddy – evidently she is not very happy with this unfortunate *spare* nurse the authorities have sent.'

Fiona popped her head out of her door. 'I think tomorrow

I'll put a lump of frog spawn into Elspeth's sago pudding. We always have sago on a Monday and . . .'

'Bed!!' Phebie cried and made a lunge at Fiona who evaded her and went running round her room shrieking with glee.

Anton smiled at the sounds of merriment. 'That little Fiona, she is heaven and hell all rolled into one. I see frogs till I am green! But, what are you doing here, Fräulein Shona? You should be enjoying yourself. I don't need anyone to hold my hand – and I have no wish to make things worse between you and Niall.'

Shona sat down by the bed. 'Ach, don't worry about us. I came over to cheer you up. I thought you would be pleased to see my bonny face.'

'Bonny?'

'A saying – it means – well – nice-looking, though not in that way exactly.'

'No, I would say more like – beautiful? Niall is a very lucky fellow – and also a very angry young man.'

She flushed. 'Ay, he is that, but not at you really, you just happened to be handy, that's all.'

'Because I'm a German. It's all right, I understand.'

'But – you shouldn't understand! How can you understand! To be hated because you are a German!'

He took her hand gently. 'It is natural, Fräulein Shona. When first I knew my family had been killed by the British I hated them. Before that they were just people to fight because fighting them was the right thing to do in war. But when the killing involves you personally it becomes a private war. Niall saw people he loved killed just a few days ago. The hate is strong within him – also he hates because he doesn't understand what has gone wrong between you and him, neither of you can. It is the baby he says you lost while he was in France. You cannot yet bring yourselves to speak about it – really bring it into the open and talk it out of your hearts. It will go on poisoning you both till you do, the mixing up of your feelings will just go on and on . . .' His blue eyes flashed and he smiled. 'And I will go on talking too much. My mother, she used to say to me, "Anton, you are like an old gramophone, wind you up and you never stop".'

Shona saw the quickening of the pulse in his neck at the mentioning of his mother and a sadness stole into her heart. 'You are a very nice person, Anton Büttger, and even yet you cry inside for the family you have lost – and – and I think you are also very brave because not once have you bemoaned the fact that some of your fingers had to come off yesterday.'

He held up his bandaged hand and looked at it. Lachlan had removed two of the fingers, hoping that the third, which hadn't been too badly frostbitten, might heal with time. 'I am not brave, Fräulein, I have lain in this bed and felt very sorry for myself indeed, but I could have been worse off. You tell me your father lost an arm in an accident . . .' he said smiling ruefully, 'I am lucky I still have an arm with at least some of my fingers attached.'

There were a few moments of silence between them. Shona got up and went to look from the window. The mist had rolled in from the sea and the moors shimmered in a thick blanket that seemed to stretch to eternity. It was an odd feeling. Rhanna was just a tiny island, isolated far out in the Atlantic, yet certain weather conditions made the great undulating shaggy blanket of the Muir of Rhanna reach out to drape over the world. During the long sparkling days of the Hebridean summers the illusion was heightened even further. The deep blue of the ocean, glimpsed between distant outcrops of perpendicular cliffs, was the cradle on which the heather-covered mattress lay, with the heads of the mountains rearing up into shrouds of gossamer mist. Then the land and the sea became as one with nothing between them and eternity.

As Shona watched a meek little puff of wind occasionally blew the mist into swirling wisps, revealing the blurred face of the moon peering in sullen anonymity through the hazy curtain.

'You look at the moon and you think of Niall and Babbie at this ceil – ceil . . .'

'Ceilidh,' Shona supplied. 'It means a sing-song and

perhaps a dance and a story. I hope you will experience one before you leave Rhanna. Ay, you are right, Anton, I was thinking, but I've had a lot of experience of that.'

'Has Babbie been your friend long?' he asked tactfully.

She shook her head and Anton could not help thinking how beautiful she looked standing against the moonlit window. 'No, not long at all. In fact I know very little about her, but enough – well, I thought it was enough – to feel as though I'd want to have her for a friend for the rest of my life.'

'She is another one who does not like Germans.' Anton said the words in a matter-of-fact way but with such assurance that Shona choked back the protest that had risen to her lips. She was remembering Babbie in the surgery, trembling, looking at the unconscious Anton with a strange, indefinable look.

'It is true, Fräulein Shona,' he continued rather wearily. 'I feel the things that people feel. I look at Fräulein Babbie's sweet and honest face and sense the battles that go on inside her head all the time. She appears calm but inside she fights many emotions. It is against her nature to dislike anyone but she dislikes Germans – and I am a German. Oh, she attends every one of my needs with devotion, but it is training – not trust or fondness – that makes her do so.'

His was such a frank assessment that Shona could find nothing to say to contradict him because she knew he would know she was putting on an act. He was watching her face with those perspicacious blue eyes of his and she found herself reddening.

'Babbie is a very mysterious sort of girl,' she said finally. 'As I say, I know very little about her so I can't tell you much about her feelings on certain matters.'

'You are kind, Fräulein Shona,' he smiled. 'You do not wish to hurt me, and while we are on the subject of people and the things they do, I believe it is you I have to thank for saving my life.'

Embarrassment made her suddenly brisk. 'Och, that is just a lot of blethers from a lot of old women. Donald and my wee

158

brother, Grant, found you. They thought you were a monster, or a ghost,' she laughed. 'And looking at your white face now I'm beginning to think they were right. It's high time I went and let you get some sleep.'

He had sunk into his pillows, hollow-cheeked and strained with exhaustion and as she tucked in his blankets Lachlan popped his head round the door and in a whisper beckoned her out into the hall.

'Shona, mo ghaoil,' Lachlan said as he put his hand on her arm, 'Niall hasn't said anything but I know all is not what it should be between you.' His deep compassionate brown eyes seemed to look right into her troubled heart. 'You must stop torturing one another, mo ghaoil, or one day you will waken up and find it is too late for either of you. You are like my own lassie and my dearest wish is to see the pair of you settled. Take heed of what I say. It's you who should be up at the Manse with him this very minute and fine the two of you know it. Sometimes I wish you were bairns again then I would have an excuse to take you over my knee and give you a good leathering!'

'Ach, you were aye too soft-hearted even to beat a doormat,' she said and they both laughed.

When Shona reached Laigmhor it was warm and quiet. Although Fergus and Kirsteen were still up in the kitchen, Shona managed to avoid them and crept wearily into bed. But she couldn't sleep. She was thinking of Niall and Babbie at the ceilidh. It would be a merry affair. The Rev. John Gray might start off with psalms and hymns but the islanders would see to it that it turned into a proper ceilidh. Niall and Babbie would dance together . . . he would hold her close . . . and then they would go back to Slochmhor together because Babbie was still staying there, though she had moved out of Anton's room. She was in the little box room – which was on the other side of Niall's room!

'Oh God,' she whispered, 'please help me to be less suspicious – and – jealous. I can't help it, I love Niall so much yet every time we meet we seem to fight all the time . . .' She snuggled into her pillows and wept. Her arms ached to hold

159

something. Tot, her faithful old spaniel, had shared her bed for years, but Tot was dead now and she felt terribly alone.

Mirabelle's rag dolls sat in a floppy row on the shelves. Whenever she looked at them she thought of the plump, homely old housekeeper who had been mother to her during the vulnerable years of her childhood. The old lady had lovingly stitched every one of the dolls and now they were all somewhat dusty and bedraggled, but on the whole they had stood the test of time. On top of the dresser was the splendid 'town' doll given to her by Fergus's brother, Alick, on one of his summer visits to the island. The extravagant beauty of the doll had taken her breath away and for a time Mirabelle's rag dolls had been cast aside. But the 'town' doll was cold and hard with none of the cuddly qualities of the others. She had never taken it to bed. Eventually it had become an ornament, a pleasant reminder of the uncle whose affection she had always appreciated though she knew he had caused so much trouble in the past. She hadn't seen Alick since last autumn. He had joined the army, surprising a lot of people except those who knew him best. He was still trying to prove himself, making up for the years of self-indulgence of his early manhood.

Shona looked at the 'town' doll with its prettily painted face. 'Poor Uncle Alick,' she said softly and, getting up, she retrieved it from the dresser, picked out her most favoured rag doll, and then padding back to bed she cuddled the toys to her like a lost child.

CHAPTER 12

When the Commandos had come to the island, expecting to round up a whole flock of German invaders, and had discovered that the whole thing was a false alarm, Dunn had quickly dispatched a message back to base to the effect that the mission would be accomplished much sooner than expected. He had used Behag's 'contraption' to send out the reports and at first she had received him into her Report Centre with utmost tight-lipped suspicion. But he was a young man possessed of fine tact, and in a few words he had dispelled Behag's guilt and made her feel an important ally in the war game.

'I need your help, Mistress Beag,' he had told her courteously. 'To be truthful, I am not acquainted enough with the machine to get the best from it. It is not exactly the most up-to-date transmitter but I am sure that is no deterrent to a woman like you . . . you are in a very important position you know, Mistress Beag . . . you and the Coastguard are probably the two best assets on the island.'

Behag had blossomed then like a wilted plant revived by water. Her jowls, which lay in several wizened layers on her neck, had unfolded one by one into taut furrows as she slowly tilted her head heavenwards and in a silent flurry of gratitude had thanked the Lord for allowing her to keep her dignity despite all the gossip she had endured since the arrival of the bomber. Later, when she could justifiably lift up her head again, the population of Rhanna was destined to hear repeatedly the story of the gallant Dunn, 'an officer and a gentleman, just', who, when her very own kith and kin had forsaken her, gave her the strength to carry on.

At first the Commandos had been disconcerted by their plight, but after a few days in the peaceful environment of Rhanna their initial irritation at the situation had evaporated quickly. Without being able to help themselves, each man had felt a reprieve from the serious and dangerous duties of the war. Despite a lack of military skill the islanders had somehow managed to net three Germans. Only one remained to be taken, and on a small island like Rhanna that seemed an easy enough task. But they soon discovered how wrong they were.

Earlier in the day Dunn had told the Commandos on guard duty at the Manse that the capture of the fourth German would almost certainly be accomplished before nightfall, but night had fallen hours ago and there was still no sign of the other Commandos and the members of the Home Guard who formed the search party. In the hours of daylight the interest of the Home Guard had been sharp enough, with each man feeling a throat-catching excitement at the idea of being the first to capture the elusive German. But the twilight had brought strange looming shapes to play on the whispering amber grasses. And when night fell, and the mist draped itself over the island like a shroud, cloud patterns danced on the aloof ruddy face of the winter moon and shadows loomed over the moor. At such time, the imaginative mind, fed from the breast on myths and folklore, saw the flapping cloaks of spooks and peat hags gliding over lost lonely places, and heard the thin voice of the sea, riding in on the wind, breathing the life of the past into the eerie shadows. These were the nights of the witching moon when fancy ran free and the crofters left the comfort of their homes only to see to their beasts or to walk a short distance to ceilidh in another warm house.

The Commandos had had a long and tiring day, but that they were able to take in their stride. The usual hazards of wide open spaces had presented no problems: they knew about peat hags and peat bogs; they were familiar with the ebb and flow of the tides and, with the added advice gladly given by Righ, had already explored many of the deep dank caverns that yawned into the cliffs surrounding the greater part of the coastline. But what they weren't so prepared for was a people so incurably addicted to the mythical legends of the moors that certain parts of it were taboo unless absolutely essential. The search for the German had been considered necessary and, on the whole, had been undertaken with curiosity. But the nearer the search got to the Abbey ruins the more the Home Guard's enthusiasm began to wane. Lusty cries of merry banter became more subdued till eventually everyone spoke in whispers and took frequent peeps over their shoulders. Much of it was exaggerated but the effect was such that even the Commandos had now lowered their voices to eerie whispers.

'Is it the German you're afraid of?' Anderson mouthed to Torquil.

Torquil didn't answer for a moment. He drew a big strong hand over his shaggy thatch and his blue eyes contemplated the craggy grey stones of the Abbey hunched together like old men sharing secrets. 'Na, na . . . tis no' the German,' he said finally without a hint of discomfort. 'Thon's the place o' the ghosts and they don't like being disturbed.'

'But it's only an old ruin,' Anderson persisted.

Torquil looked at him with pity and said heavily, 'And all you know, eh? Thon's the place o' the tomb, man. Underneath these hillocks is caves full of coffins. Walk on the turf above and waken the dead beneath!'

'And you all know where the openings of these caves . . . or tombs – are?'

'Some, ay, some no',' was the general agreement.

'But they're all grown over and mustny be disturbed,' old Andrew, who was one of the best Seanachaidhs on the island, and who was possessed of an imagination that turned the most mundane event into a thing of magic, whispered. He looked hastily over his shoulder and added, 'The mist is gathering. Look now! It's creeping in from the sea and the Uisga Hags will be hidin' on the rocks near the shore. Sometimes they come right ashore in a mist and before you know where you are they are lurin' you out to sea where you will be after drownin'.'

'The – Uisga Hags?' came the Commandos' query.

'Ay, ay, the green water witches,' old Andrew explained patiently. Thoughtfully, he gathered a gob of spit into his cheeks which he inflated several times before spitting to the ground with an expertise that left no traces on his lips. Staring at the frothy strings dangling on a grassy tussock he went on in deliberately dramatic tones. 'They're the spirits o' witches cast out o' the island hundreds of years afore, an' they have just hung aboot haunting us ever since. Beautiful mermaids they be one minute but if you are out at your lobster pots an' dare to take your thoughts away from your work, one look into the wicked green eyes o' a mermaid

163

witch an' you're done for. There she changes into a wizened crone wi' whiskers an' warts an' she carries you off to the bottom of the sea to show you off to the other hags.' His rheumy blue eyes twinkled mischievously. 'Hard up for men they are down there on the bed o' the ocean, an' the first thing they do is take your trousers off. It's the surest sign a man has been taken by the hags when his trousers float all limp and empty to the surface o' the sea!'

It was the cue everyone needed to let out a subdued bellow of laughter, for there, on the open moor, with the wraiths of haar curling into the hollows, the tale and the tone of old Andrew's voice sent shivers up the spine. But the Commandos were in no laughing mood when not long afterwards most of the islanders drifted away in twos and threes as silently as their stoutly-booted feet would allow. And so, left without the willing guides they needed, the soldiers abandoned the caves and the moors, and now narrowed the search to Nigg and the Burnbreddie estate.

On the hill track to Nigg they came upon Dodie leading Ealasaid home to her byre. The old eccentric had by now learnt to tell the difference between Germans and Commandos and at sight of them he began to gesticulate wildly and babble in Gaelic. He was in a pitiful state with his grey-green eyes sunk into his face like currants in a wizened treacle dumpling and the grey-black stubble on his chin heightening the illusion of a fungus-covered reject. Fortunately some staunch, if not daring, members of the Home Guard had remained and it soon transpired that Dodie had spent a harrowing, sleepless night.

'The big Hun was here,' Robbie translated for the Commandos. 'Poor auld Dodie says the man burst into his house like a raving bull, took all Dodie's food, and then slept most of the night and part of today in a chair by the fire. He went away only a wee whily ago and Dodie just galloped off to look for his cow . . . he loves the beast more than anything else in the world.'

'Ask him if he knows which way the German went.'

Dodie was now weeping into his big calloused hands, his

stooped shoulders shuddering with long-drawn-out sobs, the tears running in dirty rivulets through his fingers. For the first time in his life Robbie thought seriously about Dodie and his lonely simple world. It was bad enough to know about things that went on in the war but to a simple soul like Dodie, his mind groping at half-formed notions and solitary imaginings, it might be utterly terrifying. Not one of them had ever spared the time to explain to him what went on in war and Robbie realized that the arrival of the big German into Dodie's innocent world must have been a frightening ordeal. Robbie felt a great lump of self-reproach in his throat and he threw a firm arm round Dodie's bent shoulders.

'Look now, Dodie, I'm here, dinna greet any more. Just tell me which direction the big Jerry took.'

Dodie waved his arms in the direction of Burnbreddie. 'I saw him goin' in there when I was looking for Ealasaid, by the wee rustic gate in the bushes!'

Dunn looked at Robbie. 'Will you stay with him for a while? He looks like he could be doing with some comfort.'

Robbie was torn. He had looked forward to the Manse ceilidh, seeing it as a reprieve from Behag who was still giving him the 'silent treatment'. 'All day I am hearin' nothing but silence,' he had told his cronies dejectedly. 'I used to think it would be heaven to hear her mouth shut; now I am thinkin' she's even more hell wi' her lips closed.'

'Ach, all right,' he said finally, 'I'll bide a whily. Look you now, Dodie, I'm comin' in to ceilidh wi' you whether you like it or no'. I have some o' Tam's whisky here and we'll have a fine old time.'

Dodie raised a tear-stained face. It was grey and utterly woebegone in the pale glimmer of moonlight filtering through the haar, but a small ghost of a smile lit his weary face. 'Will you really stay wi' me, Robbie? My, it would be right nice so it would . . . for a wee whily just. I'm – I'm feart o' being alone till the big German is caught but at least . . .' he blinked away the last of the tears, 'I found my Ealasaid and will get some milk to drink, for that big mannie took all I had in the house.'

It was an easy enough matter after that to trace Zeitler to one of the big haysheds inside Burnbreddie. His face was haggard and he succumbed quite meekly to the Commandos, though his look of arrogant disdain said quite plainly that he was proud of the trouble he had caused everyone in the last few days.

Thomson was back in his place outside the Manse door, shakily lighting a cigarette, when old Angus drove the trap containing Zeitler and the Commandos up the steep brae. Madam Balfour of Burnbreddie had kindly and willingly loaned both her groom and the trap to the Commandos.

'We must all do what we can in these troubled times,' she had imparted graciously, looking with disdain down her nose at Zeitler. She had fussed greatly over the Commandos since their arrival, inviting them to meals and at one point lending them her precious car that they might get about the island quicker. But the car had been of little use on the stony island roads and had got stuck in a bog on the Muir of Rhanna two nights previously where it still remained because no one had had the time to get it out.

'You have been very kind,' Dunn had said, taking the old lady's hand. 'First your car, now your trap. Thank you for all your hospitality.'

'A pleasure, I'm sure,' the old lady had fluttered, her veneer falling away for a moment to show a lonely old woman, but just as quickly she had been herself again saying, 'I'll get Angus my groom to drive you over to the Manse. He detests work you know but then, these people have no ambition, none at all! There's talk that they're brewing their own whisky, you know! Oh, I wouldn't put it past them, drink all day if they could . . .'

Old Angus had chortled wickedly as he guided the horses up to the Manse. 'The old bugger has done me a favour sendin' me out for I'll be gettin' to this ceilidh after all. I was rackin' my brains all night for an excuse to come.' He now glanced at Zeitler huddled in the back seat. 'We'll be showin' the Jerries a bit o' life right enough but I'm hopin' this one

166

will be changing his clothes and scrubbin' himself. He smells terrible just!'

When the crowd piled into the Manse Jon Jodl was playing a gay little melody which brought forth smiles of appreciation from the new arrivals. In the hubbub Carl Zeitler was whisked away to the wash tub in the scullery. There, watched over by two soldiers, his urgent need for hygiene was speedily undertaken. Mrs Gray, glad to get away from the hymn singing for a while, presided over gallons of water heating on the range in the kitchen while in the scullery the men divested Zeitler of his repulsive-smelling layers of outerwear. Sounds of merriment came from the drawing-room and Mrs Gray smiled to herself. It was going to be a good ceilidh after all.

'I will just heat this – er – gentleman some food,' she said politely, glancing at Zeitler's brooding face. She looked up at the two Manse guards, Thomson and Cranwell, whose faces were rather haggard in the light of the lamp. 'Poor lads,' she murmured sympathetically. 'You look done in . . . but never mind, there's enough hot water for you all to have a nice wash. I've made lots of lovely food so nobody will starve.'

Torquil Andrew came into the kitchen, a pretty dark-haired girl hanging on one arm and a basket of food on the other. 'Some bannocks and scones,' he explained with a flash of his white teeth. 'I told Mother I was coming over to the Manse to sing hymns and she was that pleased to think I've changed my ways she started baking right away.'

'Oh, Torquil, you shouldn't,' Mrs Gray beamed in delight while in the scullery Zeitler was making strangulated sounds of protest because someone had left the door open and he sat in his zinc tub for everyone to see.

After Torquil there came a stream of people all bearing a little offering of some sort. Mairi handed over a pot of crowdie cheese. 'It will be nice on the bannocks – the way Wullie likes it,' she explained sadly before her brown, rather vacant, gaze came to rest on Zeitler. 'My, my,' she said with mild astonishment. 'You would never think he was a German without his clothes – I suppose it's just you expect that funny wee Hun sign to be everywhere on them – even their bodies!'

The earlier arrivals breathed sighs of relief when the familiar faces of the more rumbustious islanders appeared through the door. In the excitement everyone forgot inward promises of abstinence in all things the minister might consider improper. Despite the restrictions caused by rationing, the generous islanders passed round packets of cigarettes while the older men lit smelly pipes. Old Andrew, who, in the first part of the evening had done everything with his pipe except smoke it, thankfully accepted a good fill of 'baccy' from old Joe then reached for his fiddle to tune it. The Germans accepted cigarettes and, after introductions, smiled in some bemusement at the various nicknames bestowed on them. A shining Zeitler was brought in to join the company, one or two children sneaked in by the side door, and the once silent and empty room was soon filled to capacity.

A rousing welcome greeted Niall's entrance, ample proof of his popularity with everyone, while Babbie received a reserved introduction together with a swift appraisal from the womenfolk and sly glances of appreciation from the men.

'Good! Good! We're all here now!' the Rev. Gray boomed, looking round the gathering with some dismay because he hadn't expected such an enthusiastic turnout for a praise meeting. 'Now we shall really raise the roof with our singing!'

The door opened once more to admit a serenely contented Morag Ruadh who came on the arm of Dugald Donaldson. Dugald, determined to follow up the activities of the German invaders, had cycled over the rough moor road from Portvoynachan, his pockets bulging with notepads and pencils. Morag, having allowed herself some time in the fuel shed to 'gather herself up', had emerged to meet Dugald at the Manse door and had surprised him thoroughly by hanging on to his arm and chattering with unusual animation.

'Ach, that is good, now!' Tam McKinnon approved at the minister's words. 'Erchy has brought his bagpipes and we'll

168

have Andrew playin' the fiddle. 'Tis a pity poor auld Todd is laid up for it's handy to have two pipers at a ceilidh. When one gets out o' breath you can just hand over the pipes to the other while the bag is still full of air.'

The minister looked at Tam with disapproval. He had told Mrs Gray to ask only teetotallers to the ceilidh and here was Tam McKinnon who, it was rumoured, was actually brewing his own whisky. In fact, on looking over the new arrivals, the minister saw only those who were notoriously fond of 'the devil's brew'.

'You cannot sing hymns to the bagpipes, Tam!' he said sternly.

Erchy grinned mischievously. 'No, but she'll play them. Wait you and you'll hear what I mean.' He patted his pipes affectionately. 'Just right she is for a good blow. I've given her some treacle to keep her supple and a droppy whisky to give her a bit of life.'

It was Erchy's habit to fondly give his bagpipes a female gender but while everyone else smiled appreciatively the minister's frown deepened. 'I have no idea what you are talking about, Erchy, but there will be no whisky-drinking women in my house. Now . . .' He turned to Morag Ruadh and smiled ingratiatingly. 'Morag is here at last and only too ready, I'm sure, to relieve this young man at the piano – isn't that right, Morag?'

Before leaving the fuel shed Morag had consumed the remainder of her whisky and she was now seeing the world through a rosy glow. She smiled charmingly at the minister, and confounded him by replying, 'Indeed, I will not! I'm for the skirl o' the pipes and a good bit story from Andrew and Joe. 'Tis a night o' fun I'm after.'

The minister's jaw fell and everyone looked at each other in astonishment.

'It's no' natural, no' natural at all! Morag Ruadh is no' herself,' was the general verdict.

Jim Jim and his wife looked at each other. 'Here,' Isabel said, 'was you thinkin' earlier that Morag was actin' a bit funny?'

Jim Jim nodded. 'Ay, indeed. I had a mind I was smellin' the drink off her, but knowing Morag I thought it couldny be. My God, would you look at the smile on her face. She's been havin' a bit fun out there and well she looks on it too. I never thought o' Morag as bein' bonny before but tonight she has the look o' a new woman.'

The blast of the bagpipes filled the room and with a mad 'hooch' Morag was the first to get to her feet, turning to pull Dugald after her.

Isabel nudged her husband. 'Look at that now. She and Dugald Ban are right friendly all of a sudden.'

Jim Jim removed his pipe from his mouth to make a faultlessly aimed spit at the coals, despite the swirling skirts that flounced wildly to the tunes of the pipes. 'Well now, there's a thing,' he said thoughtfully. 'A fine thing, just. Dugald Ban would be just right for Morag and him wi' his ambitions will maybe become one o' they famous people wi' plenty money.'

Jon Jodl and Ernst Foch had risen to their feet and were clapping their hands and stamping their feet in time to the pipes. Only Zeitler remained staring broodingly into the fire but even he could not resist the music and one foot tapped almost automatically on the hearth.

Niall gripped Babbie's arm. 'Well, what do you think of the praise meeting?'

Her green eyes were sparkling. 'It's – it's magic, I shouldn't be feeling like this, all happy and bubbly inside, but I can't help myself. Oh, I wish Shona had come. People will be wondering. Already we're getting some queer looks.'

'You, you mean, the men can't keep their eyes off you. Shona could have come if she had wanted. She's behaving like a spoilt baby!'

'Och, c'mon, Niall, you know that's not true! You were horrible to her today and fine you know it.'

Niall's brown eyes were full of misery. 'I know, God, don't rub it in! But it was seeing her with that – that German. If he hadn't been in bed so badly broken up I swear I would have punched him. Don't tell me either that you particularly like the idea of mending a German or have you changed your mind about that sort of thing?'

She put her fingers to her forehead and shook her head angrily. 'Of course I haven't. When I saw him in Lachlan's surgery I thought for a moment that I wanted him to die!' She looked up suddenly and continued in a shocked voice, 'Isn't that a dreadful thing for a nurse to admit! I hated myself at the time and I hate myself now for ever having thought it! For three days now I've looked after him and now I don't know what to think. I look at him and I see only a wounded young man who has lost all his family in the war. I have to force myself to be cool to him and all the time he's so quiet and grateful for everything I do.'

Niall's nostrils flared. 'The best killers have the nicest smiles. He's a German and that's all there is to it!'

'Well, there's Germans here, aren't there? Why did you come tonight? After all, Niall, this ceilidh is in honour of them!'

Niall looked contemptuously at Jon and Ernst who were now jigging round the room with the utmost enjoyment. Commandos, islanders, Germans, all mixed together, 'hooching' and skirling, caught up in the irresistible wild rhythm of the pipes and the fiddles. 'I shouldn't have come.' Niall sounded defeated, with all the fight suddenly gone out of him. 'I shouldn't have done a lot of things today, but I did, and because of it Shona's not speaking to me and I'm damned if I'm going crawling to her to say I'm sorry! *I* wasn't the one fawning over a German!'

'You're jealous, Niall, so jealous you can't even think straight! I think it might be a good thing if I leave Rhanna by the next boat! Heaven knows what Shona must be thinking about you and me, first finding that we know one another then coming here tonight together and leaving her out in the cold. I'm too fond of her to hurt her!'

'And by God, no wonder. Both red-haired witches with tempers like devils! It would be fine of you to leave the island now with Biddy laid up, a spare nurse that's got one foot in the grave, and my father with so much to do he looks ill on it!

Granted I could hit him for taking that German under our roof but he is my father and he needs all the help he can get!'

They were both shouting at one another but above the noise of the pipes no one heard except for those sitting close by. Old Isabel leaned forward confidentially. 'Where is our Shona tonight, laddie? I had thought that we would all be comin' to your weddin' soon and here you are, at a ceilidh wi' another lass. It's no' right, no' right at all.'

In Niall's present mood it was fortunate for Isabel that the pipes stopped playing just then and everyone flopped exhausted into chairs. Jon Jodl came over to where Babbie was sitting and addressed her quietly in German.

'He is asking how his Commander is keeping, Miss Cameron,' the minister said.

Babbie reddened as all eyes turned towards her. 'Oh, tell him he is improving. He was very badly wounded but the doctor brought him back . . . from the dead. He has lost some of his fingers from frostbite but – otherwise he is perfectly whole.'

'Ach, the soul,' Kate sympathized solicitously. 'We are hearing that he brought his plane over the village and took an awful risk jumping out over the mountains so that he wouldny harm anyone.'

'Ay, he's no' bad for a Jerry,' Tam said enthusiastically.

'Speakin' the English too,' put in Erchy somewhat breathlessly. 'But we are after teachin' him some o' the Gaelic. Already he can say a few words.'

Tam looked at Ernst and Jon. 'These lads are no' like the real Nazis – except for the big Hun in the corner.'

Ernst looked over at Tam and said carefully, 'Uisge-beatha?'

Tam's mouth fell open and Torquil said, 'I think he's asking for some o' your whisky, Tam.'

Tam grinned delightedly. 'Well, damn me – and using the Gaelic name for it! These Jerries are clever right enough . . . here, Bullhead.' He held out his hip flask. 'Take a real good swig – you ugly big bugger,' he added in rapid Gaelic and everyone roared with laughter.

Ernst took the flask, but passed it to Jon. 'You first, Jon.' Jon took the flask and raised it high. 'Slainte!' he cried and the islanders took up the cry.

Mrs Gray was coming into the drawing-room with a tray of tea. Behind her tripped a merry procession bearing plates of food. The room was in a happy uproar. An exhausted Andrew had handed his fiddle to Jon whose long, delicate fingers extricated tunes that were unknown on the island but were so irresistibly gay they invited hands to clap and feet to tap. The Commandos and the Germans had all partaken freely from the brown cough bottles such as might be found in any medicine cupboard on the island, and an air of comradeship existed between everyone. Only the Rev. John Gray remained soberly reserved and his mood wasn't improved by his first sip of tea which Torquil had laced with whisky while it lay steaming on the kitchen table.

'Hannah, this tea tastes terrible,' he said tightly, but Hannah was beyond caring.

'Well, John, if you don't like it . . . away through and make some more,' she told him flippantly, but he was of the breed who believed the kitchen was only a woman's domain and he had no intention of domesticating himself now. Several minutes later he held out his drained cup and requested a refill.

'Ach, you enjoyed that,' Kate grinned, going off to fetch the teapot into which Tam had poured a good measure of whisky. 'There now,' she said, handing the minister the replenished cup. 'It is tastin' a wee bit funny but the water is that peaty the now it canny be helped.'

Babbie's face twitched and she let out a smothered laugh. Niall too could not contain himself and he let out a great guffaw of mirth that seemed to release all his pent-up emotions. 'Will you dance with me, Babbie?' he twinkled. 'We might as well enjoy ourselves now that we're here and if I don't grab you Erchy or one of the others will do it for me.'

They whirled merrily into the crowd while the minister, his face somewhat flushed after consuming three cups of tea, leaned towards Kate and gave her a conspiratorial wink.

'Good tea, my dear, very good! I must say there's something to be said for peaty water! By jove, it has really warmed me up and I am hoping you can squeeze another cup from the pot.'

Kate obligingly 'squeezed' the pot and put her lips close to his ear. 'There now, it's as dry as a fart in a corpse!' she imparted in a bubble of merriment.

'Mrs McKinnon!' the minister exploded, but the ghost of a smile hovered at the corners of his mouth. 'You know, for the first time since I came to Rhanna I feel really close to you all. I am very glad I held this ceilidh tonight, very glad . . . Would you care to dance with me, my dear?' he added as Jon broke into the wildly stirring *Czardos*.

A hotch-potch of an Irish jig made the floorboards jump beneath the rugs; everyone had reached the stage when anything with a rhythm made their feet itch to dance. Nearly all of the men present saw to it that they danced with Babbie. She was wearing a dress of softest green wool which complemented her amber-flecked eyes and luxuriant red curls. She had a knack of making every man she danced with feel as if he were the only man in the room, and when Niall finally managed to get to her he said with a teasing little laugh, 'You're a flirt, Caillich Ruadh. You've got all the men making sheep's eyes at you and all the women throwing daggers! I can see clearer than ever that it would be a very easy thing for any man to fall in love with you.'

'I'm in no position for anything like that ever to happen,' she answered, a little frown creeping into her radiant smile.

'You like Anton, don't you?' he said, curtly and unexpectedly.

'Niall, for heaven's sake, what's got into you?' she said in hurt bewilderment. 'It's perhaps just as well we didn't know each other too well in Glasgow because I don't like the Niall I'm getting to know better now. Don't complicate matters any more for me! You keep on and on about Anton. I don't like him and I don't hate him! Does that satisfy you?'

He shook his head as if to clear it and looked at her with the shadow of fear darkening his eyes to black pools of misery. 'I'm sorry, mo ghaoil. I'm not myself, that's for sure. I'm saying things I don't mean to say. They just come out and I canny seem to stop them. Forgive me, mo ghaoil.'

Babbie said nothing but squeezed his hand reassuringly. He smiled and put his lips close to her ear. 'Would you look at our minister. That rascal, Tam, has been putting whisky in his tea!'

The Rev. John Gray was snoring on a hard wooden chair, his hands clasped over his chest, his legs stretched like pokers; he was in danger of sliding off his perch. 'The Lord is my – Psalm twenty-six – I have trusted also in the Lord; therefore I shall not slide – tea terrible . . .' he muttered insensibly.

'To hell wi' Psalms,' Robbie chuckled. He had arrived late at the ceilidh and was determined to enjoy the rest of it. 'Away you go over to the Headquarters, Tam, and be bringin' up some more of your cough mixture. It's early yet and I'm no' goin' home to have Behag sniffin' at me like a ferret and shoutin' at me wi' her eyes.'

'Ay, I will that,' Tam responded willingly, whereupon Kate set about collecting the bottles. Tam stuck out his large square palm and cocked his eye at the company. 'Cross my hand wi' silver and I'll be bringin' back full bottles.'

'Ach, you're worse than my Aberdeen cousin!' old Angus exclaimed. 'He looks for change out o' a farthing.'

'Well, it's more than a farthing I'm after,' Tam smirked, and though everyone grumbled they handed over their money willingly enough. Tam closed his hand and winked at Mrs Gray. 'You won't be saying a word in the wrong ears, mo ghaoil?'

'Tam McKinnon!' she said sternly. 'If people want to buy your cough mixture it is nothing to do with me.' She put her hand in her pocket and then slyly put some coins into his hand. 'And I'll be having a drop too. I think Morag must have passed her cold on to me. I'll never get the chance of medicine like yours again.'

Tam looked at her with reverence. 'Mrs Gray, this will not be your last ceilidh on this island,' he intoned in a respectful whisper. He stretched out his hand and dropped her coppers back into her pocket. 'Be putting them in the kirk plate for me next Sabbath,' he said benevolently, then turned to follow the sound of Kate's clanking bottles outside.

CHAPTER 13

Niall turned restlessly in bed and wakened abruptly at the sound of stealthy footsteps climbing the stairs. Then he heard a faint exchange in German and realized that the Commandos had taken Jon to Anton's room to say goodbye. The three healthy captives were due to leave that morning, and Niall found himself fuming, unable to get back to sleep though he was still tired. Dawn was filtering over the night sky but his room still lay in darkness. He lay on his back, staring up at the ceiling, thinking about the German lying on the other side of the wall from him, comfortably lying under the roof of Slochmhor with his German companions coming to bid farewell to him. But hardly comfortable! Mixed up as Niall's thoughts were he couldn't deny even to himself that Anton most certainly must be suffering a good deal, though there was hardly ever a cheep of complaint out of him. 'But why should there be?' he argued with himself. 'His set-up couldn't be more perfect: a doctor at first hand to mend him with absolute skill and then to be right on the spot should anything go wrong; an attractive young nurse to tend him hand and foot, wipe his nose for him if need be; bed, board, all laid on with hardly even the snap of a finger to fetch him attention. The snap of a finger! The poor bastard had hardly any fingers left to snap!'

The door opened softly and Fiona crept in, a ghostly little wraith in her long flannelette nightdress. 'Niall, are you awake?'

'Ay, and you should still be asleep, you wee wittrock!

What ails you at this hour of the morning?' The next moment he felt the slight weight of her on his bed.

'Ach, don't grump at me, Niall. Mother and Father are still in bed and Father being so put upon this whily back I didn't want to waken him in case he would grump at me too. In a way you're the next in line as head of the house so I thought I would ask you if it would be all right for me to get up and go over to Aosdana Bay to see the Jerries off. I'd be back in lots of time for school and if I ran and ran I could catch up with the traps taking the Jerries from the Manse and get a lift. All my friends are going over – '

'*No!*' Niall bawled out the refusal even as his uninjured left arm shot out to grab his little sister by the shoulders and shake her till her teeth rattled. 'Don't you *dare* ask such a thing of me, you wee bitch!' he gritted furiously. 'Do you think it's a picnic? Haven't you had enough of Germans on the island without wanting to go and wave them goodbye? Wave them good riddance more like. Don't you know what they've done! Do you never listen to *anything*? No wonder old Murdoch feels like belting you round the lugs sometimes! It's likely you never take in a word of anything he tries to teach you!'

Shock froze the child's reaction for several stunned moments, but then she opened her mouth and gave her lungs full throttle. Fiona was a little girl who could throw tantrums at the drop of a hat. They were so devilish and noisy that Niall always dreaded them and was never quite sure how to handle them. He was usually the quiet one of the family, the complete opposite of self-willed little Fiona. Occasionally he smacked her bottom, mostly he simply left her to shout herself out of a temper. But this time it was neither temper nor stubbornness that made her cry. It was pure hurt at him for flying out at her for no reason that she could really understand. Her yells brought him swiftly to his senses and in a mixture of anxiety and shame he pulled her into the cradle of his strong good arm and crushed her soft little mouth against his face. She smelt faintly of lavender soap from her bath of the night before. 'There, there, my babby,' he soothed. 'Weesht, weesht now. I'm sorry, I'm sorry I shouted at you. It's just – some unpleasant things happened a few days ago in Glasgow and I can't seem to forget them. I'm being an irritable old tom cat to everybody.'

'Please don't ever get like Elspeth,' Fiona sobbed against his neck. 'I know she's lonely and that makes her peckle her nose into everybody's business like an old woodpecker and snap at me because I'm the littlest in the house. I can stand it because I have Mother and Father and you when you come home. I look forward like anything to you coming back here because you smile a lot and like all my pets but you're not smiling this time and I hate it!'

He nuzzled her soft fragrant hair and cuddled her closer. 'I promise I won't get like Elspeth,' he chuckled. 'It would be too difficult anyway since she's a woman.'

She giggled. 'Is she? I mean, you would never think it because she's hardly got any bosoms or anything, has she, *and* she's got whiskers growing, they stick out of her face like little stiff pins on a pin cushion. Still . . .' she sniffed, 'she's better than that other old witch that's come in Biddy's place. She and Elspeth are becoming friends. Can you think what life will be like for me then? Old Elspeth biting my head off and Prune Face waiting around like an old Peat Hag for me to take an illness so's she can jag me on the bum! She loves jagging people. Old Malky of Rumhor got bitten on the leg by one of his pigs and Prune Face has already jagged him twice . . . and always on the backside. He says it's no' decent, an auld wife like that looking at men's private parts though I don't know what he means by that 'cos with him being the father of six children his parts couldn't have been all *that* private!'

Niall choked with laughter into her hair. 'You know too much, you wee devil. Look, hush now and coorie in beside me till it's time to get up for school. You can bring me up a cup of tea when you go down.'

As Niall and Fiona rested quietly and watched the day slowly dawn, a bleary-eyed and very subdued Rev. John Gray rudely awakened old Angus, sound asleep under the

178

sofa in the drawing-room, to take charge of Burnbreddie's trap. They were to take the prisoners and soldiers over to Portvoynachan when the Commandos returned with Jon. 'Ach, but her leddy will be wonderin' where I am lost,' Angus grumbled, but the minister would have no excuses and Angus went stiffly to get the horses ready.

When Angus was out of the house, the minister shuffled into the kitchen and sat down at the table, his voice full of self-recrimination and dismay as he divulged to his wife that certain parts of the ceilidh were a complete blank in his mind.

'We all have our weaknesses, John,' Mrs Gray intoned prudishly while her heart surged with delight. 'You are only human after all.' In a neat, grey wool dress, her hair in a prim bun, she was Mrs John Gray, the minister's wife once more, instructions ringing in her ears about the church flowers and other such sober affairs. But nothing could keep the twinkle from her eyes. The ceilidh had opened doors that hitherto she had been too wary to enter, and now she knew that the cloak of convention would never again stifle her individuality.

'But I drank only tea!' His voice was almost a wail. 'You know that, Hannah!'

'Of course, dear, of course,' she said soothingly but in such a way as to leave doubts in his mind which would never be dispelled.

'Whisky was in that tea, Hannah,' he said accusingly.

She patted his arm kindly. 'Then knowing that you shouldn't have touched it, John. Take your breakfast now before it gets cold.'

Soon after the Rev. had sullenly gulped down his meal, old Angus rapped on the door to say that the Burnbreddie trap and the minister's own were ready to go. The Commandos and Jon appeared then and the minister insisted on squeezing the prisoners and all of the soldiers into the two vehicles for the trip across the island. Mrs Gray had prepared an early but abundant meal for the departing group, and she watched rather wistfully as the Commandos with their stomachs full and the Germans with theirs empty, for they had not felt like eating much on this uncertain morning, rumbled out into the hazy morning light. She had grown quite fond of her charges and would miss their presence – and the attention they had brought her.

Early though it was, half the population of Rhanna had contrived to be at Portvoynachan on some pretext or other. Because school hadn't yet opened, many of the children, too, were at large, and the normally deserted stretches round Aosdana Bay were reminiscent of a Sunday-school outing.

'My, my, would you look at what's coming now?' old Joe commented, looking up from mending a fishing net draped over a large boulder near the edge of the cliffs.

Jim Jim looked up, his netting needle poised in his hand. 'Ay, ay, the Jerries must be goin' away,' he commented with a bewitching show of innocence.

Canty Tam looked out to sea where, in the soft mist of morning, the grey ghost shape of a naval patrol vessel lurked. 'I wouldny like to be goin' out there in one o' they rubber balloon things,' he intoned, leering at the pearly turquoise of the early sky. 'The Uisga Hags have long claws for tearing things up. Yon rubber is no' safe, no' like a real clinker, the Caillichs will just rip the bottom out on them.'

'Ach, be quiet, man,' spat Jim Jim. 'Or it's your bottom will be ripped. Get hold o' one o' they nettin' needles and make yourself useful for a change.' As the traps came nearer Jim Jim suddenly abandoned his task to move closer to Morag Ruadh. 'You were a long time outside wi' these soldiers last night,' he said conversationally.

Morag examined her long fingers with great interest. 'Ay, you're right there, Father.'

'They wereny doin' you a mischief, mo ghaoil?'

'Indeed, hold your tongue, Father! You mind your own business!'

Jim Jim looked crestfallen but pursued the matter grimly. 'Now, now, Morag, as my daughter you *are* my business. I am hoping you are remembering the identity o' the men you were wi' last night – just in case,' he finished in a daring rush.

Morag tossed her red head haughtily. 'Your mind is blacker than the peats you damp all day. I will not be listening to another word!' She flounced away down the stony track to the bay.

Old Joe watched her and gave Jim Jim a conspiratorial wink. 'She'll have her man yet, Jim Jim. Look now, there she goes, straight to Dugald Ban. These two were more than a mite friendly last night.'

Jim Jim looked at his daughter talking animatedly to Dugald and a smile creased his brown face. 'By God, you're right, Joe,' he said happily, and leaving his nets once more, went down to join the crowds on the white sands below. When he arrived, the Commandos were retrieving the dinghies from the deep, dry caves that pitted the cliffs. Soon Dunn emerged, a frown creasing his brow.

'One of the dinghies appears to be missing,' he informed the crowd in general.

'Ach, is that not strange now?' Ranald shook his head sympathetically.

'Are you sure you have looked right? It is easy to miss things in these caves.'

'Hardly something so obvious,' Dunn said dryly.

'Maybe it was taken away by a water witch,' Brown said with a smothered laugh. But he hadn't reckoned with the islanders who immediately met the suggestion with an eager barrage of superstitious comments.

'All right! All right!' Dunn cried. 'We'll make do with what we have. C'mon now, lads, get cracking!'

There was a general bustle to the water's edge and the dinghies were lowered into the speckled green shallows. Dunn looked at Tam McKinnon whose undoubted popularity singled him out as the unofficial leader of the island's Home Guard. 'You will keep an eye open at the doctor's house,' Dunn instructed. 'I am relying on you, Mr McKinnon. I know McKenzie of the Glen is the Chief Warden, but his farming duties take up a lot of his day. In a few days' time the military medics will be back to see how the German officer is progressing.'

181

Tam's face was red with importance. 'We will do a good job, you can be sure of that, sir. We will make damt sure Mr Bugger will no' run away.'

'And we will make sure that Behag is getting her signals right in future,' Robbie put in, his round face completely cherubic.

'You will *all* get your signals correct in future!' Dunn said sternly. 'No more crossed wires . . . do you hear?' His face relaxed suddenly into a wide grin. 'Thanks, lads, for a great time . . . we'll maybe come back one day for a drop more of the water of life.'

'You'll no' be tellin' a soul – over there,' Tam said anxiously, nodding towards the horizon as if he were referring to another planet.

'Not a soul – scout's honour,' Dunn said solemnly.

Jon Jodl was sitting quietly beside Ernst in one of the dinghies. He looked at the green water lapping the edge of the sand. It was a peaceful morning filled with the tang of peat smoke and salt. Even the seabirds were in a placid mood. A curlew poked for small crabs in the shallow pools; a colony of gulls flopped lazily on the gentle swell of the waves. Above the cliffs the sheep cropped the turf with unhurried intent and two Highland cows watched the scene in the bay with silent interest. Jon looked at it all and swallowed a lump in his throat. For a little while he had found peace on the island. He felt lulled in mind and body. No matter what his future held now, he knew he would never cease to bless the reprieve that the landing on Rhanna had given him. The warmth of tears pricked his eyelids and he swallowed again. 'Farewell Paradise,' he thought sadly. The memory of Anton strayed into his mind. Dunn and Anderson had escorted him over to Slochmhor before dawn. For a brief moment Anton had opened his eyes as Jon stood over the bed. 'You take care, Jon,' he had whispered. 'I'll see you – sometime.'

'Soon – soon, sir,' Jon had said and left quickly with the Commandos to meet the traps coming down from the Manse. In a way, Jon envied Anton his prolonged stay on the island but he was immediately ashamed of himself for thinking in such a way. Anton was still very ill. The doctor had made a fine job, but Anton had lost some of his fingers. That was not a thing to envy. It could have been him lying there, his fingers gone . . . a musician needed all his fingers to play the piano, the fiddle . . . 'God forgive me,' Jon thought. 'And let Anton get better so that he can enjoy this place the way I have enjoyed it.'

Suddenly he got to his feet, making the dinghy tilt alarmingly. 'Slainte!' he cried wildly. 'To Anton!' His blurring gaze swept over the homely faces of the people who had been so kind to him, and a sob caught in his throat. 'Slainte!' he cried again and Ernst was beside him, echoing the words, quietly at first, then in a great surge of sound.

'Heil Hitler,' Zeitler muttered, but no one heard him because Jon's cry was echoing out joyfully from the gathering on the shore. 'Slainte, Jon! Slainte, Mr Foch!'

Dunn was politely thanking the minister for his hospitality but the great swelling of the Gaelic 'Health!' bouncing from the pillars of the cliffs and reverberating through the caves, drowned his voice. Dunn turned and stepped into the nearest dinghy and he too took up the cry. Then the crowd rushed to the water's edge to wave and shout and the Rev. John Gray stood alone.

'Slainte!' He heard Jon's voice above the rest, and a hot flush of shame darkened his face. He had been on Rhanna for more than twenty years and never in all that time had he uttered one word of the Gaelic. Jon's stay had been a matter of days and he was proudly shouting the Gaelic to the skies. The dinghies were now little dark blobs on the sun-flecked sea, yet still the cry of 'Slainte' tossed back at the crowd surging round Aosdana Bay.

'Slainte,' the Rev. John Gray whispered and turned abruptly on his heel to hide the red face of humiliation from the world.

Having forgotten now about the goings-on at Portvoynachan, Fiona snuggled against Niall contentedly and thought about Anton alone in the adjoining room. She opened her mouth to tell him how much she liked the young German but her better senses warned her against it and she said instead, 'I like Babbie being here, she's nice and she says funny things. I let her see some of my spiders and she didn't scream like some of these silly big girls do. That stupid Agnes Anderson screams all the time, especially if there's boys around. I love Shona for that too. I'm glad she's home. It means she'll be here a lot because you're here too. I'll hate it when you're married though and likely leave Rhanna. It's a pity people have to get married all the time. I don't think I ever will, you have to do awful things like wash your husband's socks and drawers and some of them have terrible smelly feet. Johnny Taylor is only nine and his feet are . . .'

'Weesht, you wee chatterbox,' he scolded gently. 'You'll wake Mother then *I'll* get skelped lugs for encouraging you.' The child's mention of Shona had brought back all his doubts and self-recriminations. He knew he was the one in the wrong. That it was he who ought to make the first move and go over to Laigmhor to tell her he was sorry. But then he would have to explain about Babbie and at that moment in time he felt he wasn't prepared for more emotional questions, upsets – perhaps even tears. He was too tired mentally and physically to sort out other people's feelings, let alone his own . . .

Half an hour later the house was up and bustling. Elspeth always came at eight o'clock sharp to help Phebie prepare breakfast. With the household's vastly increased numbers there was more work than ever to be done. Elspeth grumbled a good deal over this but her efficiency couldn't be denied and Phebie shut her lips and let the housekeeper ramble on.

A sparkling-eyed Fiona danced up to Niall's room with tea and toast. 'Mother is walking with me to school because she wants some things at Portcull. Elspeth's moaning about the rationing again so Mother's going to try and wheedle some stuff from Merry Mary. Babbie's going over to Tina's to see to her ankle. I think really she's getting out the house quick before Prune Face turns up. When she does you've to tell her to go over to see Todd and Biddy. Mother says it will serve you right for lying in bed!'

'Won't Father be here to tell her?'

'No, he's been called out to Old Malky at Rumhor who sent word that he thinks his leg is going to drop off at any minute with pain . . . so you'll be in the house with Prune Face and Elspeth.' She snorted with ecstatic laughter at the look on his face and didn't hear him mutter, 'Not forgetting Jerry next door.'

Babbie looked in a few moments later to bid him a hurried goodbye and then went to Anton's room, staying there for quite some time before her footsteps clattered away downstairs.

With everyone gone the house seemed very quiet. It was a dewy morning with banks of mist lying in the hollows of the moors and clinging to the mountain tops like big lumps of fluffy cotton wool. Niall felt very peaceful lying there in his own familiar bedroom at Slochmhor. It was what he needed, to be alone, to have time to sort out his thoughts and feelings . . . but it would have been more peaceful still if Anton hadn't been in the next room. Returning from the ceilidh the night before Niall had been tired and drunk yet unable to sleep. Shona, Babbie, Ma Brodie – Anton – they had all crowded into his mind till his head had whirled and he had felt sick, hate curling his stomach into a tight knot. He had never hated anyone before and the things it did to him had frightened him. Yet all through the feeling he had reasoned that he didn't know Anton enough to hate him, it was what the young German stood for that he hated: Britain was at war with the Germans; the Enemy were to be despised for the things they did; Anton was the Enemy – he was to be despised . . .

A terrific thud from the room next door shattered his thoughts. He sat up in bed, his heart hammering into his throat. There was the sound of scrabbling now, and the unmistakable moans of someone in pain. Niall quickly got out of bed, rushed out to the landing, and threw open the door of the spare room. Anton was on the floor, on his knees,

185

his hands clawing frantically at the bedclothes in an effort to get back into bed.

'Christ Almighty!' Niall exploded. 'What in heaven's name are you playing at, man?'

'Playing – no – and certainly not on my knees – praying!' Anton gasped. His face was a ghastly white colour. 'I reached – for a glass – of water – I fell.'

Niall was across the room in seconds, trying frantically to pull Anton upright. Once deposited back on his bed, Anton lay sprawling and panting, his mouth twisted in pain, his bandaged hand groping inadequately for something to hold on to to aid himself upright. Niall saw with alarm that blood was seeping through the wadding across his middle and he said harshly, 'You've hurt more than your pride, Jerry! You're bleeding!'

Anton closed his eyes as he struggled to regain his breath but a bitter little smile twisted his fine mouth. 'Do not concern yourself for me. No doubt it hurt you very much to have to lower yourself to help a Jerry, as you call me, but you do not have to go beyond the call of human decency to do any more for me. Leave me alone now.'

'Too bloody right I will!' Niall said, but with uncertainty rather than anger. In a flash he saw not a German but a fair-haired, blue-eyed youth, very badly injured and undoubtedly in great pain. Then he saw the Iron Cross on the bedside table and his hatred returned anew. 'At least you're lucky you're alive and bleeding! Dead people don't bleed! It congeals too damned quickly once the heart stops beating! You've spilled plenty of blood in your time, now it's your turn! It's called poetic justice!'

As Anton struggled for breath, he allowed Niall to go raving on and heard the words being lashed out at him but did not really take in their meaning. His head felt light, there was a queer sensation in his belly, a feeling of nausea, of burning, of tearing apart. At first his mind was filled only with the sufferings of his body, but at Niall's last words the sufferings of his emotions took precedence. He could take no more: no more hate, accusations, rejections. He felt himself trembling but could do nothing to control it. He shook his head from side to side on the pillow in a demented silent torture of body and soul and gritted his teeth to stop from crying out, but it was useless.

'Will you stop it!' He screamed the words at the ceiling. 'You talk about justice! What the hell do you know about justice? Was it justice that killed my mother, my father? Two little girls who were too young and innocent to think they would ever be killed by a bomb? I loved my family, I still love them! Only they are no more! I will never see their faces again! I will never hear my mother singing or watch my father working in the fields – ever, as long as I live. Heidi – my youngest sister – she was like yours – playing with spiders and frogs and loving her life! I go to bed at night and I see her face, her smiling face! I hear Olga talking about her ambition to be a nurse, to help people who are suffering! I see, I hear – and I cry . . . do you hear me? I cry!' The tears were running unchecked down his face, drenching his neck. He struggled to sit up and even though his eyes were swimming the blue hurt and pain in them seared Niall's soul. 'You are a very angry young man, Niall McLachlan! But I too am an angry young man . . . angry and lonely and wishing at this God-forsaken moment that I had crashed to my death up there in the mountains! What is left for me? Tell me that! Tell me that if you can, damn you!'

Niall put his fist to his mouth and squeezed his eyes shut. 'Oh God! God!' he whimpered in utter despair. He fell to his knees by Anton's bed and buried his head into his plaster-encased arm. His sobs were harsh and dry at first, but then the tears came, flowing endlessly, while his shoulders shook and he rasped for breath. His heart was so full that it felt like bursting, but the tears were like a balm, and the more he cried the calmer his heart and mind became. They cried together for what seemed eternity but what in reality was but a few minutes, Niall on his knees by Anton's bed, Anton lying back on his pillows letting the pent-up tears of many months course freely till the pillows and the collar of his pyjamas were soaked in them.

Anton drew a shuddering breath and choked out, 'Our cup runneth over. We are indeed a lucky pair of fellows.'

The remark was both apt and silly. Niall choked on a mixture of laughter and tears. He lifted his head and looked at Anton's swollen eyes beginning to twinkle in his chalky white face. 'Not a word to anyone about this – do you hear?' Niall said. 'If the lads of the island heard about it I'd never live it down.'

'Do you take me for a fool?' Anton returned, drawing a hand over his eyes. 'Am I going to tell – Babbie for instance – or Doctor McLachlan that while they are out of the house I cry my eyes out . . . "Oh, don't worry about me, Doctor, I pass my time nicely while you are gone – I weep like a baby." He would think I am insane above all else.'

Niall got up from the floor and sat shakily on the edge of the bed. 'You know, old Mirabelle was right,' he said thoughtfully. 'She used to say, "A good greet cures a host of ails", and she's right, it does. I feel as if a lot of poison has just been washed out of my system.'

'A – good – greet?'

Niall laughed, his brown eyes, though swollen, shining for the first time since his return home. 'A Scottish way of saying a good cry cures a lot of troubles. You know, maybe that's how girls get things into better perspective than we do, they cry a lot and seem to see the world through a clearer pair of lenses.'

'Then – perhaps Fräulein Babbie would be the better for a good cry. She smiles her smiles of sunshine but inside – she bottles up.'

'You see a lot of people's feelings, Büttger.'

'I see in her what is inside myself – too much keeping in the thoughts that hurt – that is, until this morning when I had my good greet.' He smiled and his keen blue eyes looked straight at Niall. 'Please, do not call me "Büttger" or, worse, "Jerry". My name is Anton. I think friends should call each other by their Christian names.'

Niall took Anton's hand and squeezed it firmly. 'All right – Anton – later we'll talk some more, keep each other company while we're both convalescing, but right now I'd better get dressed and get downstairs to meet Prune Face and give her the morning's instructions.'

'Prune Face?'

'Nurse Millar,' Niall chuckled. 'Fiona christened her Prune Face which is appropriate if unkind.'

'Ah, yes, I know the one. She came up to look at me yesterday and I really mean *look*. She just stood in the doorway with her hands folded very primly over her stomach and just *looked* at me. I felt like some sort of exhibit, tagged and laid out for inspection.'

Niall shuffled uncomfortably. 'Ay, well, Nurse Millar isn't the only one guilty of prejudgement – anyway, I'd better get washed and dressed or Mother will come back and clout me on the lugs for being lazy.'

But Babbie's arrival into the room delayed his departure. She looked at the sheepish, tear-stained faces of the two young men and knew immediately that they had made up their differences. She was surprised at the relief she felt, and it added to the sense of well-being she had come away with after her visit to Tina's cottage. The young woman had greeted her with easy-going pleasure and had admitted her into a cluttered small world of lazing animals, jumbled furniture and drowsing peace. But Babbie's professional composure had almost failed her when, over a strupak, Tina had observed casually, 'I am hearing that you are doing a grand job sleeping wi' the German laddie.'

'Not sleeping *with* him,' Babbie had spluttered into her tea, 'sleeping *beside* him, in the same room, to be near him the first night he was so ill.'

'Ach, well, is it no' much the same thing?' Tina stated placidly. 'And working so close to him, healing him and talking with him you will be seeing another side to him that maybe no' even his Jerry friends ever saw when they were all fightin' together. He is just a human being like the rest o' us and though some of them are real Nazis and never think about anything else except killing and winning, this one is quite a young gentleman from what Matthew was after

189

telling me. He will likely be more an ordinary laddie than he is a Hun. It will make it easier for you to forget he is a Jerry, him bein' so nice – and good-lookin' too from all accounts . . .' Tina's eyes sparkled. 'You had better watch out or he will be after fallin' in love wi' you. Men always fall for good-looking young nurses.'

Babbie had said nothing but unworldly Tina had given her much food for thought. They were true, the things Tina had said. Babbie *was* beginning to forget that Anton was a German. In fact she was at the stage when she had to keep reminding herself of the fact in order to remain impersonal towards him. With the passing of the days she knew all too well that his charm was bewitching her, and doubly so because it was a natural rather than a calculated charm, a personal charisma that seemed to reach out and embrace her every time she entered his room. But she had to keep herself aloof, there was no room in her heart for sick young men, no matter how handsome or charming they might be.

Anton's face had lit up at her entrance and his blue eyes had become bluer and deeper as he gazed at her.

'I bumped into Nurse Millar downstairs,' Babbie said lightly. 'She was full of moans about the walk from Biddy's house and told me that she ought to be staying here to be right on hand and that I, if I had any common decency, should pack my bags and move back to Laigmhor. I didn't think poor Phebie or Lachlan would take too kindly to the idea of Nurse Millar under their roof, and just stood there, not knowing what to say, when old Elspeth came to the rescue. She said Nurse Millar was welcome to stay at her house, which isn't too far from here, and the old dear jumped at the offer. I think really she feels too isolated at Biddy's house and as she and Elspeth seem to have become friendly, the arrangement suits them both. They can moan at one another to their hearts' content. Now Nurse Millar is away over to see to Todd and Biddy with something on her face that could actually be described as a smile!'

'Fräu Morrison is a very soft-hearted old lady underneath

her steel,' Anton observed, holding up his hand to ward off the barrage of disbelieving comments with which his words were met. 'It is true, she hides it well under a face which shows nothing, she complains about everything – yet – she finds time last night to come up to my room with a bowl of something she calls Benger's food. She frowns at me and tells me I look like death then sits on my bed to spoon the food into me as if I was a little boy.'

'*Never! !*' Babbie and Niall cried simultaneously.

'Oh, but yes. She is a very lonely old woman with a great capacity for love. It is squashed away inside her heart but occasionally – it shows.'

'You are quite the young philosopher,' Babbie said dryly.

'Nothing so grand, Fräulein. I just observe people, that is all, and lying here, with nothing to fill my time, I observe more than ever.' A spasm of pain crossed his face and Babbie was immediately alert.

'Observing you I would guess something is wrong,' she said briskly. 'Where does it hurt?'

'It is nothing,' he said weakly.

'I found him crawling about the room and saw blood on the bandages round his middle,' Niall volunteered somewhat sheepishly.

'And you sit around gossiping like a couple of old women knowing that!' Babbie scolded angrily. 'Och, men! What makes you all think it's brave to tear yourselves apart and then say nothing about it?' She threw back Anton's covers and saw at once the blood seeping through the bandages. His hand was over the wound, as if trying to staunch the blood which was profuse enough to seep steadily through his fingers. 'Oh, let me look!' Babbie cried furiously. 'A philosopher you may be but certainly not a wise one! You've probably gone and burst your stitches. Niall, go down quickly and ask Elspeth for a bowl of hot water . . . and bring some bandages from the surgery!' she yelled after his departing form.

'Fräulein . . . Babbie . . . don't be angry.' Anton laid his bandaged hand on her arm. 'There was something that had to be settled – something far more important to me than a few burst stitches. Do you understand?'

'Ay, well enough,' she replied shortly. 'Now lie back and be quiet, you've talked enough for one morning.'

With the bandages removed and the wound cleaned up Babbie soon saw that the damage wasn't as bad as she had imagined. Only two of the stitches had torn apart but even so, Babbie was in an awkward position. She knew she couldn't get Anton down to the surgery to administer to him properly, but he read her thoughts.

'Do it here,' he told her, 'and please, without ether, it makes me sick and stupid and I've already had enough of it.'

'Oh, but . . .'

'Please – Babbie. I am just beginning to enjoy food again . . . and . . .' he looked at Niall. 'I have some company around me that is just getting interesting.'

'Father has some of Tam's whisky in his cupboard,' Niall said. 'I'll go down and get it.'

Niall fed Anton the whisky while Babbie repaired the damage. He watched Babbie's sure, steady fingers gently but firmly closing up the raw, gaping aperture in Anton's belly and was filled with admiration for her coolness. Anton said nothing. He spluttered on the whisky, gritted his teeth and held on to Niall's arm with such force that the mark of his fingers lay on Niall's flesh in a vivid white pattern. Only when Babbie was finished did she show some reaction, and to steady the trembling of her legs she raised the whisky bottle to her lips and took a good draught.

'God bless Tam McKinnon,' she choked, and Niall followed her example.

'Slainte!' he cried.

'Slainte,' Anton muttered feebly though he had no earthly idea what it meant.

They all looked at one another and smiled.

'Well done, Nurse Babbie,' Niall said softly.

'And Niall McLachlan,' Anton muttered with a little laugh.

Babbie gazed for a moment into Anton's eyes which,

192

though dazed with pain, still shone in his face in all their startling acuity. 'Well done, Anton Büttger,' she said huskily. 'You deserve a medal.'

A flush stained his pale face. 'No more medals, please. Just a good strong "cuppa" as you say, with plenty of sugar . . . that is . . . if it can be spared, of course.'

Later that day Niall went up to Anton's room armed with a pack of cards and an account of an exploit that had happened over lunch and which had almost sent Elspeth away from Slochmhor for ever. It transpired that Fiona had danced home from school simply because sago pudding was on the menu that day and it was her favourite. Phebie had entirely forgotten her daughter's threat of the previous evening about doctoring Elspeth's pudding with frog spawn, and had not been even suspicious when the little girl had volunteered to go into the kitchen to fetch the pudding. But when Fiona had returned, proudly bearing the dish, and had placed it in front of Elspeth, the old woman had stared for a long moment at the lump of white jelly dotted with little black spots wobbling on top of her sago, and then let out a wail that made everyone jump. Without being able to help themselves the entire company had erupted into spasms of agonized mirth, all except Nurse Millar who had glowered at everyone and commiserated with Elspeth in a nasal, monotonous flow of useless adjectives. Phebie had bulldozed Fiona out of the room and into the hall with the intention of spanking her soundly, but on looking at the child's unrepentant grin she had instead collapsed on to the stairs where both mother and daughter had clutched each other in an ecstasy of pure, unadulterated, silent mirth.

The unfolding of the tale made Niall bellow with renewed laughter while Anton clutched his stomach. 'Please, no more, I want to keep my stitches for a while yet. Ah, she is truly a devil, your little Fiona. But, why did she do it?'

'A build-up of many things, but mainly for you.'

'Me?'

'Ay, she was mad at Elspeth for going on about rationing and you being here eating all the food that we don't have and which you were too ill to eat if we did have. But, Fiona's like that. She always protects those who can't speak up for themselves.'

'She is a little girl who goes for the underdog, eh?'

'She is also very fond of you.'

'Then, she is an angel. Heidi – Fiona – little devils with haloes, in Heidi's case perhaps even more appropriate now. But, poor Frau Morrison, she talks only for the sake of listening to her own voice. It is perhaps the only thing she has sometimes to keep her company.'

'Ach well, never mind that now, how about a game?'

'Fine, but you should be with your Shona at this moment.'

'Should I?' Niall said sharply.

'You know it or you would not shout.'

'You know too much, or you think you do!'

'Don't you love her? If she was my girl I wouldn't lose sight of her for a moment. She is very beautiful.'

'Perhaps I – love her too much.'

'No one can ever be loved too much. Listen, Niall, I don't give a damn whether you take your feelings out on me or not, but don't take them out on that lovely child you call your sweetheart. Because – she *is* a child, Niall,' he went on earnestly. 'You have only to look at her to know that. Eighteen, it is very young, she hasn't yet learned to say "sorry", but you, you are a man, a boy in many ways but the war makes people grow up quickly, with too much of a jolt perhaps, but it does the job a lot quicker than nature intended. So, stop behaving like a spoilt little boy and go and get off your chest whatever it is that makes you moon about by a German airman's bedside instead of facing up to reality.'

'You cheeky Jerry bastard!' Niall grinned.

'I know,' Anton said simply.

'Girls,' Niall said ruefully.

'What would we do without them? So, today, games; tomorrow, Shona. All right?'

'You win,' Niall laughed. 'But I hope not at cards. Hell!' he glanced at his plastered right arm then at Anton's bound fist, 'look at us, like a couple of Egyptian mummies! Bugger it! How are we supposed to deal with these useless things?'

But Fiona, popping her head round the door at that moment, solved the problem. 'Cards! Can I play?'

'You can deal,' Niall said promptly, and he and Anton squealed with joy which was lost on the adroit Fiona who proceeded to deal, called on all the games which she knew best to play, then completely foiled her partners by winning time after time till, exhausted, the men declared themselves well and truly beaten.

'We really ought to play for money,' dimpled the little girl as she whirled out of the room with a triumphant whoop.

CHAPTER 14

Early next morning Niall met Fergus at the gate of Laigmhor. Fergus looked at Niall's plaster-encased arm and his dark rugged face broke into a smile. 'We have one thing in common – for a time at least.'

Niall leaned against the dyke and looked towards the sea gleaming in the sun-bathed morning. 'There's a lot we have in common, Fergus, though at one time no one would have thought it. For one thing we both love the same girl – with one difference – you know how to get the best out of her. There was a time I thought I could do that too, but growing up has brought changes to us both . . .' He shook his fair head, at a loss how to explain further.

Fergus lit his pipe and stood puffing it for a moment, his thoughts on the last two difficult days during which both he and Kirsteen had talked to Shona about the foolishness of wasting time on petty quarrels and how she had only to cast her mind back to the precious years he and Kirsteen had wasted to realize how time could slip by too easily through pride and misunderstanding. Shona had listened, quietly and respectfully, without any fight or argument whatsoever, which very fact had puzzled and worried both Kirsteen and Fergus because it was so unlike spirited Shona. In the end Fergus had lost his temper and told her she was behaving like a spoilt child and if she ever wanted any happiness out of life then she would first have to learn to grow up and do a bit of giving as well as taking. Losing his temper had been a mistake, of course, because then Shona lost hers also and more or less told him to mind his own affairs. He had been able to sense the misery engulfing her and had wanted to take her to him and hold her close but the barriers had been too firmly up for that and it was with a sense of relief that he now handed the problem over to Niall.

'Take a bit of advice, lad . . .' he said, 'I haven't had a lot of experience with women – God knows I mucked up my own affairs pretty thoroughly – but I've learned that it's no use hanging around waiting for time to sort things out for you, you've got to do it yourself. Time has a knack of changing things, sometimes not to very good advantage. I know my daughter. She's a stubborn wee bitch at times . . .' He smiled. 'What else can you expect from a girl with a father like me? You'll have to show her who's boss, be a little domineering! She's in there now, mooning around, waiting for you – get in there and be firm with her! She can't go running off into tantrums for the rest of her life!'

It was a big speech for someone usually so thrifty with words, and Niall sensed the caring that had prompted it. He gripped Fergus by the shoulder. 'Thanks,' he said briefly then went through the gate and up the path.

Shona was putting away the breakfast dishes. She had seen him at the gate and kept her back to him as he came through the door. She knew it was a foolish gesture. She had waited for this moment for what seemed eternity. Now it was here and she didn't know quite how to handle it.

'Right now, we'll have no more of your sulks!' Niall said firmly. 'It's a lovely day, just right for a brisk walk over the moors!'

She turned a crimson face, opened her mouth to speak, but he gave her no chance. 'Be quick now, get your peenie off.

196

You'd better wear your wellies, for the dew is still heavy on the grass.' With that, she flew upstairs, her heart singing, and was back in minutes with a blue cardigan over her shoulders.

'Put your coat on too,' Niall told her sternly. 'There's a bite in the wind despite the sun.'

'You sound like Mirabelle,' she laughed happily and they went out into the sunny morning. He put his arm round her shoulders and they walked in silence to the hill track that wound over the high moors. The wind blew against the tough sedge grass, rippling it into tawny waves; green fern curls prodded through the tangle of dead bracken and nebulous webs glistened on the rich carpet of moss at the edge of the track.

On the ridge of a hillock a small group of islanders were already skinning fresh peat hags. Laughter and banter went hand in hand with such work because it involved both sexes. Peat skinning meant a lot of hard work yet a casual observer might have been forgiven for thinking the fun-loving islanders were literally having a picnic. Yet, despite the banter, the hags were worked with a skill that could only be carried out by a people imbued with generations of self-sufficiency. While the men cut deeply into the banks with the broad bladed rutter the women expertly skimmed off the top layer of turf with flaughter spades. At regular intervals the workers fortified themselves from the milk luggie into which they simply plunged a ladle to fill with thick creamy milk.

'It's early for the skimming,' Niall commented.

'The weather has been so fine here,' Shona said almost apologetically. 'There's a good skin on the hags.'

'Ay, it has been warm for the time of year,' Niall said absently. 'Though I canny say I noticed too much blue skies. Smoke hangs about a long time after the fires have died down.'

Torquil Andrew's voice came floating down and they looked up to see him waving his spade. 'Were you enjoyin' the ceilidh last Sunday, Niall?'

Niall waved and answered in the affirmative.

Shona's head went up. 'So, you had a fine time the other evening, Niall McLachlan!' she said.

'Indeed I did so,' he said defensively.

'And Babbie too, no doubt?'

'I think so. She went home earlier than the rest.'

'And you went with her?'

'No, I did not. Nancy and Archie saw her along. She was tired with one thing and another!' He stopped and faced her squarely, the wind tossing his fair hair into his eyes and whipping at the old kilt he always wore when he came back to Rhanna. 'If you must know, you wee spitfire, I got well and truly drunk at the ceilidh. To put it rudely, I got pissed! And all because of you! Good God, you little bitch! I've longed to see you for months – when I do I find you hanging over a German airman as if you never knew Niall McLachlan was born!'

She stared. 'You're jealous, Niall McLachlan!'

'All right, I'm jealous, dammit! I have a right to be jealous. If I could look at you without trembling I might not be jealous! But I am, and I do, and if that sounds like a lot of seagull shit you can throw it back in my face if it makes you feel better . . . go on then, start throwing!' he finished passionately.

'It was your attitide to Anton,' she said gently. 'I know he's a German – the Enemy – but he's first and foremost a human being and you spoke to him as if he were a bit of cow dung!'

'I know.' His voice was subdued with shame. 'I apologized to him yesterday. After I got home from the ceilidh, I was in my room, drunk as a lord, hating the thought of a German through the wall from me! I spent a good long while feeling sick and hating Anton. I wanted to go through and spew on him! Then the next morning I heard a thud and went in to find the poor bugger had fallen out of bed trying to reach a glass of water. He burst some of his stitches and Babbie had to sew him back up again – all without ether. Later we talked for ages . . . about the war, what it does to people. He's all right is Anton.'

Shona reached up and pushed a lock of hair from his eyes. 'When I saw him, lying so hurt and helpless, it was you I saw on a bloody beach in France. His face was your face. I had to help in every way I could because, in a way, it was you I was helping. I suppose that sounds silly.'

He laughed then, his brown eyes crinkling with joy. 'The daftest thing in the world, but I love you for it!' He drew her to him and kissed her harshly, his lips forcing hers apart till the warmth of his tongue briefly touched hers.

'Oh God.' Niall breathed into her silken hair. 'I've dreamt of this moment for so long. I want to kiss you forever! Do you think people are allowed to kiss each other in heaven? If not then I'm never going to die!'

Shona laughed gaily. 'I think people kiss all the time in heaven. How else would they know they were there?' She lay against him for a moment then murmured casually, 'And what about Babbie?'

The question took him unawares as indeed she had meant it to do. He blushed and drew away from her, not meeting her eyes. 'Babbie, ay, we must have that out. It's what I brought you out to talk about really.' He sat down on a mossy boulder and idly pulled at the dried heads of dead heather. 'We weren't lying when we said we knew one another only briefly in Glasgow . . . on the other hand we weren't being exactly truthful either. We met on a blind date and before we really knew what was happening had poured out all our troubles to each other. I think we both had wanted just a shoulder – you know the sort of thing. I found out she was married . . .'

'Married! But she doesn't wear a wedding ring!'

'It's on a chain round her neck. Babbie is a very private person. When I met her she had just had word that her husband had been reported missing, believed killed. They had been married only six months when he went to war. At this very moment she is in the most private hell of all . . . not knowing if he is alive or dead. That's why she doesn't wear her ring for all the world to see, she can't bear all the questioning.'

'Oh dear God! Poor Babbie!' Shona cried in anguish. 'I know only too well what she's going through, the terrible suspense, the hoping when you've almost given up hope. It's cruel, so cruel you wish that half the time you were dead yourself yet you have to keep hanging on . . . in case . . . just in case there might be a chance . . .'

'Oh, my darling,' he murmured huskily, 'you understand it all so well. In a way I wish you didn't because it makes the next part so difficult to tell.'

He turned his head suddenly and the rays of the searching sun vividly betrayed the deep purple scar beneath the golden fuzz of hair on his neck. A sob caught in her throat and she had to press her fists to her mouth to stop from crying out that she loved him no matter what he had done. But first she had to know! To hear it from his own lips.

Niall went on talking, his voice barely audible. 'On that date, Babbie and I got a bit drunk. We went back to her flat . . . and went to bed. I wanted to make love to her, I tried to make love to her . . . but I couldn't – my body wouldn't let me betray you. I kept seeing your face and hearing your voice . . . and – anyway – we both sobered up and felt horribly ashamed but glad that neither of us had betrayed the people we really loved – Oh God,' he lowered his head and hid his face in his hand, his voice breaking on a sob. 'That sounds such a poor way of wriggling out of the fact that we tried to make love!'

Shona didn't look at him or speak and eventually he burst out, 'Aren't you going to slap me . . . or – or shout or *say* something!'

'No.' Her voice was taut with unshed tears. 'I'm going to cry. I try never to cry! It's so silly to cry! Girls cry far too much and I always vowed that I would never be silly – and – and – cry . . . but now I can't help myself.'

And cry she did, the tears pouring down her face, the sobs breaking in all their harsh misery. She cried and sobbed and trembled and he rushed to hold her to him and cradle her head under his neck. 'Weep, my babby, let it all go. Remember what Mirabelle said. Cry, my lovely darling for, –

200

I am crying with you,' he soothed brokenly while his own tears washed down unchecked over his face.

Shona gave a watery sniff. 'Don't, please don't love me too much at this moment because I have something to tell you too. When I was in Aberdeen I went out with a couple of boys – one of them I liked very much – so much in fact I began to doubt my love for you. I thought perhaps that we had made a mistake, that when we thought we were in love it was only really a physical thing we had discovered when we grew up. We were so young then, without any experience of any kind. After our little baby died I really began to feel that I would never want you to make love to me again so I started to wonder if I really did love you. I enjoyed the company of this other boy and we went out a good deal. Then one night he tried to make love to me and I was so shocked and horrified that I had let it get to that stage that I bawled at him like a fiend and went into one of my worst tempers. He got such a fright I never saw him again, but I knew after that it was you I loved and always would . . . but I did kiss him and let him pet me a bit – and that's all.'

'So, the odds are even, then.'

Niall's tone was so strange that she looked up at him and giggled.

'So, it's all right for you but not for me. You can be jealous of me but I can't be jealous of you!'

He chuckled. 'Ach, you win, mainly because what you say is true. Will – will any of this make any difference between you and Babbie? She thinks the world of you and was so upset by meeting me on Rhanna that she was all for leaving that night at the ceilidh though I persuaded her against it.'

'If it hadn't been Babbie it would have been someone else,' she said wisely. 'You were ready for the comfort of someone else's arms – we all were. Naturally I will look at her and think of the pair of you together but I'll get over that. In a way I love her more than ever after what you've told me. Of course I won't let on I know about her husband, but at least I can understand better when she goes into one of these queer green-eyed moods of hers.'

'Ay, I've noticed them, too, and the habit she has of going off to Aosdana Bay. It's one of her favourite places.'

'The Bay of the Poet,' Shona said slowly. 'Yes, one or two people have seen her walking there – alone – always alone. Some of the old folks say she is drawn there by the spirit of the young man who died there long ago.'

'She goes there to have a good think more like. You see, I have an idea she is falling in love with Anton. She doesn't really know it herself yet or is only half-conscious of it and is having to fight with herself to stop it happening. I watched her with him yesterday, all very cool and nurse-like, but when she thinks he isn't watching she watches him with the eyes of a girl who is in love.'

Shona leaned back against a heather-mound in despair. *That* makes everything a hundred times worse. Her loyalties are with her husband who might be dead and her heart is with Anton who is alive but who will eventually have to leave Rhanna and go off to a prison camp somewhere. Oh, sometimes I wish I was a wee lassie again because being grown up is so complicated and makes everyone else around you complicated too!'

'I know, and we still have one very complicated matter to sort out. Right now I want you to come somewhere with me.'

'Och, Niall,' she scolded happily. 'You know I'd go anywhere with you.'

'Even to the – cave at Dunuaigh?'

Shona immediately recoiled from him. 'No, no, Niall! Don't ask that of me!'

'Please, Shona,' he begged earnestly. 'I have my reasons.'

'Very well,' she faltered unhappily. 'But there are nicer places on a beautiful day like this.'

In days gone by they had sped to the cave on swift, carefree feet but now she was pale and apprehensive as Niall put his arm round her firmly and led her towards the long heat-hazed stretches of the Muir of Rhanna. The sun beat down warmly, the dry heather rasped under their feet. Niall was very quiet. Shona looked at his boyish profile and wondered

202

why he was taking her to a place that had no meaning for her now. They were skirting the edge of Burnbreddie Estate. Very soon they topped a rise and stood looking down at Dunuaigh with the Abbey ruins nestling in a hollow. It was very peaceful. The shaggy sheep of the hill cropped the new, sweet grasses; contented cud-chewing cows sat in the cool shadows of rock outcrops; and in the distance the deep blue of the Atlantic sparkled to the boundless horizon. Shona drank in the scene avidly.

'It's so beautiful here,' she said wonderingly. 'I'd almost forgotten the enchantment of it.'

'Come on,' he said softly and they ran then to the sun-drenched hollow where the silence of forgotten places descended on them in a thistle-down blanket of peace.

'Oh!' Shona was staring at the little birch tree that Niall had planted to mark the entrance to the cave. It was less than a year since her last tortured flight to this place of memories. How eagerly she had looked then for the little birch tree and how near to panic when her desperate gaze had nearly missed the twisted little sapling that had weathered the terrible winds that howled over the moors. She couldn't miss the tree now. Though warped cruelly by the weather it had grown bigger and sturdier, its silver bark shining in the sun, its slender bare branches throwing shadows among the gorse.

Niall glanced at her. 'It's weathered the storms all right. Can we say the same, mo ghaoil?'

But Shona didn't answer. She was running to the cave, pulling back bramble and bracken, snagging her clothes, pricking her fingers, pulling and tearing while the tears choked up into her throat. 'Hey, steady on!' Niall said as he rushed up to her, but she wasn't aware of him. She sat on her heels gazing into the cool, dry cave, going over every little detail that was etched in her memory. Mirabelle's dolls flopped on the shelves, jostling with cups. The cruisie, containing the remains of the candle that had given her light during the agonizing hours of her labour, still hung from its chain; the wickerwork chairs, carried over the moors on a far-off morning of childhood, still sat, one on either side of the rough stone fireplace. And in the corner, the roughly-hewn bed of stone, piled with cushions and a sheepskin rug now grey with dirt. Everything was covered in cobwebs. It was neglected and forgotten, but she looked and remembered: the happy echo of childish laughter; the whispered hopes and dreams; the discovery of carefree young love. She tried to push her mind on further but couldn't. The agony of her lonely childbirth was a blank in her mind and the lifeless body of her tiny son a dim blur almost beyond recall.

Niall slid his arm round her waist. 'Well, my darling little girl, what now are your strongest memories of this place? Sadness or happiness?'

'Happiness . . . oh, so much happiness I can hear the laughter now!' She buried her face into his neck. 'I can look down the years and it's all so real – you and me and dear old Tot . . .' She pulled away to look at him and continued slowly, 'The only thing that isn't real to me is – the – the last time! Oh God! I feel so guilty! It's my last experience of this place, yet it's the dimmest. In my mind I can see Tot with her golden ears covering her white muzzle – yet – I can't see the face of our little baby! Why, oh why can't I?'

'There now,' he soothed. 'I had an idea this place would get things into perspective, that's why I brought you. You can see the old spaniel because she lived before she died . . . our little boy didn't,' he finished gently.

They were quiet for a long moment, and then he asked, 'Well, am I going to be a bitter bachelor all my days or an old married man?'

Shona reached out and touched the scar on his neck. 'An old married man, so long as you're married to me. You didn't have to bring me here to make up my mind. We've already wasted too much time looking back to things that can't be undone, and we're not going to waste any more. I did a lot of practical thinking while I was waiting for you to come out of the raids and praying you would be safe. Rhanna will give me back my health . . . When I'm ready to go back to nursing – I want to take my full training – and what better place than Glasgow? Being married means terrible things like bills. We'll need money for all that – so don't tell me I can't do it.'

Niall smiled wryly. 'Who ever tried to stop a McKenzie? But I won't have a wife of mine being the sole breadwinner. Glaikit wee Niall will find himself a weekend job . . .'

'And we have Mirabelle's legacy to tide us over at the beginning . . .' Shona caught her breath. 'I wish she was here now, I owe her so much. Oh God! It's wonderful not to feel guilty about the baby any more!'

'He'll come back to us.' Niall took her hands and looked at her with quiet joy. 'We'll have other sons – and daughters – lots of them – we'll fill the world with our children!'

As their shouts of laughter echoed through the cave, he embraced her and they sank to the heather as one, their mouths meeting over and over. His tongue touched hers and she responded wildly.

'My dearest, dearest love,' he murmured unsteadily. 'I feel so lucky to have you back again.' He caught her again and she tilted her head for his kiss, delighting in the firm strength of his young body. Her face was cupped in his hand and she could feel a small pulse beating in his thumb, the rhythm of his life throbbing steadily. She heard a sob catching in his throat and saw that his eyes were clouded with tears, those beautiful brown eyes of his that mirrored so many of his emotions. Now the look was one of tenderest love, his love for her, and she felt herself drowning in his tears, in his love. She had thought she would be afraid to give her body to him again, but love, tears, joy, washed away fear and carried her swiftly on a tide of pure ecstasy. The days of the fumbling, inexpert Niall were far in the past. His body was hard and demanding against hers and his lips moved over her face to her neck and then to the soft flesh above the swell of her breasts. He was no longer an unsure boy. His touch was masterful and certain. He was warm, flushed and powerful in the silence of his searching passion.

His plastered right arm made him momentarily clumsy as he unbuttoned her dress, and they both laughed, but softly, burning with the fires that consumed them. She helped him to undress her and for a moment he drank in the loveliness of her creamy-white body, marred only by the little stretch marks of pregnancy on the soft curve of her belly. With reverence he kissed them, and the feel of his lips on those parts of her made her cry out and close her eyes in an anguish of longing. She wanted to reach out to heaven and take all the pleasures of the universe swiftly and without measure of time. But he had yet to rouse her to a pitch that would make his own the doubly satisfying. The first time he had entered her body roughly, with thoughts only of himself and his needs. But now, though parts of him were hard, his limbs were tensile and he made her relax too and wait for the exquisite moments to come.

The sun wandered in through the opening of the cave, warm and fragrant with the scents of the moor captured in its rays; an early bee buzzed restlessly in a search for nectar. Far out on the open moor, a curlew bubbled out a song of pure joy, which reached deep into their souls where it was magnified a thousand times till it became a rhapsody to love. And then he went into her, pushing and seeking, while his mouth played with the delicate shells of her ears and he pledged his love for her over and over. They moved together, in the sweet delirium of their joining, washing away all the doubts and hurt of the last few months in soundless tears, and little cries of untamed excitement. The song of the curlew grew in intensity till it reached notes of highest perfection which carried them with it, up, up, to the top of the world, till together they touched the stars, and their cries ringing out, the echoes mingling, and in her greatest moment of agony he kissed the little dew of sweat on her brow and stroked the silken strands of her burnished hair. When it was over they lay together, trembling with reaction till they grew calm and slept, still as one flesh, to one another as a foetus is in its mother's womb.

Later, when Shona opened her brilliant blue eyes, Niall was watching her, studying the composure of her relaxed little face.

'Why are you staring at me?'

'Not staring, admiring. And congratulating myself for having the good taste that I have. Beautiful children with bodies like goddesses are not thick on the ground, my darling . . . at least, I haven't found it to be so. Now, tell me. You say – or rather you said – you thought you might be afraid to love me again. What are your feelings now on the matter?'

'I think – that we've given in to ourselves again and it's just as well we're going to be married because this sort of thing can't go on . . . but, it was wonderful . . . and . . .' she laughed sleepily, 'you're a young stallion. I couldn't wait – yet I wanted it to last forever.'

His eyes held hers intently. 'It will, my darling, when we're married I'll show you that today was just the beginning – but – no more till then. It's enough at the moment that your fears have been taken away. We'll keep the rest of the treats till there's a ring on your finger. But I warn you now, after our honeymoon you'll be wishing you could have a holiday away from me!'

She shrieked with laughter and smothered his face with a cushion then they both got dressed and walked hand in hand into the sunshine.

'Will folks *know*?' she wondered aloud. 'I mean, do we *look* different?'

'Yes, daftie, we do,' he said tenderly. 'We look happy.'

Dodie was coming along the moor track from Croynachan, carrying a laden creel. He gave a start when he saw them and looked somewhat guilty. 'It's too early yet to be gathering in the peats,' Niall joked.

'Ach, I know that, laddie,' the old eccentric rebuked gently, 'it is hardly even time for cuttin' them. Are you forgettin' these things living in the big city? I am hearin' the fumes o' they motor cars can poison folk's brains and make them forget easy.'

'I was only pulling your leg,' Niall grinned. He paused and looked at Dodie's lumpy face with concern. 'You're looking a bit thin, Dodie. Are you all right?'

Dodie seemed embarrassed by the question and for a long

moment looked with sorrowful reproach at the tawny slopes of Sgurr nan Gabhar before stuttering quickly. 'Ay, ay, right enough.'

'Father was saying he hadn't seen you for a while,' Shona said kindly. 'The wee lambs are beginning to come and you always help him at lambing time.'

'Ay well, I've been busy,' he answered evasively, his dreamy eyes raking the far reaches of the moor with unusual impatience.

'I'll help you to carry your creel,' Niall offered, reaching out a hand, but Dodie backed away.

'Ach, no, it is kind you are but I'll be managing fine by myself. I'm after lookin' for Ealasaid too and she might no' come to me if there's a crowd to hand.' Then he galloped away and was soon just a black shape flapping in the distance.

'If it's possible, I'd say old Dodie is acting queerer than usual,' Niall commented thoughtfully, but Shona laughed and linked her arm through his once more.

'He lives in his own wee world and has his secrets like the rest of us. We'd better hurry too for it must be near lunch time . . . and wipe that smile off your face before we get home or folks *will* know we've been up to something!'

Almost a week later Fergus leaned against the dyke and looked beyond the bridge to the hill-track leading to Dodie's house. 'I thought Dodie would have been down to help out,' he said to Kirsteen, Shona and Niall rather irritably. 'We're getting busier here and could be doing with an extra pair of hands. Bob and myself have other things to see to forbye the ewes.' Kirsteen stood beside him, nursing an orphan lamb, giggling as it slobbered greedily into a feeding bottle.

'You're holding it like a *real* baby,' Shona said, smiling as she reached out to stroke the lamb's curly fleece.

'It *is* a real baby,' Kirsteen laughed. 'It's how you must have sooked your bottle, and how Grant did too. He was so greedy he used to have most of the milk finished before I knew he had hardly started.'

'Shona and myself might take a walk over to Dodie's house,' Niall volunteered. 'I'm beginning to wonder about him myself and folks in the village are saying they haveny clapped eyes on him for some time.'

'You usually sit with Anton about now,' Shona pointed out.

'He's getting up today and Babbie is supervising so I thought I'd best keep out of the way.' He crooked his arm to Shona in a dashing manner. 'Will you do me the honour, my leddy?'

They went off giggling and Kirsteen smiled at Fergus. 'They have made up beautifully wouldn't you say, Fergus?'

He kissed a lock of her golden hair. 'Almost as well as we did on a certain night not too long since. I only hope . . .'

'Fergus,' she reproved quietly, 'everything is all right. They are very young and very much in love. You haven't forgotten what that is like, have you?'

'Ay, I'm beginning to . . . let me see, it must be nearly two nights now and *that* seems an age away. You wouldn't fancy a quick scrub in the tub before dinner, would you? I could always do your back . . .' They hugged each other with delight, and then he grew serious, his eyes dark with his love for her. 'Every day I watch you and I thank God for my happy life. Each morning I love you more than the one before which means all our tomorrows will be better than our yesterdays . . . and Good God! Here is me a farmer, turning into a poet. Get on your way, woman, and take the bairnie with you before it bursts with all that milk you're feeding it!'

Shona and Niall walked over the hill hand in hand, occasionally breaking into a run to chase each other like children, and by the time they reached Dodie's cottage they were hot and breathless.

'For goodness sake! What on earth is *that*?' Niall cried, pointing to a ramshackle creation of wood and metal huddled into the bushes near the cottage. The wind soughed through it, rattling metal against metal, eerily whining into cracks in the wood. They didn't need to look too closely to realize that Dodie had built himself a 'wee hoosie' using materials from the wrecked German bomber. The tail piece of the plane served as the roof with the bold symbol of the swastika breathtakingly displayed to the world. Niall and Shona gaped in astonishment, then sped over to examine the monstrosity at close quarters. The door scraped open on ill-fitting hinges. In the middle of the black cavern sat Dodie's large chamber pot, looking like the proverbial pea in a drum. On a small wooden shelf a large assortment of aircraft equipment jostled with a pile of neat newspaper squares. To the right of the chamber pot the control column was stuck into the ground at a crazy angle; propped in a corner was the broken barrel of a gun; under it, decoratively arranged, a band of ammunition,

Shona pointed at the control column and hissed, 'What is *that* for?'

'The mind boggles – but that's not all – look at this! Dodie is certainly going to be well amused when he's using his wee hoosie!' Affixed to the back of the door was an array of plane's instruments looking decidedly incongruous in such odd surroundings.

'Och, he's the limit!' Shona giggled. 'He's made his wee hoosie like the inside of a plane so that he can pretend to be flying when he's in here!'

Niall let out a bellow of mirth which coincided with a terrible bellowing that suddenly erupted from the cow shed. Ealasaid stood in her stall looking greatly distressed and Niall saw immediately that her udder was so distended the veins stood out like knotted rope. 'She hasn't been milked,' Niall said, frowning. 'Something's wrong with Dodie. He would never let Ealasaid suffer like this.'

They raced to the cottage and tiptoed in. They hadn't visited the place since they were children but it hadn't changed. Threadbare curtains covered the tiny windows, ashes spilled from the grate, treasures reaped from sea and land lay everywhere, lovingly gathered by the old eccentric who saw great beauty in the simple things of life. But one difference was immediately apparent. The old rickety chairs had been replaced by two well-upholstered car seats. They sat, one on either side of the fireplace, comfortably ridiculous-looking. Various other car accessories were scattered round the room and Shona held her breath in delight. Madam Balfour's car was one of two cars on the island; the other was owned by Lachlan.

He had been talked into buying it by a doctor acquaintance who was shocked to find his colleague still using outdated modes of transport. After much persuasion Lachlan had acceded to the suggestion of a car, but he felt embarrassed and out-of-place in a vehicle that made all eyes turn, and he began to find the car more trouble than it was worth. Machines of any sort were regarded with amused suspicion on Rhanna. Few of the men were mechanically minded, including Lachlan himself who found it easier to manipulate a horse or a bicycle than he did a contrary starter motor. Moreover, with the advent of war, fuel became difficult to obtain and the car had since lain in a shed, and was used only for the most urgent cases on the farthest corners of the island.

Like Lachlan, the young laird, a keen horseman, seldom used his car, which had been purchased at his mother's insistence that 'people of our standing ought to have a car'. But unlike Lachlan, Madam Balfour revelled in the attention paid her when her son drove her round the bumpy island roads. However, with his going she could find no one else willing to drive the vehicle. Angus, the aged groom, had been shown how to drive, 'Aying' his way through a course of instruction, but he had tucked the knowledge away in the farthest recesses of his mind in the hope he would never have to use it. Used to a lifetime of caring for horses, he resented the space the car took up in the stable buildings. Madam Balfour had been furious when he had refused to recover the car after the Commandos had left it near Croynachan, and by the time she had coaxed Lachlan into fetching it, it had been completely dismantled. Only the chassis and the body shell had been left to rot on the Muir of Rhanna.

It had been difficult to lay blame at any one door, and finally Madam Balfour had tried to enlist the services of Dugald Donaldson who was a retired policeman. But he had refused to get involved and eventually she had contacted the Stornoway police, from whom she was now awaiting an official visit. Rhanna was visited seldom by a policeman. The one who usually came was related to nearly everyone on Rhanna and spent his time ceilidhing at relatives' houses. But it had been rumoured that 'Big Gregor' had been transferred to Mull, and when Madam Balfour's plans became known there had been a scuffle to cover up any little misdemeanours that might warrant investigation. Tam McKinnon had been particularly disturbed by the news and had made haste to transfer his 'still' back to Annack Gow's secret room inside the blackhouse. A delighted Annack had been only too willing to oblige, and once again her secret room was fully operational, as it had been in the days of her forebears.

Thinking back on all those events, Shona smiled to herself as she looked round the room. She knew that no official being would hazard a visit to Dodie's cottage and she hugged herself with glee at the idea of his getting away with a large share of the spoils.

'Are you about, Dodie?' Niall cried and was rewarded with a soulful 'He breeah' from a door leading out of the kitchen. They went up a short passageway, hung with driftwood cupboards, and came to the bedroom. Dodie's particular odour pervaded every cluttered corner. His old mackintosh hung from a hook on the door over a layer of tattered oilskins. Under the window stood his huge wellingtons and Shona rushed forward to throw open the sash, allowing the fresh, clean air from the moor to swoop in and absorb the smell.

'Ach, dinna open that window!' Dodie cried in alarm. 'I'm just about dead wi' cold as it is!' He was terribly embarrassed, cowering under the threadbare sheet like a frightened animal. He was a pathetic sight with his gaunt, grey face covered in stubbly little patches of hair. On a locker by his bedside a Delft cup held ancient dregs of tea, and on a saucer beside it two mouldy crusts adhered to a festering slice of cheese. Grimy tears coursed down the sunken indentations of his face, his mouth was twisted in pain and a band of perspiration glistened beneath the rim of his greasy cap.

'I have a terrible bellyache,' he wailed, scrubbing his tears with one hand and rubbing his middle with the other. 'It's been on me for a time now but it has just got worse this whily back. I'm near dyin' wi' the pain . . . and – Ealasaid, my poor beastie, is ill too. I havny been able to rise out my bed to milk her. She's roarin' in pain and breakin' my heart hearin' her.'

'I'll go and milk her now, I saw a bucket in the shed,' Shona said, thankfully escaping the room.

'And I'll go and fetch Father before he finishes in the surgery,' Niall added quickly. He eyed a heap of gay patchwork quilts lying on an antiquated bride's kist. 'Would you like some of these quilts on the bed, Dodie? You're shivering.'

Dodie looked terrified. 'No, no, I dinna want them! Just shut the window.'

Exasperated, Niall banged the window shut and turned out of the cottage. Leaving Shona to keep an eyes on things he ran back over the hill track to Slochmhor. He found his father at once, and having managed together to get the neglected car started, they hurtled over the narrow track, the sound of the roaring engine making the crowd at the peat hags stop work as one.

'An emergency, just,' commented Erchy.

The others nodded in sad agreement. 'The doctor is having a busy time these days,' was the general verdict.

'Who will it be?' wondered Kate.

'Lachlan will see them along,' Jim Jim said with conviction.

'If the Lord spares them,' Isabel sighed sagely.

There was a move towards the milk luggie where creamy milk was amiably dispensed, together with much speculation about the 'emergency'.

When Lachlan arrived the hens were squawking dismally in the kitchen while Shona boiled a rather sparse 'hen's pot' over a fire made up hastily with cinders and kindling. She knew Dodie would be embarrassed by her presence and Lachlan went alone into the bedroom.

'You dinna have to look at me, Doctor,' the red-faced Dodie sobbed. 'I know fine what ails me.'

'Indeed, and what might that be, Dodie?'

Dodie looked with horror at the pile of patchwork quilts. 'It's *these*! I know it's these! I've been *smitted*, Doctor!'

'Smitted with what?' Lachlan saw how distressed the old eccentric was and his voice was gentle.

'With *Shelagh*! You mind, Doctor, she always said it was the winds she had, but I know fine what killed her.'

'But, Dodie, that was years ago,' Lachlan protested. 'I don't see what it has to do with your condition.'

'I have it, Doctor, the cancer! The same as Shelagh. Before she died she told me I was to have these lovely quilts made by her very own hands. After she passed on I took them . . . just to please her because she was always my good friend. My, but they were warm right enough but I havny used them since my bellyache started.'

Lachlan sat down on the bed which sagged alarmingly under the extra weight. Patiently he explained. 'You don't catch cancer, Dodie. It isn't a germ like a 'flu or cold. Please believe that. I'll examine you and tell you what I think you've got.' Despite vigorous protestations he proceeded with the examination, inwardly shocked when he was how thin Dodie was. A few minutes later he looked up, a warm smile lighting his face. 'Stop worrying, Dodie, you don't have cancer but you do have an ulcer, probably a duodenal.'

Dodie looked terrified. 'Ach, Doctor, that sounds worse than the other!'

'It won't be with proper treatment and diet. What on earth have you been eating, man?'

'Nothing, Doctor.'

'*Nothing!* But you must be eating something!'

Dodie turned his face to the wall and his big calloused hands worked nervously on the sheet. Lachlan felt a great surge of remorse and compassion for the old man. His life had been one of misfortune from the start. Against all odds he had battled on, catering for his simple needs by the sheer hard work that had been his lot since he was old enough to hold a spade. Everyone on the island genuinely liked him, but his fierce independence made charitable acts difficult and he was more or less left to his own devices. It never occurred to anyone that the show of independence might be a form of pride born in a man deprived of the basic things in life that everyone else took for granted. His was a big heart with a great capacity for loving all the creatures, great and small, that God had put on the earth. In his simple world he had created for himself a life far happier than that of many who had all the obvious requisites. But it was a lonely existence and no one needed to be that lonely.

'Come on, Dodie,' Lachlan coaxed, taking one of his big hands and squeezing it reassuringly. 'You can tell me, I'll understand.'

'Och, Doctor, I'm starvin' so I am! I used my ration book to help light the fire one morning – I didny know what it meant for I canny read things in the foreign language. When I went to Merry Mary's for my messages, she asked me for it and I didny like to tell her I burnt it. She would think I was daft, and it bein' a Government thing I thought I would get into trouble so I just stopped goin' to the shop. My tattie crop was a bad one last year and all but ran out on me after the New Year. Then that big Jerry wi' the square head burst in on me and ate everything that was left . . . even the few neeps that I had. My poor hens have gone off the laying without the right food – it's terrible to see them starvin' to death.'

'You could have boiled one to yourself, Dodie.'

'Och, no, never! I wouldny kill the poor beasts!' Dodie was horrified at the suggestion.

'So, you had only Ealasaid's milk?' Lachlan said quietly.

'Ay, but never even that sometimes for she has never been the same since that big German chiel hurt her udder tryin' to get milk out o' it.' He put out a big hand. 'Doctor, it's my baccy I miss most. You wouldny have a wee bit – would you now?'

Lachlan extracted a tin from his pocket. 'You keep this, Dodie, but don't chew any till you've had a bite to eat. It's not the best thing for an ulcer but it will do wonders for your peace of mind. Now put your clothes on. I'll take you down in the car to Slochmhor.'

'But . . . what about Ealasaid?' came the inevitable wail.

'One of the lads will drive her down.' Lachlan's smile lit up his boyish face. 'How would you like to go and stay with Mairi for a wee while?'

Dodie's face glowed through the tears. 'Mairi,' he breathed happily.

'Ay, you know how she loves looking after people. With Wullie away she's at a loss . . . You and Mairi get on fine together, and she'll put Ealasaid in with Bluebell.' Lachlan was rewarded by Dodie's radiant eyes. He knew he wasn't taking a liberty, because Mairi had often confided to him her desire to give Dodie 'a good bit loving care and plenty food.'

Lachlan went out to explain matters to the young people who were tidying the kitchen.

'Poor old Dodie,' Shona breathed.

'It's up to all of us to see this never happens again,' Lachlan said. 'He could have died up here and no one the wiser.'

Niall swallowed hard. 'Surely – Erchy must pop in sometimes with the mail?'

'What mail? I don't think Dodie has ever had a letter in his life. Just now I noticed a picture postcard above his bed. It was tattered almost out of recognition by continual handling . . . probably the only postcard he's ever had.'

They went outside and stood silently, each appalled and saddened by their thoughts. Niall looked at Dodie's pitiful attempt to build a 'wee hoosie' in order to be like the majority of the islanders, and he said huskily, 'Come the summer Dodie will have the finest wee hoosie on Rhanna. I asked Wullie the Carpenter last night if he could give me a job during my summer holidays. I should learn how to knock a few nails into wood. I'll get some of the lads to help me. We

216

can scrounge some bits and pieces from Tam. He has a shed full of junk.'

'Good idea,' Lachlan approved.

Just then Dodie appeared, apologetic because he had taken some time to gather together his most treasured possessions into a large, spotted hanky.

'My hens, what about my hens?' he whispered, holding on to a gatepost for support.

'They'll be looked after too,' Lachlan said patiently and bundled Dodie into the car.

When they arrived at Slochmhor, Dodie underwent the rigours of a steaming carbolic bath, but the comforts that awaited him more than made up for such indignities. For the first time in his life he was made to feel cherished and important and was the first to admit he owed it all to a 'leddy'.

PART V

RHANNA
Spring 1941

CHAPTER 15

Shona walked quickly over Glen Fallan to Slochmhor. Anton was leaving the island next day and Niall had asked Shona to come over to the house early because he had planned some sort of outing. They were all sorry that the young German was going. Lachlan had kept the military medics at bay with various plausible excuses but there was no denying that Anton was now fit enough to go.

The April sun cascaded over the countryside, the heat of it abundant for the time of year. The air was fragrant with the scent of clover, crushed by the frolicking hooves of the lambs scattered in the fields, and Shona lifted her bright head and breathed deeply. She loved the spring, with each day bringing the promise of the long, golden summer ahead. The last few weeks with Niall had been full and happy. In a way, they both seemed to be getting to know each other all over again. Sometimes the past loomed very near, at others it was so far away it was like a dream, a mad jumble of hurried moments in which everything happened too quickly for there to be any lasting impressions.

Shona's thoughts drifted as she went up the path to the house. As she expected, it was very quiet. Phebie had worked so hard the day before, preparing for the surprise ceilidh they would hold that night, that Lachlan had decided to leave his patients to the tender mercies of Nurse Millar and take Phebie away for a day off. They had gone off with Fergus and Kirsteen to picnic in one of the sheltered coves near Croy. Elspeth, too, was away. She had passed Laigmhor earlier on her way to the shops at Portcull, and now Slochmhor looked rather deserted nestling against tall green pines.

When Shona reached the kitchen she saw Niall standing outside the kitchen door with Babbie in his arms, her head resting on his shoulder. He was stroking her fiery hair tenderly and she was leaning against him crying quietly. In her hand fluttered a buff envelope and Shona remembered that Erchy had gone whistling away ahead of her up the Glen. That envelope! Those tears! So unlike cool, self-possessed Babbie to cry. A pang of jealousy shot through Shona's heart at sight of her friend in Niall's arms but she knew she was being unreasonable, that something had happened to cause the scene.

Niall looked up suddenly, saw her standing there, and pushed Babbie, who hadn't seen Shona, gently into the house. Then he came dashing back to grab Shona's arm. 'Listen, something's happened. I can't tell you now because I want this morning to be special for everyone.'

Shona looked into his honest brown eyes and wanted to tell him that she knew, that he didn't have to pretend, but instead she said, 'All right, Niall, let's make it special. What do you want me to do?'

'Just behave normally, that's all . . . No, listen, Shona, we're all going away for the day . . . you, me, Babbie and Anton. We're all going over to Portvoynachan in Father's car. Babbie wants to go to Aosdana Bay.'

'The Bay of the Poet again. Yes, Niall, I understand, but who will drive the car? Anton isn't quite up to it with half his fingers gone.'

'I will – I learned in the army.'

'But – your arm . . .'

'Never mind my arm, I'll manage.' He looked at her pleadingly. 'You saw me with Babbie just now but I want you to trust me, darling – and – and no matter how you feel right now act as if you're having the time of your life! Laugh, sing – anything. I'll tell you why later!'

They collected the bulging picnic hamper Phebie had left on the kitchen table and then went to the shed where Lachlan kept the car.

'Does your father know you're taking it? Shona asked quietly while a strange feeling of dread squeezed icy fingers round her heart.

'No, it only really occurred to me after he left and Babbie

222

mentioned Aosdana Bay. I had intended getting one of Ranald's boats out for the day, but don't worry about Father, he'll understand – he always does.'

Babbie came out of the house with Anton leaning on her arm and she remembered suddenly the first day she had got him out of bed, surprised at how tall he was, how the trusting feel of his thin arm round her shoulder had made her quite suddenly want to cry. He had laughed a little and been embarrassed at having to rely so much on her help. His smile had reminded her of another young man, the fleeting, anxious smile of a very new and youthful husband leaving her behind at the station, the sight of his beloved face at a window, a million years of love in his eyes . . . mixed with fear and doubt as they both wondered if that farewell kiss might be their last . . . then the whistle blowing, his eyes gazing into hers wordlessly as the train pulled away . . . his hand raised – and soon the face that she loved just a dim little white blur framed in the carriage window of the train taking him out of her life. His body had been hard and strong – as Anton's was now, now that he was recovering his strength a little bit more every day . . .

'I will give you money for your thoughts.'

His voice brought her out of her reverie and she forced a laugh. 'Only a penny. They might be worth more, but only to me.'

They all piled into the car, Babbie and Anton in the back, Shona beside Niall at the front.

'I'll steer with my left hand,' Niall told Shona laughingly. 'And you can work the gears . . . Don't worry,' he stemmed her protests. 'Fiona could do it, it's so easy. I'll be working the clutch with my foot. It's a simple matter of coordination, mo ghaoil.'

She forced the laughter he had requested, but as they got going on the journey she found herself responding to him with a spontaneity that was entirely natural. Niall was in a wild, abandoned mood. His head was thrown back, his brown eyes sparkling as the car hurtled over the rough moor road. Just outside Portcull, the road was no more than a horse track over high cliffs whose basalt columns dipped into the swirling sea far below. At times the way was so narrow it seemed a certainty that the offside wheels would career into thin air. Natural corrosion had eaten away the soft crumbling earth on the clifftops, which were now held together by only a tangle of roots. To the nearside was a deep soggy ditch flanked by stony turf, and on the narrow grass verges groups of cud-chewing sheep stared unblinkingly into the distance. Rhanna sheep gave no precedence to anything on wheels. The island was theirs to roam as they liked and the noisy motor car was just another intrusive object to bleat at with disdain.

Niall weaved the car around potholes and seemed not to notice the horrific drop to the sea. For a time everyone was silent but soon the road began to wind over the moors and they all began to sing, the jolting of the car distorting their voices and choking the merriment in their throats. Anton and Babbie clutched each other, the former lapsing into German in his excitement. His pale, handsome face sparkled, and he chuckled as Babbie, thrown against him time after time, finally gave up the effort of trying to stay upright. She leaned against him and they both jolted in unison.

Niall began to sing a Gaelic song and immediately everyone else took up the tune despite the fact that they didn't know the words. It was a discordant mêlée but no one cared. They were all mad and young together, their voices careering out over the moors, tossed by the fresh spring breezes into a wild concoction of sound. Crofters stopped work to watch the passing 'contraption', and rosy-cheeked children stood by the wayside to wave at it solemnly.

'This day will last forever!' Anton cried, his arms embracing the world.

'Forever and ever!' Babbie echoed, while tears of sadness and joy clouded her mysterious green eyes.

Soon they reached Aosdana Bay, which was drowsing in the quiet of morning, its silver-white beaches inviting them towards the effervescent blue sea.

'C'mon, I dare you all to have a paddle!' Niall said sitting down on a rock to pull off his boots and stockings, and in minutes a variety of footwear dotted the sands and everyone was dancing to meet the foaming surf, shrieking in agonized ecstasy as the freezing water splashed their naked skin. They joined hands and ran to meet each wave, and though skirts were tucked into knickers and trousers rolled to knees, the hems were soon soaked.

For a time the world was theirs to command. Blue sky and sea reeled round as they danced. Aosdana Bay belonged to them. The beauty of youth reflected gloriously in each bright face in those carefree moments. Two fiery-haired girls, two fair young men, pranced together like children and though one of them was a German it mattered to none of them.

'Oh, I'll have to stop,' Babbie gasped eventually. 'Remember, you're just babies compared to me. I can't keep up.'

'I am twenty-four, Fräulein, older than you,' Anton pointed out soberly.

Babbie smiled carelessly. 'Men are slower to grow up. To me you're just a boy.'

'The day I joined the Luftwaffe I became a man,' he said with dignity but she merely smiled because he looked like a small boy in the huff. When Niall went with Anton to retrieve the hamper they had left in one of the cool caves, Shona said quietly to Babbie, 'You'll miss Anton when he's gone, won't you? You've been closer to him than anyone else these past weeks.'

'He has to go sometime,' Babbie said before turning away to spread a rug over the sand.

Niall and Anton returned shortly, and then they all feasted on chicken sandwiches and fluffy scones, and afterwards lay down on the warm beach. Shona turned her head to look at Niall and his hand came out to squeeze hers till it hurt, the strength of his love reaching out to her, but a moment later he jumped to his feet and pulled her up with him. 'C'mon, lazy,' he said lightly. 'You know we said we would pay Alasdair Robb a visit.' Shona began to protest but he led her away, saying casually over his shoulder, 'We'll see you two about an hour from now. Don't be running away, Anton. Remember you're in my charge.'

When they reached the top of the cliff Shona turned on him. 'Niall, if I didn't know you better I'd say you were going a bit daft! I thought we were out for a picnic.'

'And it seems I don't know you at all, Shona McKenzie. I credited you with a pretty keen sense of perception.'

'You mean – it's true about them then?'

'It's so obvious I thought the whole of Rhanna knew. Mother and Father saw it long ago. They're daft on each other though neither has yet admitted it to the other. She's mad on him – yet her heart is breaking because – of circumstances.'

'Oh God, I love you, Niall!' she breathed, drawing him into her arms and laying her warm cheek against his.

'We're lucky, my darling,' he said softly. 'We've had time to know what love is like. And how much better it will be with the passing of each day . . . They have only a little time left, which is why I wanted them to make the most of it. Can you imagine what it's like? To be in love and never to be alone together?'

'There is something else, though, isn't there? That letter in Babbie's hand earlier? It brought back a memory to me, one I want to forget . . . a letter in a buff envelope telling me you had been reported missing, believed to be killed. I was in Slochmhor alone, it was quiet and deserted, the way it was this morning when Babbie got her news . . . It was about her husband, wasn't it?'

'Ay, it was to tell her that he had been definitely classified as killed in action. The waiting for her is over but it doesn't stop her feeling as if she is breaking in two – one part of her crying for the young husband who is dead now – the other loving Anton but everything in her fighting against it because to admit it will make her feel a traitor. She's got a lot of loyalty in her has Babbie.'

Shona felt drained with sadness. 'And we thought we had troubles,' she whispered.

He kicked the ground fiercely. 'Life can be a damned cruel

thing sometimes. She comes to a remote Hebridean island to nurse her hurt and anxiety over her husband and ends up falling in love with a German airman. Ironic, isn't it?' His brown eyes were dark pools of compassion and she drew him into her arms once again. They clung together in the warm, sweet heather and cried for two young people with so little time left to love.

Anton watched Shona and Niall disappearing over the line of the cliffs and then twisted round to take Babbie's cool little hand. 'You are shivering, Fräulein. Are you cold?' he asked in his attractive broken English.

She shook her head, her oddly mysterious eyes clouding with the sting of tears. 'Not cold – happy in a sad sort of way. It's been a wonderful day . . . thanks to Shona and Niall.' She looked down at his hand resting in hers. The three little stumps of his lost fingers had healed beautifully but the sight brought a sob to her throat. 'What will happen to you, Anton?'

He shrugged. 'I do not know. A camp, in Scotland or England. It doesn't matter. My home was in Germany with my family. I don't pine for a place where they are no more.'

'Poor Anton,' she breathed softly.

Anger flashed out of his blue eyes. 'I hate pity! Please don't pity me!'

'I don't pity you, Anton, I was thinking how strange everything is. In a way we are both orphans. No family for either of us to go home to.'

'Babbie.' His voice was soft again. Very gently he touched her hair where the sun turned it to fire. 'Your hair, it is like summer. Whenever I think of you I will think of a summer sun blazing red at the end of the day. These weeks you have nursed me like an angel.' He smiled. 'You also make jokes like a little devil. I have laughed – and looked – and – loved . . . *Liebling*.' The endearment made her heart beat rapidly and she couldn't trust herself to look at him. '*Liebling*,' he said again, his voice barely audible. 'I love you and you know it. Niall gave us this time alone together – you know that, don't you?'

'It – it looks that way. He came to Rhanna like a young warrior – now he plays at Cupid,' she whispered, looking up then at the clear-cut structure of his handsome young face so that she would remember it for the rest of her life.

Slowly, he leaned towards her and she shut her eyes to feel his lips caressing her eyelids and when his mouth came down on hers she made no resistance. Instead she put up her hands to trace the curve of his ears, tenderly urging him to kiss her harder. They were timeless moments. The gulls mewed softly, the sun beat down warmly, the creamy foam of the incoming tide rattled the tiny shells of the smooth white sands.

He undid the top of her dress and played absently with the little gold ring attached to a chain round her neck. 'Did it belong to someone you loved?' he asked tenderly. 'My mother had a ring her grandmother gave her and she, too, wore it round her neck on a chain.'

'Yes, someone I loved,' she said tensely.

'*Liebling*.' His voice was taut with passion. He touched the softness of her breasts and she cried out, wanting him to love her but afraid that he would hurt himself. A soft dew of tears shone on his fair lashes. 'Please, Babbie, let me love you – tomorrow I go away – let today last forever.'

She was unable to resist his pleas. 'All right, Anton, but gently – for your sake.'

With trembling legs they walked to the great columns of rock beside the caves. There, in the shadow of the sentinel pillars, he made love to her with such tender devotion she had to press her knuckles between her teeth to stop from crying out in those exalted moments. When it was over they lay quietly, Anton in Babbie's arms, his head pillowed on her breasts. The peace of Aosdana Bay, that had, in years gone by, inspired love, hope and finally tragedy in a lovelorn young poet, washed into the souls of the two lovers with so little time left to love. They listened to the timeless wind and tide that had swept the Bay for aeons past and both of them knew these were the memories they would carry into eternity.

But their time together was coming to an end and Anton finally broke the spell of silence. 'Babbie, I want to ask you to be truthful to me. Our aquaintance has been very short yet my feelings for you are so deep it seems you have always been in my heart. If I am lucky enough to be sent to a Scottish camp then we wouldn't be so far apart. Could you – would you – wait for me?'

The welling of her tears drowned out the world for a moment and it was while she couldn't see the love shining in his eyes that she managed to say lightly, 'Och, c'mon, now, Anton, be realistic! You'll forget all about me in a little while. Young men always fall in love with their nurses. It's a part of convalescing.' Still she couldn't see him but she heard the deep hurt in his reply.

'Forget you, Babbie! How can I forget today – yesterday? You can't forget love! But perhaps – I just imagined that you loved me too.'

'You will forget, Anton, and some day you'll meet a really nice girl.'

'I don't want a nice girl – I want you!' he cried passionately.

She smiled through the mist of tears. 'That's not very complimentary, Anton.'

He was angry now, his blue eyes bewildered. 'You know very well what I mean! Good God, Babbie . . .' He spread his hands in appeal. 'Don't play games with me now. Tomorrow I must leave this island – I want to know what you feel for me!'

She turned away from him because the pleading in his eyes was taking away all the resolution in her breaking heart. 'I – my dear Anton – I feel a great affection for you, but . . .' Her voice broke on a sob. 'That's not enough for the thing you ask of me.'

He slowly got to his feet and stood looking down at her. 'Thank you, Babbie, at least you are truthful,' he said huskily. 'I will always remember today – even though you may forget.' He lifted his head proudly and she stared up at him outlined against the blue sky, tall, slim, fair threads of hair glinting in the sun, already a million miles away from her.

Niall and Shona appeared on the skyline then and Anton cried brightly, 'Hey there, you two, you are just in time! I was beginning to miss my escort. You have grown on me like a bad habit!'

It seemed that the whole of Portcull was crowded into the parlour at Slochmhor for the ceilidh. Most of the menfolk had donned kilts for the occasion, anxious to show Anton what a real island ceilidh looked like. Todd had recovered sufficiently from his appendix operation to be there complete with bagpipes though Lachlan warned him not to blow on them too hard or he would do himself an injury.

'Ay, and we're no' wantin' any more of the Ballachulish bagpipes for a whily,' put in Biddy who had hobbled along on sticks and was back to her usual grumbling good nature.

Todd looked uncomfortable. The 'Ballachulish Bagpipes' was Biddy's quaint way of referring to an enema, and the memory of Nurse Millar 'wi the tubes' was still keen on his mind.

It was a laughing, carefree gathering and Anton looked round at all the faces that had become so familiar and so dear to him and he felt a lump rising in his throat. This ceilidh tonight was in his honour and he felt like laughing and crying at the same time. The room was cosy with a peat fire leaping in the hearth and lamps burning softly, giving a glow to the colourful array of tartans. The womenfolk had changed out of rough homespuns and were wearing dresses of softest wool in a variety of rainbow hues. Some wore tartan shawls, caught at the neck with Cairngorm stones encased in silver. The skin of these island women was, in almost every case, soft and dewy, flushed into rosiness by generous amounts of good, clean Hebridean air which was about the only 'cosmetic' that any of them had ever known. Even the men had this fine complexion, a sparkling look about them that made their faces come alive and their eyes glow with the joy of their living. The freshness was not taken away by advancing years and indeed many of the old ones had only snowy locks and wisdom in their eyes to show for the years they had been on earth. Agility was another thing common to both old and young and it was no surprise to anyone that old men of ninety still worked a croft and old women of the same years ran a home with complete thoroughness and tended their animals into the bargain. If one of their kind was taken from their midst at the comparatively young age of sixty, heads would shake sadly and they would tell one another, 'And him in his prime, wi' all his life in front o' him.'

Anton had noted all these facts long ago and he sat in the midst of the Rhanna folk and wished that he could stay with them for the rest of his days, to discover the secrets that made for contented minds and to be rewarded with the elixir of youth that the simplicity of life on Rhanna seemed to bring.

Tam had brought along a good supply of 'the water of life' and glasses were filled with the amber liquid, chinked together solemnly in those first sober moments, while cries of 'Slainte' filled the room.

Babbie had not wanted to come down but had been persuaded to do so by Shona, and now she sat in a corner, hardly daring to look up for fear she would meet Anton's blue, questioning gaze.

The fiddles began to play and soon the room was filled with haunting melodies that spoke of the ocean and of young men who had died in treacherous seas while out with the fishing boats. After the fiddles came the rousing tunes of the pipes and soon everyone was up dancing, 'hooching' with wild abandon, a swirling mass of tartan kilts, fine hairy legs and flouncing skirts.

Fergus whirled Kirsteen round in a gay eightsome reel, his deep laugh booming out, so unlike the Fergus of yesteryear who had sat alone in corners during times like these, brooding over the girl he thought he would never see again. Now, here she was, one minute out of his reach, the next, warm and desirable in his grasp, her golden hair shining, her white teeth flashing.

'Don't whirl me so fast, Fergus,' she protested at one point. 'I'm dizzy enough as it is.'

'Do you think it's true then?' he murmured delightedly, 'the thing you told me on the thirteenth night of last month?'

'If it isn't then my name is not McKenzie!'

Everyone seemed to have a partner and the two who might have made the happiest partners of all sat miserably alone in their respective corners, pretending to be enjoying themselves, smiling without the smiles reaching their eyes – apart, yet so aware of each other's presence they might have been locked in the other's arms, whispering the words of love that so overflowed in their hearts.

'You'll be having another dram, Mr Bugger?'

Anton smiled up at Tam and accepted a fill of the Uisgebeatha. 'Thank you – Tam, and please, don't call me that – my name is Anton. You are Tam, I am Anton.'

'Ach, of course you are, son. Slainte, Anton, and get up off your backside and dance. There's a fine wee lass over there in the corner. Our very own Nurse Babbie.' Tam leaned forward confidentially. 'I would ask her myself but Kate would have me out of here by the skin of my lugs before you could blink.'

But just then everybody flopped down exhausted and it was time for the Seanachaidhs to tell their strange tales of myth and legend. Jim Jim had been watching his daughter with Dugald Donaldson and as soon as the red-faced Erchy stopped to gather breath, he spoke in a voice so mysterious that all eyes in the room turned towards him.

'I am thinking of a very odd story told me by Black Ewan that time I was over in Barra helping wi' the mackerel shoals.' At the very mention of Black Ewan the atmosphere in the room was charged with a subdued excitement. Black Ewan of Barra was well known throughout the Western Isles for his strange powers of second sight and his spine-chilling tales that went hand in hand with his 'seeing eye'.

'It was a gey queer tale but true – true according to Black

Ewan,' Jim Jim went on, pausing to let his words take effect in the intervening hush. Erchy's heavy breathing and the sparkling of the peats in the grate were the only sounds that filled the silence for a few moments.

'Go on now, Jim Jim,' Bob encouraged, his curiosity getting the better of his resentment of Jim Jim's taking the limelight away from himself and Andrew, the two recognized Seanachaidhs in the room.

'Well, it was about the time o' the Great War,' Jim Jim continued slowly. 'And you mind Black Ewan was out at sea wi' the Naval Patrol vessels?'

'Ay, ay, that was the time he found the barrel o' rum floatin' in the sea,' Ranald supplemented with a beaming smile, 'and was so drunk on it his mates tied him to a chair in the wheelhouse because it was the safest place for him.'

'Look you, that has nothing to do wi' my story,' Jim Jim said scathingly. 'It is about one o' the lads on the boat who was always boastin' about the amount o' women he managed to have and never after marryin' one o' them. Black Ewan warned the chiel to stop his mischief and with his seeing eye he foretold the man was going to seduce the daughter o' a witch. If he wasny after marrying her he would have a fate that no mortal could foretell it would be so evil. Well, it happened right enough and worse than anyone imagined. Out at sea, with no land expected for miles, an island just appeared out of nowhere. On it was marooned a lovely young maiden, hair black as night and eyes like the black peats on the moor. All the men on the vessel were terrified but no' the seducer. He landed on the island an' promised himself to the maiden if she succumbed to him. Well, she did right enough, the bad bad lassie, but then he was all for leavin' her to go back to the ship. Just then a fearful hag rose out o' the sea, green wi' slime and black wi' warts. She screeched an evil curse on the seducer that was terrible to hear. He remembered his mother tellin' him "Never look into the eyes of a Green Uisga Caillich and their curses might no' work", but he was so taken aback he stared straight at the hag. There and then he was turned into a lump o' black rock, all twisted like he had died in agony. On the top was a black skull wi' two empty sockets where his eyes had been.'

Jim Jim paused for breath and a round-eyed Mairi said wonderingly, 'Och my, the poor mannie, it must have been sore on him.'

'Ay, but that's the kind o' things that happens to men who go around seducing innocent women then leave them in the lurch,' Jim Jim nodded with a meaningful look at Dugald Ban, named so because of his mop of white hair.

Morag Ruadh threw back her head and gave a shout of laughter. 'Ach Father, you'd best stick to damping peats with your spit for you're no use at all as a story-teller . . . as Bob and Andrew will be after tellin' you from the look on their faces.'

'I did not understand it all but I think it is a very interesting story,' Anton said courteously.

'Will you tell us a story about the legends of Germany?' came eagerly from Ranald. 'I was reading a book about it and there's a lot o' strange things happen there . . . other of course than thon funny wee man, Hitler.'

Anton smiled. 'Not a story about Germany, Ranald, but something that I remember and always brings my home back into my thoughts.' He sat with his hands between his knees and slowly looked round the company. 'I am not one for too much talking and never could I tell a story like Jim Jim. These are memories I tell you now. When I was a little boy back home in my father's farm in Berlin, he used to say to me – round a fire like this, "Love each season for they are God-given. Love each day for each day is a gift. Love each moment, like moments in heaven . . . love, never hate for life is too swift." I have never forgotten these words and though I did not fully understand them at the time, I do now. I have not always found it easy – never to hate – but here, tonight on Rhanna, among people who have become my very dear friends, I understand fully the meaning of my father's words. Tomorrow I leave you all and never have I been so loath to leave a place as I am now.'

There was complete silence with all eyes on the young German whose boyish figure was outlined against the glow of the fire. He raised his head and smiled warmly at Lachlan and Phebie standing together. 'To you I raise my glass and say, Slainte – good health in return for mine. If all doctors were like Lachlan and all doctors' wives were like Phebie, then the world would be filled with health, and peace . . . and, most important of all, love. To Shona and Niall I give thanks for many things – friendship, companionship, for laughter when I didn't want to laugh . . . to my little Fiona I am deeply indebted for keeping me supplied with pets till my bed jumps with them and I almost undo all of Lachlan's good work leaping about after them. Frau Morrison I thank for her Benger's food and for keeping my bed so tidy I am almost afraid to lie in it – and . . .' he looked straight at Babbie, 'to Babbie, who nursed me like an angel, I give thanks for memories that will go with me for the rest of my life. To you all I give my gratitude for making the days of a German airman those that he will never forget. To all of you I say, 'Slainte' and God bless you all!'

The silence in the room had deepened till it was something that could be felt. The islanders did not like sentiment openly displayed and were always careful to hide their deeper emotions in frivolous words and happy banter, but at that moment there was hardly a dry eye in the room. Elspeth rose hastily and rushed into the kitchen to stand with her hands planted firmly on the table in an effort to stop her gaunt frame from trembling with all her suppressed tears. Lachlan and Phebie held on to each other and smiled with eyes that were too bright. The rest of the gathering shuffled in embarrassment. And when Anton looked at Babbie's corner he saw that she had fled, taking his heart with her.

'Ach, you are a good laddie, right enough,' Biddy sniffed gruffly. 'The Lord will spare you wherever you go, I'm damt sure o' that.'

'Ay, indeed just,' was the general murmur round the room.

Niall jumped to his feet, raising his glass to the ceiling. 'Slainte to you, Anton! I never thought I'd ever say that a Jerry was – is – one of the best friends I ever had – but I'm saying it now – tonight! To Anton I say, haste ye back for auld lang syne!'

The room rose as one. 'To Anton, haste ye back!'

'And God bless you, Anton Büttger,' Phebie whispered shakily and buried her face in Lachlan's shoulder.

The island gave Anton a good send-off. Cries of good wishes for his future well-being filled the harbour at Portcull. He stood for a few moments, observing it all, the spring green on the mountains, the smoke that drifted as dreamily as the people of Rhanna, the bronzed slopes of Sgurr nan Ruadh that reminded him of a girl with hair the colour of a fiery sunset. He looked at the water remembering eyes that were like pools of amber-flecked sea, and he smiled and felt like weeping. In his pocket were several packages, one a bottle of Tam's Uisge-beatha, the other a small parcel which Elspeth had pushed brusquely at him when he left Slochmhor for the last time.

'Some tablet to put strength in your feets,' she had told him sourly. 'With the sugar on rationing it wasny easy but we must all share what we have – after all – we are all alike in the eyes o' God though sometimes I think He must be needin' specs.'

He had surprised her by taking her hand and saying quietly, 'Mein Frau – thank you – and it is not God who is needing the spectacles – it is ourselves. He will bless you for your thoughtfulness – Elspeth.'

His pronunciation of her name was beautiful and, with crimson staining her cheeks, she had hurried quickly into the house to dab at her eyes with the corner of her apron.

Fiona also had given him a present, a glass jar containing a large hairy spider. 'For luck,' she said briefly for it had cost her a lot to part with her most prized specimen. 'His name is Geallachas, which is the Gaelic for faithful, so mind you take care of him. Keep the jar open so's he can catch flies and get a parcel of midgies together. Mind give him a drop of water too for spiders get gey thirsty.'

Anton had laughed and stooped to look into the child's bright eyes. 'Thank you – *jungfrau* – that is the German for maiden. I know Geallachas will bring me luck – perhaps enough for me to come back to this island and marry a beautiful princess called Fiona McLachlan!'

'Ach, you'd be too old!' she told him, but her smile was coy and she threw her arms round his neck to kiss his forehead.

The military escort were impatient to be on their way but Anton's blue eyes were scanning the harbour hoping to catch a last glimpse of Babbie. She hadn't said goodbye to him, she had barely spoken a word to him since yesterday. There was no sign of her at the harbour and his heart lay like a pebble in his breast.

He extended his hands to Shona and Niall who had come down with him. 'Fräulein Shona,' he whispered, 'my beautiful maiden who rescued a monster in distress.'

'A monster who changed into a handsome young airman,' she said as lightly as she could, hardly able to bear looking at the pain of hurt in his eyes.

'Hey, enough you two, Niall laughed, 'jealousy is rearing its ugly head again!'

Anton turned to him. 'Thank you, my friend, for yesterday. It is a day I will remember. Will you tell Fräulein Babbie I give to her my love. Thank her also – for healing my body – just say that, Niall.'

Niall gripped Anton's hand so hard he winced. 'I'll tell her, Anton.' Desperately he tried to think of something comforting to say but there was nothing. 'She couldn't come to see you off,' he said as the young German turned away. 'She said you would understand.'

A pink stain touched Anton's pale cheeks. 'Perfectly,' he said shortly and walked quickly to the waiting boat.

In the distance a figure came flying down Glen Fallan. Shona saw it first and hope fluttered in her breast. A few seconds later she saw the unmistakable gleam of red hair as Babbie ran past the War Memorial near Murdy's house.

'Anton . . . wait!' Shona's voice was a strangled little sob of sound.

Anton turned and in that split second the despair in his eyes was replaced by a jostling welter of emotions, with hope, that bright spark which buoys up the spirits in their most flagging state, struggling upwards from the depths of his being.

'Babbie.' He murmured the name huskily. 'Babbie.'

She came fleeing towards him without pause, straight into the water to wade towards the boat, without heed for anything or anyone.

'Anton!' His name soared towards the heavens. 'Anton! I love you!' she yelled in an ecstasy of joy. She fell into his arms and he caught her, laughing into her hair, burying his face into her breasts. Their tears mingled as they kissed and the military turned discreetly away.

'Anton, I couldn't let you go,' she sobbed almost incoherently. 'I thought about you all night long . . .'

He smothered her words with another kiss and she struggled to say breathlessly, 'I have so much to explain to you, Anton – all the reasons why I thought I couldn't love you – but I do – I do! You must send me your address and I'll tell you all in a letter . . . and I'll wait, I'll wait my darling . . . forever if need be!'

'I don't think the war will last that long!' he said, sparks of joy flashing from his blue eyes. 'And time will go quickly. I'll write you twice a day . . .'

'Once will be enough,' she laughed. The engine started up and they clung together. 'Oh, my darling, I don't want to let you go,' she cried. 'I want to hold you and love you and touch you.'

They drew apart, hands clinging, eyes saying a million things as yet unvoiced. Briefly he touched her hair, her face, then almost roughly he pushed her away from the boat. His eyes sought out Shona and Niall on the shore. 'Goodbye, my friends,' he breathed, while the man in him fought back the tears of such a bitter-sweet parting.

The boat's engines whirled the water into foam and pulled

it steadily out of the harbour yet still Babbie stood up to her knees in the sea with tears coursing down her face. Anton's head was now a golden crown, a minute later just a bright gleam far out in the water. 'I love you, Anton, I love you,' she sobbed into her hands.

Niall waded out to fetch her back to shore. 'That's right,' he said gently. 'Greet your heart out. It will do you good, myself and Shona found that out a whily back. Take my hanky and give your nose a right good blow.'

She obeyed with such ardour that the sound of her blowing her nose was like a miniature foghorn and all three burst into subdued laughter.

Babbie gave a watery sniff. 'Fiona told me she gave Anton a spider for luck – and it worked – that and the pair of you going off yesterday and leaving me alone with him.' She twisted round to look at the boat which was now just a black speck in the water but Shona took her firmly by the hand and led her past a gaping throng of islanders towards Glen Fallan and the welcoming banner of smoke from Laigmhor's chimneys.

PART VI

RHANNA
Summer 1941

CHAPTER 16

Rhanna droned lazily in the heat of high summer and Shona ran swiftly over the green fields of Laigmhor. Out on the Sound of Rhanna the ferry sounded its deep mournful horn and she stopped to watch it gliding into the harbour before she walked into the cool, silent woods that skirted the road. Pine needles rustled beneath her feet, the sunlight dappled the rich brown earth. She sat down on a mossy tree stump to hug her knees while she waited for Niall the way she had waited countless times before. She was wearing a dress of palest green which was a perfect foil for the deep gold of her suntanned limbs and the luxuriant auburn hair which she had swept upwards and pinned carefully into place.

She had taken overly long to get ready that morning, exasperating both Kirsteen and Fergus by running downstairs during breakfast, deciding to change from her white dress into a yellow one before the meal was over, deciding she liked neither and changing to the green. She had wondered whether to wear her long hair up or down and when Fergus said, 'I like it flowing down your back the way it was when you were a wee girl,' she had answered, 'I am *eighteen*, Father!' and had gone immediately upstairs to pin up the thick waving curls.

'You're too grown up for me to *talk* to now,' Grant told her disgustedly.

'And you're too much of a baby for me to care!' she had snapped at him. She was tense and irritable as so often happens when a keenly anticipated event is nearly reality.

Sitting among the cool trees she was ashamed of her outburst. The atmosphere at Laigmhor was usually one of happy contentment and it was wonderful to live in a house where laughter prevailed above all else. The weeks since Niall's going had been calm and uneventful except for an outbreak of measles which had affected a good part of the island's population. At Laigmhor, Grant had gone down with the rash first, followed by Kirsteen, who had laughed and felt ridiculous contracting measles at her age. Shona and Fergus had administered to the invalids but it was a mild form of measles and both Grant and Kirsteen were soon up and going about as normal. There was going to be another child in December. Kirsteen had confided the news to Shona and Grant a fortnight ago and they had celebrated by holding a gay ceilidh.

Grant's feelings were mixed on the matter. He dreaded the idea of a 'silly wee sister' and half-heartedly decided a brother might come in useful 'once it grows from a smelly baby into a real human'.

'Are you pleased, Father?' Shona had asked.

Fergus's black eyes had regarded her for a long moment. 'Ay, delighted,' he had said eventually. 'But no matter how many bairns may come along there will never be one to match you.'

'That could mean a lot of things,' she had answered with a smile.

'You know what I mean, mo ghaoil,' he had said with an intensity that made her put her arms round his neck and nuzzle his thick dark curls.

'I know, my dearest father,' she had said gently. 'It's easier for me, I have only one father to adore . . . you have more than one child – and you must love them all equally.'

Shona clasped her knees and thought about her father. The years they had spent together at Laigmhor had been stormy but beautiful years in her life and she knew she would always treasure the memory of them. But always there had been Niall. All through her tempestuous childhood he had been the other prop in her life and undeniably an even stronger one than her father whose pride had been the cause of unhappiness for a lot of people.

She watched a baby mole ambling blindly among the moss. A squirrel washed its whiskers on a branch above her head and she held her breath, loving the peace of the pine-scented wood, treasuring it even more because it was a part of Rhanna, the island she loved with every fibre of her being. Yet soon she must leave it if she wanted to remain with the man she loved. Niall had given her an ultimatum. 'When I come back to Rhanna in the summer I want your answer, Shona. You must decide when we are going to be wed.' Those had been his parting words when he left to go back to his studies at the vet. college.

A jaunty whistle came faintly on the breeze. Niall! At last, Niall! The thought of him so near quickened her heart. That whistle! It suddenly came to her that she hadn't heard it for many months. It had always been part of Niall yet on his last visit to Rhanna she hadn't heard it once. The gay sound of it came closer and she got to her feet. Niall was back! The Niall of the carefree years before the war! The dear, sweet Niall of her early memories. She saw him through the trees, tall, sturdy, his hair gleaming like a field of summer corn. His hands were deep in his pockets, his stride firm and sure as he walked on past the woods and into Glen Fallan.

'*Niall!*' She burst from the trees in a breathless flurry and he turned, holding out his arms to embrace her. He held her away and looked at the graceful beauty of her golden limbs and slender body. The upswept hair enhanced the curves of her delicate neckline and showed to perfection the symmetry of her pointed little face.

'Hey!' he laughed joyously. 'You're all grown up! My God, you're beautiful. I won't tell you that too often though in case you get big-headed. And that tan – you make me feel like a ghost!' Tenderly he tucked away a small tendril of fine hair. 'You've got your hair up again, I see.'

'Yes, do you like it? I did it especially for you.'

'It makes you look – sophisticated – the way some of the town girls look. I always thought of my Shona as a tom-boy, hair flying all over the place.'

'You don't like it!'

'I never said that – Caillich Ruadh!'

'Don't call me a red witch again, Niall McLachlan! You know I hate it!'

'Temper! Temper!' he scolded, his eyes dancing. 'Now, if

you were Fiona I'd take down your knickers and skelp your wee arse!'

'You're a barbarian, that's what you are – and a glaikit one at that! I don't know why I bother with you!' she cried, her cheeks red with rage.

'Because I'm irresistible, that's why.' He grinned delightedly. An ancient van trundled towards them on the dusty Glen road. Behind the windscreen two heads bobbed in unison, one a flaming red, the other a startling white. Morag Ruadh beamed at them, her ruddy face radiant, and Dugald Ban peered out, nodding in acknowledgement.

'*That* was Morag Ruadh!' Niall gasped. 'What is Dugald Ban doing riding around with that Caillich Ruadh?'

'It *was* Morag Ruadh,' Shona said politely. 'Now Mrs Dugald Donaldson, mistress of Dunbeag, Portvoynachan.'

'Never – never Morag Ruadh! How did she do it?'

Shona couldn't help laughing. 'In the same way as her cousin Mairi, only Morag Ruadh, the one-time saint of Portcull, was far more blatant than poor Mairi. Old Behag says she's never seen such sinful flaunting in anybody – but of course she says that about everyone who strays from the narrow path . . . I got it all, too . . . and from Morag as well, the besom.'

'But how did poor old Doug get caught? I thought he and Totie were pretty thick!'

'They were – up until that time the Commandos came and there was a ceilidh at the Manse. It seems Morag and Doug were very friendly that night. When Morag knew she was pregnant she blamed him, and Isabel and old Jim Jim gave him no peace till he took Morag to the altar. The baby's due in December. The cailleachs are saying that the Manse ceilidh was no more than an excuse for drunken lechery.'

'One up for Morag,' Niall grinned. 'Though I'll never know how poor old Dugald Ban got himself into that one.'

'Neither can anybody else. The gossips' tongues are red-hot, for some say that Doug wasn't the only one with a hand in the affair. When Jim Jim first asked Morag who was the father of the bairn she said calmly, "Will you take your pick,

Father? I have been a loose woman." When Jim Jim heard that he nearly went up in a puff of peat smoke and said he hoped the father, wasn't a Jerry. After that Morag pinpointed Doug. Morag was such a confirmed saint Doug just took her word for it so he must have been *one* of them.' She giggled. 'All these years, Morag without a man and suddenly we are to believe they are queuing up!'

'Totie must be furious! She kept Dugald dangling long enough.'

'She doesn't mind at all. Morag is kept so busy typing all Doug's notes and looking after the house she doesn't have time for the kirk organ so she signed it over to Totie. Doug got himself that old van and takes Totie's goods all over the island. She's delighted but Behag and Merry Mary are furious because it has taken business away from them.' They arrived at the gate of Laigmhor in a merry state.

'Let's go off on a picnic,' Shona suggested. 'I'll go in and get some stuff together while you go up and change into your Rhanna clothes.'

'Good idea, I'll see you in twenty minutes.'

They met at the dyke outside Laigmhor. He put his arm round her and led her towards the long heat-hazed stretches of the Muir of Rhanna. The sun beat down warmly. Needle-whin and broom nestled among tawny tussocks of sedge, and banks of butterwort popped shy violet faces through the leaves of the more boisterous marsh trefoil whose dazzling white-flower spikes carpeted the moor bogs. A Hebridean rock-pipit winged overhead, muttering deep in its throat; bees, already laden with little sacs of pollen, prodded frenziedly into the bell heather; and delicate moths fluttered uncertainly over the wild flowers, restlessly roaming from one clump to the next.

Niall sniffed deeply. 'You know, I really love coming home to Rhanna. I used to think it was quite exciting going away to new places but I've got that out of my system now. This is where I really belong. I feel it more and more strongly each time I come back. We'll settle to live here one day.' He said the words with conviction but she looked at him with both doubt and hope in her eyes.

'But – how can we? You're going to be a vet. You would never find enough to keep you going here.'

'I've already thought about all that,' he said happily. 'I could divide my time up between Rhanna and some of the other nearby islands. A kind of travelling vet. I'd be here maybe four days out of seven – the rest of the time I'd be away . . . but it would be worth it – don't you think so, mo ghaoil?'

'Too wonderful to believe,' she breathed. 'It would be a dream that might never come true.'

'Dreams do come true if you work to make them real. It's a thought for the future anyway.'

'Oh, yes, yes, Niall,' she cried and threw herself into his arms to kiss him till they drew apart to look at each other longingly.

'Enough,' he said shakily. 'Two minutes of you and I'm shaking like a leaf.'

A sprite of mischief danced in her eyes. 'It's a good job you've got your kilt on, Niall McLachlan! Being the bull you are you wouldn't have room in your trousers.'

His brown eyes glinted. 'Remember old Burnbreddie? In the hayshed rutting at some old yowe? He wore nothing under his kilt then. How do you know I'm decently covered? Would you like a quick peep?'

She got to her feet in an outrage. '*Niall McLachlan!* You dirty bugger!' She ran and he chased her, in and out of the crumbling pillars of the Abbey.

He caught her and held her head between his hands. 'I love you! And I wish we were married right now because this waiting takes a bit of doing.' He studied her intently for a few moments. 'Something's missing! That beautiful hair, sliding through my fingers like silk! Let me unpin it so that it flies loose and wild like it used to. We'll be children again for a while! We'll dance and sing like idiots and we won't grow up till we're ready! We have the whole lovely summer ahead of us!'

For a brief moment their hands entwined, and a playful

breeze lifted the loose strands of her hair, blowing it over her face, throwing it into a ruffled bronze mane behind her back.

'Race you!' he shouted. Their feet took wings and they were running, children again, their breath catching with laughter in the mad flight over the perfumed shaggy moors.

They were married when the soft, golden days of the Hebridean summer were growing shorter. The island waited with a subdued excitement for the event while Laigmhor and Slochmhor bustled with unhurried preparations.

The Rev. John Gray spent many hours rehearsing the wedding ceremony in Gaelic while his long-suffering wife sat with her knitting and made automatic sounds of approval. In her opinion his loud, booming voice was entirely unsuited for the soft pronunciation of the Gaelic language. Once she said mildly, 'You must speak softer, John, and you need some lilt. If you listen to the islanders you will hear the lilt.'

'I *am* lilting, Hannah!' he roared indignantly. 'Your trouble is you don't listen properly. Put those knitting needles away and you will *hear* my lilt!'

It seemed as if the whole of Rhanna was crowded into the Kirk on the Hillock to watch the ceremony. Mary, Alick's wife, was there with her twin sons. A letter had arrived from Alick. 'I can't be at the wedding of my favourite niece but my spirit is with you, mo ghaoil. I will picture you looking beautiful in front of the altar. For God's sake try to keep your temper for once and when the toasts are being made at the reception say one for me. God be with you both and may you be blessed with the thunder of many tiny feet.'

Babbie had arrived the day before, a new kind of radiance in her dancing green eyes. Anton had kept his word and letters had come for her every other day, tender love letters full of an impatience to be with her again but a certain contentment between the lines indicating to her his deep happiness that one day they would be together.

With Biddy's full approval Babbie had applied for the post of assistant nurse on Rhanna. The 'galloping hairpin' had long ago departed the island, glad to escape Biddy's criticism and the eccentricities of the older inhabitants.

'You're up on your feets I see, you auld cailleach,' had been Babbie's laughing greeting to Biddy. 'If things go right I should soon be having the pleasure of hearing you telling me how to give enemas properly.'

'I will never utter the words,' Biddy had growled while her old heart glowed. Babbie had become like a daughter to her and they were able to argue without animosity and hug each other with laughter over all the funny little happenings that could not be avoided in work such as theirs.

Shona was radiant in a simple blue dress with white marguerites braided into hair that tumbled down her back in rich thick waves. At the altar Niall stood tall and straight in a lovat tweed jacket and McLachlan kilt, his fair skin flushed with a mixture of pride and nerves. Strong, rugged Fergus wore the McKenzie kilt with pride but he felt a moment of panic at the idea of walking into kirk and all eyes staring as he gave his daughter away. Then Shona was beside him and he braced himself.

'Well, Father,' she whispered, 'another man will have to put up with my tempers now.'

He nodded slowly. 'Ay, you're right there, lass. Not only your tempers but those awful dumplings you make and your cheek at the breakfast table . . .' His black eyes were very bright. 'And your singing when you're doing your chores and your wee voice bidding me good night . . . these are all the things I'm giving away to another man, together with a million other things I love about my lass.' He gave a wry smile. 'You didn't know your old man could make speeches like that, eh?'

'Not my old man,' she said with a little sobbing intake of breath. 'My handsome big boy, remember? I haven't called you that in years but I still think it.'

Behind them, Fiona and Grant fidgeted impatiently. 'I'll *never* marry,' hissed the former, pulling disgustedly at the frills on her dress.

'Nobody would want to marry *you*,' Grant returned. 'You're more like a boy than a girl.'

'I'm glad of that; even though boys are horrible they're better than silly girls. I'm going to be an explorer when I grow up and live in a tent in the jungle.'

'I'm going to be a fisherman like old Joe and sail all over the world. I'll never get married either 'cos it's stupid. Mother and Father fight one minute then make goggle eyes at each other the next – *and* they have babies all the time,' he finished in aggrieved tones.

Inside the kirk, Totie pedalled energetically in an effort to get the bellows of the ancient harmonium fully inflated before she began to play and in the red-faced fight with the instrument she wondered, not for the first time, why Morag Ruadh had put up such a struggle to remain the kirk organist all these years. Totie pedalled and puffed, the harmonium wheezed into life, spluttered for a few nerve-shattering moments, and then graciously the notes soared forth, sweetly and beautifully, and Totie knew once more the reasons for Morag's reluctance to let someone else play. The Wedding March soared majestically to the roof, the door opened and the ceremony began.

The Rev. John Gray had listened to his wife after all. His subdued tones lacked the 'lilt' but his Gaelic was perfect, and the old Gaels looked at each other with a mixture of surprise and delight.

'Ach, he's speaking the Gaelic in English,' Jim Jim muttered.

Isabel poked him in the ribs. 'The man is doing his best. He means well right enough. Just you leave him be, Jim McDonald.'

Despite the lack of the lilt, the ceremony was beautiful. The Gaelic words echoed round the old kirk and the ancient walls seemed to soak them in for a moment as if joyfully savouring a familiar tongue, then they were released again to go bouncing from wall to wall, one upon the other.

'Oh God,' Phebie gasped, dashing away a tear. 'I promised myself I wouldn't cry.'

Lachlan moved closer to her. 'Lend me your hanky,' he said with a watery sniff. 'Men aren't *supposed* to cry at weddings.' He gripped her hand. 'If they have a marriage like ours – then they couldn't ask God for more . . . my bonny plump rose.'

'Ay, you're right, Lachy – my darling,' she said huskily and blew her nose as quietly as she could.

Kirsteen felt a strong movement inside her womb and glanced towards Fergus, tall and dark, handsome in his kilt and tweed jacket. It seemed just yesterday that they had stood at the altar taking their vows, and now here she was, his flesh growing inside her, growing from the love and the happiness they had shared since their marriage. He caught her eye and smiled, an intimate secret smile, and she felt her heart glowing.

When it was over and they were all moving outside, Erchy and Todd stood one on either side of the door, and the bagpipes wheezed into life, the gay tunes filling the air. Laughing, the islanders linked arms and began to dance. The ceilidhing was already starting.

Shona and Niall were accosted from all sides, but Biddy, her ancient box camera at the ready, was the most persistent. 'Look you now, will you be standin' away from these gravestones,' she commanded. 'Todd, get out of the way! I'm no' wantin' your hairy legs in my picture.' Dodie galloped up, knocking her elbow just as the shutter clicked. Turning, she clouted him on the ear as if he was a small boy. 'You are just like a herd o' elephants!' she scolded. 'Now I have nothing but a fine picture o' the clouds!'

'Ach, I'm sorry, Biddy!' he wailed. Mairi had restored him to such a degree of good health that his cheeks popped out from his face like wizened brown apples and his bony frame had filled out considerably. But he was a creature who needed the freedom of wide places. After weeks of cosseting he was glad to escape to his lonely cottage in the hills though he showered Mairi with such a continual flow of simple little gifts it had been suggested to her by the opportunist Ranald that she should open up a craft shop for the summer tourists.

Dodie turned hastily from Biddy, knocking her hat off in the process and amid a stream of abuse he shouted to the newly-weds, 'Will you be waiting a minute. I have a wee wedding gift for you, that I have.' It was a dewy spray of harebells, bog myrtle and white heather, lovingly wrapped in a square of toilet tissue such as was used at Burnbreddie.

'It's a lovely present, Dodie,' Niall said gratefully.

'Ach well, it will be mindin' you of the moors when you are being gassed by the smelly smoke in the city. The heather will bring you a lot o' luck. I had a job findin' it but I wanted to give you something after the fine job you made o' my wee hoosie.'

'Is it all right then, Dodie?'

'Ay, lovely just.' His grizzled face shone with pride then he looked ashamed. 'I am after putting back my own roof wi' the nice pattern.'

'But, Dodie,' laughed Niall. 'That's the sign of the swastika – the Nazi sign!'

Dodie's face showed no comprehension. 'Ay, ay, a lovely sign it is! I like it fine,' he enthused.

'Daft, daft, he is,' Canty Tam smirked. 'The British planes will be shootin' his wee hoosie down in flames else the Peat Hags will haunt him for takin' the pattern away from them.'

Shona had stolen away from the crowd to the part of the graveyard that held the remains of so many who had been her dear friends in life. Pausing at each grave she laid a single white rose on the grassy earth, each one plucked from her wedding bouquet. The only person she had never known was the one who had given her life and for a long moment she stood looking at her mother's headstone, then she stooped to lay her garland of marguerites on the mossy brown earth. 'Thank you for my life, Mother,' she said simply and turned to walk down to where her father was waiting quietly a few yards away.

'She would be proud if she was here today,' he said softly.

Shona looked straight into his dark eyes. 'I think she is here today, they're all here, Mother, Mirabelle, Hamish, old Shelagh . . . everyone – and – ' she smiled, 'just think, what a grandstand view they must get of everything.'

Babbie was standing on the fringe of the crowd. Off her

guard for a moment she looked alone and vulnerable. Shona raised her arm and threw her bouquet – straight at Babbie.

'Oh – I caught it,' Babbie said with such surprise that Shona chuckled.

'I didn't mean it to fly to the moon, daftie.'

'If all goes according to plan I should be where he left me when the war is over.'

'What! Up to your knees in the middle of the sea?'

'Ach, you're even madder than usual,' Babbie giggled. 'All this excitement has gone to your head.'

The Rev. John Gray was standing at the kirk door and Shona went over to take him warmly by the hand. 'Thank you for such a lovely service. The older Gaels were able to understand every word. You will of course be coming to the ceilidh?'

'Well, I . . .' he began then stopped. 'I'll look forward to it my dear.'

Shona stood on her tiptoes and planted a kiss firmly on his cheek then did the same to a beaming Mrs Gray. 'The flowers were beautifully done, Mrs Gray. You have both given me a day to remember.'

A hard lump that had come suddenly to the Rev. Gray's throat made him cough and he stared after Shona's retreating back with eyes that were very bright.

'You know, John,' Mrs Gray said thoughtfully, 'I'd say that you have seen more than one kind of light in the last few months.'

He took her by the arm. 'Hannah, my dear, I do believe you're right. I have wasted a lot of years with my head in the clouds with the result that I couldn't see what was under my nose. These islanders are a fine people and for the first time I feel that I have taken a wee step closer to them . . . however, I warn you, Hannah, no more of that peaty tea tonight, I have to set a good example, you know.'

They chuckled and went off arm in arm to the Manse to get ready for the ceilidh.

That evening Tam's Uisge-beatha rocked the foundations of Laigmhor with its happy effects. At ten o'clock

Niall and Shona stole away and sped hand in hand over the dark fields to the harbour where Ranald was waiting to take them out to a fishing boat. It was sailing with the tide to Stornoway where they were to spend their honeymoon.

Ranald's face beamed at them in the darkness. 'I kept a special boat for you,' he confided. 'I've been waitin' for a chance to use it and it bein' your weddin' night you must have everything done proper.' He led them to the dark blob of a rubber dinghy floating in the shallows. 'In you go now, mo ghaoil,' he said, courteously helping Shona aboard. 'If you feel like you've been walkin' all day on air then now you're goin' to be floatin' on it.'

'But, Ranald, this dinghy belongs to . . .' She stopped short and chuckled. 'Ranald McTavish,' she finished and the wily Ranald said a polite and utterly innocent, 'Right enough, now,' and began to row away from the shore.

Shona looked at Rhanna slipping away. The rugged peaks of Ben Machrie and Sgurr nan Ruadh were outlined in the remnants of a deep golden sunset that still hovered in the north-western sky. Sounds of merriment came faintly on the breeze; on the sands skirting Port Rum Point a family of gulls squabbled quietly; the dark shape of a lone heron glided on silent wings, uttering a sharp 'Cra-ack' as it passed over the dinghy. Shona's heart rose into her throat but Niall's arm came round her and his warm lips touched hers.

'Slainte – Mrs Niall McLachlan,' he murmured softly. 'You belong to me now.'

'We belong to each other,' she said firmly, dashing away the tears that had sprung to her eyes. 'Always you seemed to leave me behind on Rhanna . . . you can't do that any more – and I'm happy to be coming with you – my darling husband . . .' She pointed upwards to where the sliver of a young moon peeped out shyly from a fluffy cloudbank. 'Look, Niall, the new moon! Mirabelle always made a wish whenever it appeared. We must each spit on a piece of silver, hold it in our hand and wish.'

Solemnly they carried out the ancient ritual. 'I've made mine,' said Niall seriously. 'I hope it comes true.'

She nodded with assurance. 'It will – so long as you never tell anyone what it was. Some of my best wishes came true on the new moon.'

High in the fields above Laigmhor a tall figure looked out to the Sound of Rhanna, watching the dark little blob of the dinghy moving over a velvet sea faintly flecked with gold. It was a lovely autumn evening, filled with the sharp tang of peat smoke and fresh salt wind, the kind of weather Shona had always loved. Fergus breathed the scent of it deeply into his lungs, looking at the picture before him till it became a blur.

'Goodbye – Ni Cridhe,' he said, so quietly it might have been the sigh of the wind.

Kirsteen came up behind him and slid her arms round his waist. 'I knew you'd be up here,' she murmured, 'saying goodbye to her. Don't be sad, Fergus. She'll be back.'

'Only to visit us,' he said huskily.

'Perhaps – she has her own life to lead now but I think one day they'll both come back – to stay. I have some news for you that will most certainly take your mind off things. I didn't say anything till now because I didn't want to steal Shona's thunder. Lachlan examined me yesterday and heard *two* heartbeats. We're going to have twins, my darling.'

Fergus let out a roar of joy. 'Heaven help us! If they're girls Grant will have a fit! We'd better break the news to him gently or he'll be borrowing one of Ranald's boats to leave home in!'

She linked her arm through his. 'Talking of Grant, I'm sure that wee devil Fiona gave him a glass of sherry. He's doing a Highland fling with Biddy and her teeth and specs are rattling like mad! Come down now, darling, and help me to get him under control or the minister will never come to another island ceilidh again.'

Turning his back on the sea Fergus put his arm round her waist and they walked over the dew-wet fields to Laigmhor. As they walked the happy sound of laughter drifted to them on the playful breezes which eternally caressed the lonely high places of Rhanna